LOOKING AT LANGUAGES

A Workbook in Elementary Linguistics

Paul R. Frommer
Edward Finegan

Harcourt Brace College Publishers
Fort Worth   Philadelphia   San Diego   New York   Orlando   Austin   San Antonio
Toronto   Montreal   London   Sydney   Tokyo

ISBN: 0-15-500123-X

The LaserHEBREW, LaserIPA, LaserKOREAN, LaserPERSIAN, and MacCHINESE Mandarin fonts used to print this work are available from Linguist's Software, Inc., P. O. Box 580, Edmonds, WA 98020-0580 tel. (206) 775-1130.

Address editorial correspondence to:
Harcourt Brace College Publishers
301 Commerce Street, Suite 3700
Fort Worth, TX 76102

Address orders to:
Harcourt Brace & Company
6277 Sea Harbor Drive
Orlando, FL 32887
1-800-782-4479 outside Florida
1-800-433-0001 inside Florida

Printed in the United States of America

4 5 6 7 8 9 0 1 2   095   9 8 7 6 5 4 3 2

CONTENTS

Preface   vii

Acknowledgments   ix

CHAPTER **3** Morphology 107

CHAPTER **4** Syntax 153

CHAPTER **5**   Semantics and Pragmatics   207

CHAPTER **6**   Historical and Comparative Linguistics   253

CHAPTER **7** Dialect, Register, and Style 285

CHAPTER **8** Writing 319

APPENDIXES 353

BIBLIOGRAPHY 361

Preface

Like the ability to play the piano, ride a bicycle, or solve a calculus problem, the ability to analyze linguistic data can be acquired and refined only through practice. Mastering general principles of analysis is necessary but not sufficient, and students can develop a sense of excitement and accomplishment by "getting their hands dirty" in the data of a wide range of languages, both familiar and unfamiliar. Only then can students fully appreciate the principles of linguistic analysis and the structure and organization of languages.

Looking at Languages is designed to provide practice in the analysis of natural languages. Written to accompany *Language: Its Structure and Use,* Second Edition, by Edward Finegan, it is nevertheless self-contained and may be used with most introductory language and linguistics textbooks. We hope that this workbook will prove useful to students and teachers in a variety of teaching and learning situations.

Besides examples from fictitious languages like Klingon and Spiiktumi, *Looking at Languages* examines data from 28 natural languages, only a few of which, like Akan and Wichita, might be considered "exotic." For most beginning students, the phenomena of Arabic, Greek, Chinese, Japanese, Malay/Indonesian, Persian, and Turkish are exotic enough, and the accessibility of speakers—sometimes sitting right next to them in class—who can pronounce the examples natively and offer their observations about them can infuse an exercise with immediacy and life.

With a few exceptions, we have arranged the problems in each chapter in order of difficulty, with later exercises generally being more involved or requiring more creative thought than earlier ones. Any ordering of problems by difficulty is to some extent subjective, so some users of this workbook may judge certain problems more challenging or less challenging than we have.

In preparing this workbook, we weighed matters of form as well as of content, considering practical questions of problem format alongside substantive issues such as language choice and range of difficulty. A glance through the book will indicate how we answered our formatting questions; here it may be useful to spell out some of the motivation for our decisions in this area.

On the basic issue of whether to include space for answers or provide only the questions—that is, whether to create a workbook or a problem book—we felt that a workbook would enable teachers and students alike to make the best use of the time spent on the exercises. From the point of view of teachers, our experience suggested that the uniform formatting of answers facilitated by a workbook with removable pages makes for more efficient grading of problems. From the standpoint of students, a workbook often eliminates the need for the tedious copying out of data, while charts, diagrams, matrices and maps that are simply to be filled in rather than created from scratch provide direction and encourage focus on the substance of a problem without irrelevant distractions. In one matter we had to choose the lesser of two evils: in order to allow any particular exercise to be handed in without also including part of another, we start each problem on a right-hand page, the tradeoff being that some facing pages remain blank.

From students and teachers alike we would welcome comments about *Looking at Languages,* especially those that may be useful to future readers.

Paul R. Frommer

Edward Finegan

Acknowledgments

Our thanks to the following linguists, language experts, and friends who read portions of the manuscript, offered suggestions, supplied data and intuitions, or tried out the problems with their students: John E. Brinkley, Paul Bruthiaux, Edward Chisholm, Larry Da Silva, Eric Du, Christine Cox Eriksson, Charles S. Fineman, Sylvia Frommer, Patricia Hunt, Larry Hyman, Min-Kyong Ju, Dino Koutsolioutsos, Martin Lo, Terry Loop, Andrew Meisel, Fred Nager, George Schlein, Donald Stilo, Terry Szink, and especially Ger-Bei Lee. Our book is a better one because of their help.

Name _____   Section _____   Date _____

C H A P T E R

1

Phonetics

1.01 TRANSCRIPTION—READING PRACTICE 1

Using standard English orthography, identify the English words represented by the following phonetic transcriptions. (*Note:* Aspiration and stress have not been indicated.)

1. ɪnstənsəz — *instances*
2. ənawnsmənts — *anouncements*
3. gɪglɱ — *giggling*
4. nɑDəd — *nodded*
5. tiðɱ — *teething*
6. notwərðinəs — *noteworthiness*
7. ɪspešəli — *especially*
8. čuzəz — *chooses*
9. ʌnhæpinəs — *unhappiness*
10. mɛnšənɱ — *mentioning*
11. lōkwešəs — *loquacious*
12. dɪspležər — *displeasure*
13. blʌǰənd — *bludgeoned*
14. ʌnθrɪfti — *unthrifty*
15. kənspɪrətɔriəl — *conspiratorial*

16. mɪsfɔrčən   *misfortune*
17. farməsuDəkəl   *pharmaceutical*
18. saykoənæləsɪs   *psychoanalysis*
19. æŋkšəs   *anxious*
20. nalɪjəbəl   *knowledgable*
21. səksešən   *succession*
22. yuθənežə   *euthanasia*
23. fɪzɪks   *physiques*
24. sɪnəsɪzəm   *cynicism*
25. fɛðərwet   *featherweight*
26. anərɛri   *honorary*
27. kənsivd   *conceived*
28. kyukʌmbər   *cucumber*
29. risɛst   *recessed*
30. əkamədešənz   *accomodations*
31. rilɪŋkwɪšt   *relinquished*
32. tərbyələns   *turbulance*
33. ɪgzæktɪŋ   *exacting*
34. homonər   *homeowner*
35. kərejəs   *courageous*
36. pətɛnšəli   *potentially*
37. æməčər   *amateur*
38. lɪjənər   *legionnaire*
39. ɔθɛntəket   *authenticate*
40. šušayn   *shoeshine*

Name _____   **Section** _____   **Date** _____

1.02 TRANSCRIPTION—READING PRACTICE 2: ENGLISH HOMOPHONES

Each of the phonetic transcriptions below represents two or more different English words with different spellings. In each case, give the possible spellings represented by the transcriptions. The numbers following the transcriptions indicate the number of possibilities that have occurred to the authors. Try to find as many of these as you can. For a few of the more esoteric vocabulary items, a dictionary may be helpful.

EXAMPLES: tʰu 3 <u>to, too, two</u>
si 3 <u>see, sea, c</u>

1. so 3   so, sew, sow
2. ber 2   bear, bare
3. brɛd 2   bread, bred
4. ǰinz 2   genes, jeans
5. rid 2   read, reed
6. sɛnt 3   sent, cent, scent
7. ruts 2   roots, routes
8. dayd 2   died, dyed
9. siz 4   sees, seas, seize, c's (cees)
10. mud 2   mood, mooed
11. rez 3   raise, raze, rays
12. hid 2   heed, he'd
13. pʰækt 2 packed, pact
14. yu 4   you, ewe, u,
15. rayts 3 rights, writes, rites
16. tʰod 3 towed, toad, toed
17. kyu 3   cue, queue, que
18. mit 3   meat, meet, mete
19. ay 3   eye, aye, I
20. sayt 3 sight, site, cite
21. fɔr 3   for, four, fore

22. gron 2 — grown, groan
23. ren 3 — rain, reign, rein
24. lut 2 — loot, lute
25. hərts 2 — hearts, harts
26. sayz 3 — size, sighs, ⬭
27. rɛst 2 — rest, wrest
28. noz 3 — nose, knows, nos.
29. ædz 2 — ads, adds
30. fıltər 2 — filter, philter (or philtre)
31. hil 3 — heel, he'll, heal
32. er 3 — aire, air, heir
33. ayl 3 — I'll, isle, aisle
34. pʰaks 2 — pox, pocks
35. rʌf 2 — rough, ruff
36. sɔrd 2 — sword, soared
37. swit 2 — sweet, suite
38. ven 3 — vain, vane
39. lagər 2 — lager, logger
40. kʰi 2 — key, ⬭
41. nid 3 — need, knead, kneed
42. flu 3 — flu, flew, flue
43. hastəl 2 — hostile, hostel
44. pʰɔz 2 — pose ⬭
45. awr 2 — our, hour
46. mayt 2 — might, mite
47. pʰuDıŋ 2 — putting, pudding
48. dıskrit 2 — discreet, discrete
49. kʰampləmentəri 2 — complimentary, complementary

Name _____   **Section** _____   **Date** _____

50. kʰɔrs 2   course, coarse

51. steš̄əneri 2   stationary, stationery

52. pʰroz 2   prose, pros

53. pʰrɪnsəpəl 2   principal, principle

54. liDər 2   leader, liter

55. dez 2   days, daze

56. frayər 2   friar, fryer

57. kʰærət 4   carrot, carat (carot) ('caret)

58. ərn 2   earn, urn

59. fayl 2   file, phial

60. ɔrəl 2   oral, aural

There are many more such examples in English. See if you can come up with three of your own:

61. _____   _____

62. _____   _____

63. _____   _____

Name _____   **Section** _____   **Date** _____

1.03   TRANSCRIPTION—READING PRACTICE 3: FILM AND PLAY NAMES

Using standard English orthography, identify the film and play titles transcribed phonetically below:

1. rɑki hɔrər pʰɪkčər šo _Rocky Horror Picture_

2. sayko _Psycho_

3. ðə dɑktər _The Doctor_

4. pʰyur lʌk _Pure Luck_

5. ɛm bʌDərflay _M. Butterfly_

6. tʰərməneDər tʰu jʌ̌jmənt de _Terminator II - Judgement Day_

7. ðə kʰɪŋ ən ay _The King and I_

8. gosbʌstərz _Ghostbusters_

9. rigɑrdɪŋ hɛnri _Regarding Henry_

10. sɪDi slɪkərz _City Slickers_

11. bɔyz ɪn ðə hʊd _Boys in the Hood_

12. ə hʌndrəd ən wʌn dælmešənz _A Hundred and One Dalmations_

13. θɛlmə ən luwiz _Thelma and Louise_

14. ritʰərn tʰə ðə blu ləgun _Return to the Blue Lagoon_

15. pʰærɪs ɪz bərnɪŋ _Paris is Burning_

16. rɑbən hʊd pʰrɪns əv θivz _Robin Hood Prince of Thiefs_

17. bɪl ən tʰɛdz bogəs jərni _Bill and Ted's Bogus Journey_

18. dõ tʰɛl mɑm ðə bebi sɪDərz dɛd _Don't Tell Mom the Babysitter's Dead_

19. čɑpər čɪks ɪn zɑmbitawn _Chopper Chicks in Zombietown_

20. dayɪŋ yʌŋ _Dying Young_

21. ðə spɪrət əv sɛvəndi sɪks _The Spirit of Seventy-Six_

22. rozənkræns ən gɪldənstərn ər dɛd _Rosencrans and Gildenstern Are Dead_

23. ðə sayləns əv ðə læmz _The Silence of the Lambs_

24. mɛžər fər mɛžər _Measure for Measure_

25. may byuDəfəl lɔndrɛt _My Beautiful Laundrette_

26. ðə fæntəm əv ði aprə _The Phantom of the Opera_
27. sno wayt ən ðə sɛvən dwɔrfs _Snow White and the Seven Dwarfs_
28. bəlaksi bluz _Biloxi Blues_
29. læst ɛgzɪt tʰə brʊklɪn _Last Exit to Brooklyn_
30. bæk tʰə ðə fyučər pʰart θri _Back to the Future Part Three_
31. tʰineǰ myutənt nɪnǰə tʰərtəlz _Teenage Mutant Ninja Turtles_
32. nekɪd gʌn tʰu ən ə hæf ðə smɛl əv fir _Naked Gun Two and ½, the Smell of Fear_
33. ɛDəpəs šmɛDəpəs æz lɔŋ æz yə lʌv yər mʌðər _Oedipus Smoedipus as Long ya Love Your Mother_
34. kʰɔl θiDər fər ʌðər pʰrogræmz _Call Theater for Other Programs_

Name _____   **Section** _____   **Date** _____

1.04   TRANSCRIPTION—READING PRACTICE 4: CONTINUOUS TEXT

Convert the broad phonetic transcription below into standard English orthography; / is used to indicate original sentence breaks. [From *The Buddha of Suburbia* by Hanif Kureishi (Penguin, 1990)]

ay ræn ən fɛčt dædz prəfərd yogə bʊk yogə fər wɪmən wɪθ pɪkčərz əv hɛlθi wɪmən ɪn blæk liətardz frəm əmʌŋ hɪz ʌðər bʊks ɑn buDɪzəm sufɪzəm kənfyušənɪzəm ən zɛn wɪč hi hæd bɑt æt ði ɔriɛntəl bʊkšɑp ɪn sisəl kɔrt ɔf čærɪŋ krɔs rod / ay skwɑDəd bəsayd hɪm wɪð ðə bʊk / hi briðd ɪn hɛld ðə brɛθ briðd awt ən wʌns mɔr hɛld ðə brɛθ / ay wazənt ə bæd riDər ænd ay əmæjənd maysɛlf tə bi ɑn ðə stej əv ði old vɪk æz ay diklemd grændli səlambə sərsasənə* rivayvz ən mɛntɛnz ə spɪrət əv yuθfəlnəs ən æsɛt biyɑnd prays / ɪt ɪz wʌndərfəl tə no ðæt yu ɑr rɛDi tə fes ʌp tə layf ænd ɪkstrækt frəm ɪt ɔl ðə ril joy ɪt hæz tu ɔfər

* Salamba Sirsasana (a name)

_____

_____

_____

_____

_____

_____

_____

_____

_____

_____

_____

_____

_____

_____

_____

_____

_____

_____

Name _____   **Section** _____   **Date** _____

1.05   TRANSCRIPTION—READING PRACTICE 5: CASUAL SPEECH

Below you will find transcriptions of the casual, colloquial English of a particular American speaker.
Write the English versions of each sentence in two ways: the first time using standard English spelling,
the second time with the kind of colloquial spellings that you are used to seeing in comic strips or in the dialog sections of a script. (Note: Stress has been indicated by an acute accent mark over the vowel [´].)

> **EXAMPLE:**   ɑmnɑ́tgʊnəgó
> (1)   I'm not going to go.
> (2)   I'm not gonna go.

1.   wénəryəgʊnəgímiðəglǽsəwɔ́Dərayǽstfɔr

> (1) _____
>
> (2) _____

2.   soiséztəmi yúənáykənmekbyúDəfəlmyúzəktəgéðər

> (1) _____
>
> (2) _____

3.   ɪfyəwúdṇmáyn knáysipʰɑ́rDəyərpʰépər

> (1) _____
>
> (2) _____

4.   tʰéləmayǰʌskʰæntʰékɪtɛnimɔ́r aymáwDəhir

> (1) _____
>
> (2) _____

5.   dyəwánəgóDuəčáynízərənətʰǽlyənréstrɑnfərdínər

> (1) _____
>
> (2) _____

Name _____   **Section** _____   **Date** _____

1.06   TRANSCRIPTION—WRITING PRACTICE 1

Transcribe the following one-syllable words and names phonetically.

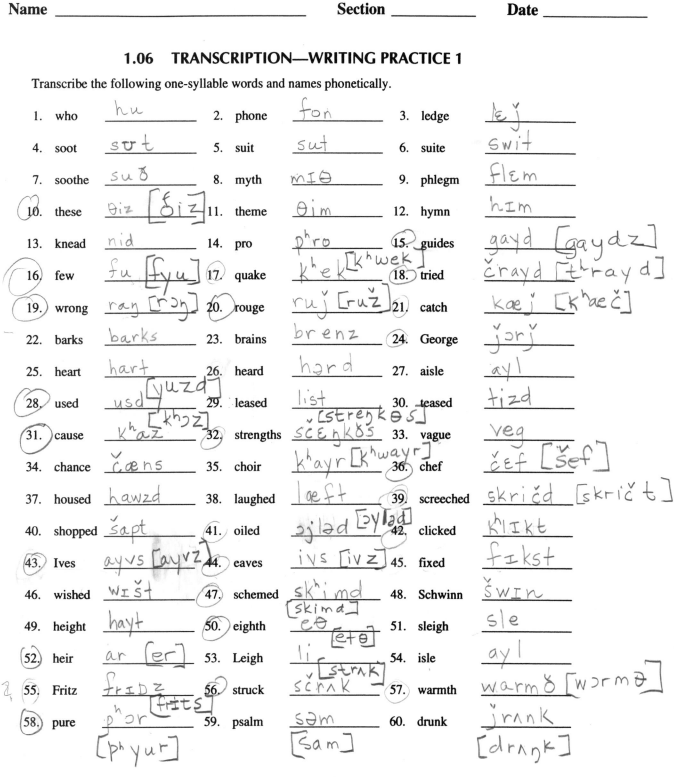

1. who ___hu___
2. phone ___fon___
3. ledge ___lɛǰ___
4. soot ___sʊt___
5. suit ___sut___
6. suite ___swit___
7. soothe ___suð___
8. myth ___mɪθ___
9. phlegm ___flɛm___
10. these ___ðiz [ðiz]___
11. theme ___θim___
12. hymn ___hɪm___
13. knead ___nid___
14. pro ___pʰro___
15. guides ___gayd [gaydz]___
16. few ___fu [fyu]___
17. quake ___kʰek [kʰwek]___
18. tried ___črayd [tʰrayd]___
19. wrong ___raŋ [rɔŋ]___
20. rouge ___ruǰ [ruž]___
21. catch ___kæǰ [kʰaeč]___
22. barks ___barks___
23. brains ___brenz___
24. George ___ǰorǰ___
25. heart ___hart___
26. heard ___hərd___
27. aisle ___ayl___
28. used ___usd [yuzd]___
29. leased ___list___
30. teased ___tizd___
31. cause ___kʰaz [kʰɔz]___
32. strengths ___scɛŋkθs [strɛŋkθs]___
33. vague ___veg___
34. chance ___čæns___
35. choir ___kʰayr [kʰwayr]___
36. chef ___čɛf [šɛf]___
37. housed ___hawzd___
38. laughed ___læft___
39. screeched ___skričd [skričt]___
40. shopped ___šapt___
41. oiled ___ɔyləd [ɔyləd]___
42. clicked ___kʰlɪkt___
43. Ives ___ayvs [ayvz]___
44. eaves ___ivs [ivz]___
45. fixed ___fɪkst___
46. wished ___wɪšt___
47. schemed ___skʰimd [skimd]___
48. Schwinn ___šwɪn___
49. height ___hayt___
50. eighth ___eθ [etθ]___
51. sleigh ___sle___
52. heir ___ar [er]___
53. Leigh ___li___
54. isle ___ayl___
55. Fritz ___frɪɖz [frɪts]___
56. struck ___scrʌk [strʌk]___
57. warmth ___warmθ [wɔrmθ]___
58. pure ___pʰɔr [pʰyur]___
59. psalm ___səm [sam]___
60. drunk ___ǰrʌŋk [drʌŋk]___

Name _____   **Section** _____   **Date** _____

1.07   TRANSCRIPTION—WRITING PRACTICE 2

Pronounce these words aloud, and transcribe your pronunciation phonetically:

1. mosquitoes _____

2. suitcases _____

3. jubilantly _____

4. bicycled _____

5. fanatical _____

6. possession _____

7. opinionated _____

8. accented _____

9. characteristics _____

10. potpourris _____

11. psychological _____

12. pneumonia _____

13. machinations _____

14. calming _____

15. introductions _____

16. thistle _____

17. requirements _____

18. persuasive _____

19. immeasurable _____

20. breathed _____

Name _____   **Section** _____   **Date** _____

1.08   TRANSCRIPTION—WRITING PRACTICE 3

American English contains a number of written forms that can each be pronounced in more than one way. Sometimes the different pronunciations reflect different regional or social dialects (*aunt:* [ænt], [ɑnt]; *root:* [rut], [rʊt]). Less often, the different pronunciations are simply in free variation (*either:* [iðər], [ayðər]; *economics:* [ɛkənɑmɪks], [ikənɑmɪks]). This exercise is concerned with a third category: written forms whose different pronunciations reflect differences in meaning and/or function.

For each of the English spellings below, give two different phonetic transcriptions representing the different possible pronunciations. For each transcription, give an example of a sentence using the word pronounced in that way. For words of more than one syllable, indicate stress. In some cases, the two pronunciations will represent completely unrelated words; most often, however, you will find that the different pronunciations reflect grammatical differences among related items (noun/verb differences, for example). In two cases, you will have to capitalize the word to find the other pronunciation!

      EXAMPLE: protests
                 a.   [prótɛsts]   The station received a number of protests from irate viewers after airing a condom commercial.
                 b.   [prətésts]   I'd say she protests just a little too much.

1. read

    a. _____   _____

    b. _____   _____

2. record

    a. _____   _____

    b. _____   _____

3. present

    a. _____   _____

    b. _____   _____

4. live

    a. _____   _____

    b. _____   _____

5. dove

    a. _____   _____

    b. _____   _____

6. conduct

   a. _____   _____

   b. _____   _____

7. bow

   a. _____   _____

   b. _____   _____

8. address

   a. _____   _____

   b. _____   _____

9. house

   a. _____   _____

   b. _____   _____

10. perfect

   a. _____   _____

   b. _____   _____

11. minute

   a. _____   _____

   b. _____   _____

12. polish

   a. _____   _____

   b. _____   _____

13. refuse

   a. _____   _____

   b. _____   _____

14. progress

   a. _____   _____

   b. _____   _____

Name _____   **Section** _____   **Date** _____

15. resume

    a. _____   _____

    b. _____   _____

16. affect

    a. _____   _____

    b. _____   _____

17. rebel

    a. _____   _____

    b. _____   _____

18. content

    a. _____   _____

    b. _____   _____

19. estimate

    a. _____   _____

    b. _____   _____

20. job

    a. _____   _____

    b. _____   _____

Name _____   **Section** _____   **Date** _____

1.09   TRANSCRIPTION—WRITING PRACTICE 4

Write in phonetic transcription:

1. She said you laid the plaid tie on the couch.

   _____

   _____

2. I'm not in a good mood, for it's no great treat to sweat blood.

   _____

   _____

3. If the bough breaks, the cradle will fall through the roof ...

   _____

   _____

4. ... but the tough little kid with asthma, although coughing, will be OK.

   _____

   _____

Name _____   **Section** _____   **Date** _____

1.10   CLASSIFICATION PRACTICE 1

A. In each case, circle the sound that doesn't fit the description.

EXAMPLE: Consonants: ž   h   (æ)   ŋ

1. Voiced stops: g   b   (z)   d
2. Affricates: (z)   č   ǰ
3. Back vowels: u   e   (o)
4. Tense front vowels: i   (e)   ɪ
5. Voiceless sounds: (m)   s   θ   h
6. Fricatives: s   ž   ð   (ǰ)
7. Nasals: m   (l)   ŋ   ñ
8. High vowels: (o)   i   u   ü
9. Round vowels: o   (i)   u   ü
10. Liquids: r   l   (y)
11. Velars: x   ŋ   (d)   g
12. Voiced labials: (m)   b   f

B. Circle the sound that doesn't belong, and name the category.

EXAMPLE: t   p   (s)   k   ___Voiceless stops___

1.   i   æ   (s)   u   _____
2.   (pʰ) n   m   w   Voiced
3.   ǰ   š   s   ž   _____
4.   a   ɔ   u   æ   _____
5.   b   g   k   d   _____
6.   f   s   (z)   š   voiceless fricative
7.   tʰ   pʰ   t   d   _____
8.   i   æ   ü   u   _____
9.   β   ð   ɸ   ɣ   _____
10.   e   (ɔ)   ɛ   ɪ   high voiced

Name _____   **Section** _____   **Date** _____

1.11   CLASSIFICATION PRACTICE 2

Give a brief phonetic description of each of the consonant sounds listed below. Then give examples, in both standard orthography and phonetic transcription, of English words that contain the sound in *initial*, *intervocalic* (i.e. between vowels) and *final* position. If there are no examples of the sound in a certain position, indicate this with a dash.

EXAMPLE:

		Initial	Intervocalic	Final
š	voiceless palato-alveolar fricative	chevron [ševrən]	nation [nešən]	rush [rʌš]

		Initial	Intervocalic	Final
b	voiced - bilabial stop	boy [bɔj]	stubble [stʌbl]	tub [tʌb]
s	voiceless - alveolar fricative	sit [sɪt]	tested tested	hiss hɪs
h	voiceless - glottal glide	has [hæs]	_____	_____
r	voiced - alveolar approximants	ride [rayd]	party [parti]	roar [ror]
z	voiced - alveolar fricative	zap [zæp]	jazzy [jæzi]	raise [rez]
θ	voiceless - interdental fricative	thrifty [θrɪfti]	_____	path [pæθ]
n	nasal - alveolar	nine [nayn]	cannot [kænɑt]	fin [fɪn]
v	voiced - labiodental fricative	vener [vɛnɛr]	heavy [hɛvi]	have [hæv]

		Initial	Intervocalic	Final
ŋ	nasal - palatal - velar	—	singing [sŋŋ]	song [sɔŋ]
ð	voiced - interdental fricative	thank [ðænk]	feather [fɛðər]	
y	voiced - palatal approximants	you [yu]		happy [hæpi]
kʰ	voiceless - aspirated velar - stop	cover [kʰəvər]	(?) mechanic [mɛkʰænɪk]	

Name _____   **Section** _____   **Date** _____

1.12   CLASSIFICATION PRACTICE 3

A.   The same consonant chart is reproduced several times below, each time with a different group of segments highlighted. In each case, give the term that identifies and defines the group of segments in the grey area.

EXAMPLE:

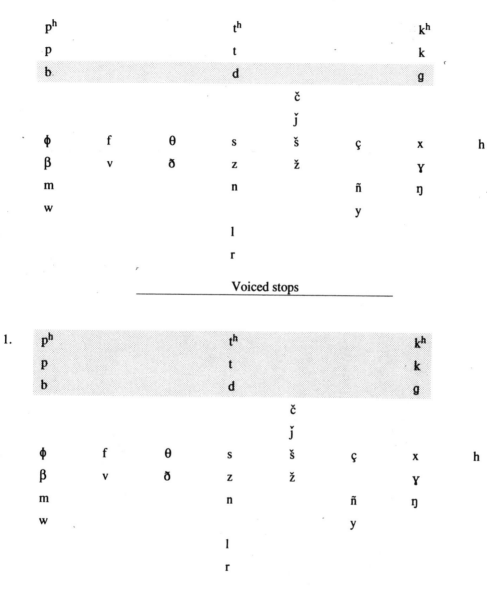

1.

2.

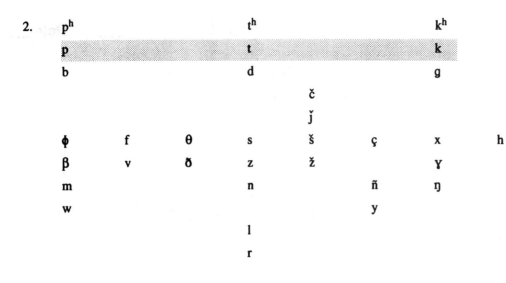

pʰ				tʰ			kʰ	
p				t			k	
b				d			g	
					č			
					ǰ			
ɸ	f	θ	s		š	ç	x	h
β	v	ð	z		ž		ɣ	
m			n			ñ	ŋ	
w						y		
			l					
			r					

_____

3.

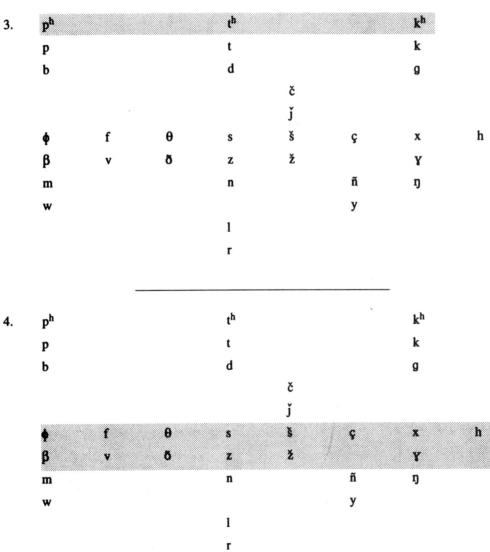

pʰ				tʰ			kʰ	
p				t			k	
b				d			g	
					č			
					ǰ			
ɸ	f	θ	s		š	ç	x	h
β	v	ð	z		ž		ɣ	
m			n			ñ	ŋ	
w						y		
			l					
			r					

_____

4.

pʰ				tʰ			kʰ	
p				t			k	
b				d			g	
					č			
					ǰ			
ɸ	f	θ	s		š	ç	x	h
β	v	ð	z		ž		ɣ	
m			n			ñ	ŋ	
w						y		
			l					
			r					

_____

Name _____   **Section** _____   **Date** _____

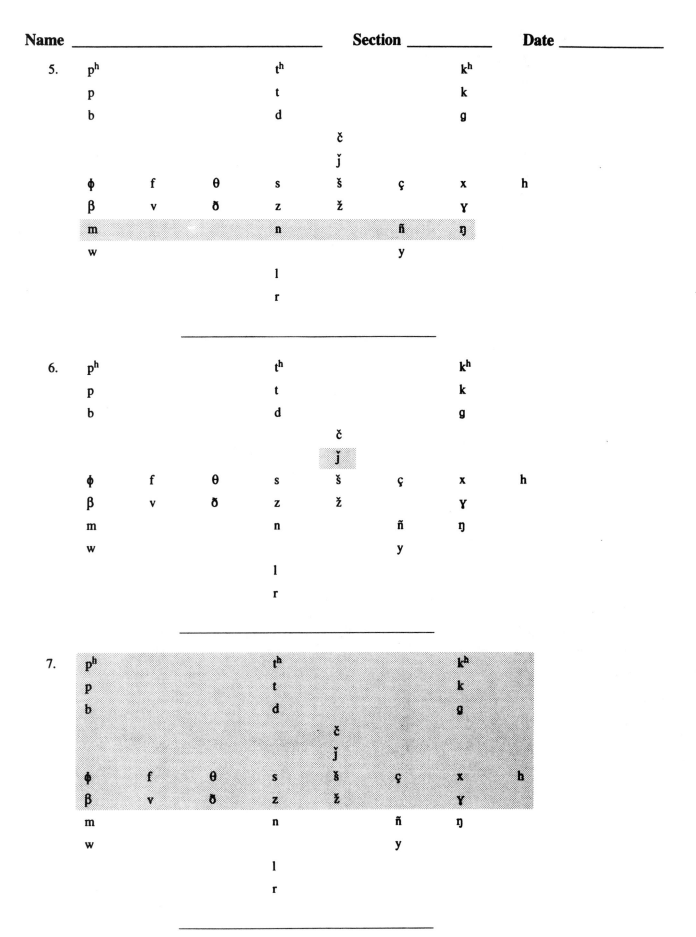

5.

pʰ				tʰ			kʰ	
p				t			k	
b				d			g	
					č			
					ǰ			
φ	f	θ	s	š		ç	x	h
β	v	ð	z	ž			ɣ	
m				n		ñ	ŋ	
w						y		
				l				
				r				

_____

6.

pʰ				tʰ			kʰ	
p				t			k	
b				d			g	
					č			
					ǰ			
φ	f	θ	s	š		ç	x	h
β	v	ð	z	ž			ɣ	
m				n		ñ	ŋ	
w						y		
				l				
				r				

_____

7.

pʰ				tʰ			kʰ	
p				t			k	
b				d			g	
					č			
					ǰ			
φ	f	θ	s	š		ç	x	h
β	v	ð	z	ž			ɣ	
m				n		ñ	ŋ	
w						y		
				l				
				r				

_____

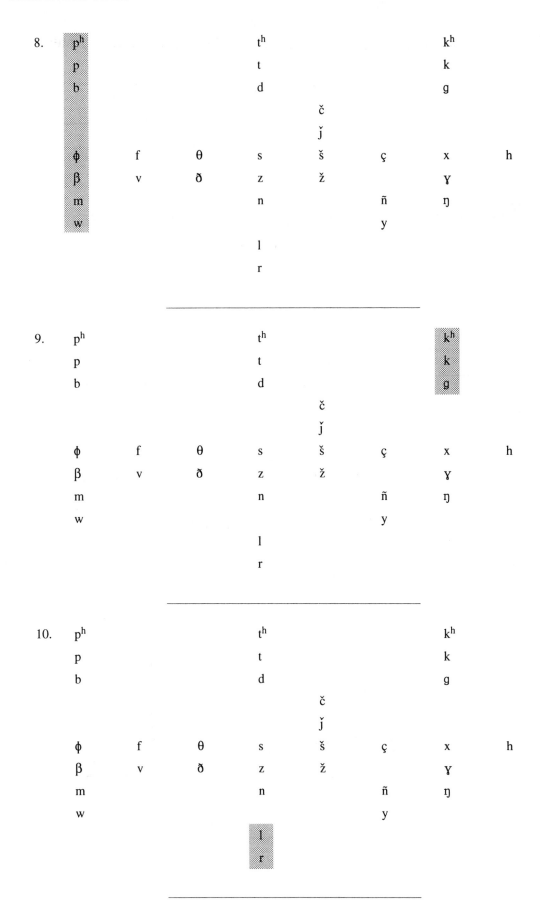

8. pʰ   tʰ   kʰ
    p   t   k
    b   d   g
                                        č
                                        ǰ
    ɸ   f   θ   s   š   ç   x   h
    β   v   ð   z   ž   ɣ
    m   n   ñ   ŋ
    w   y
                  l
                  r

_____

9. pʰ   tʰ   kʰ
    p   t   k
    b   d   g
                                        č
                                        ǰ
    ɸ   f   θ   s   š   ç   x   h
    β   v   ð   z   ž   ɣ
    m   n   ñ   ŋ
    w   y
                  l
                  r

_____

10. pʰ   tʰ   kʰ
    p   t   k
    b   d   g
                                        č
                                        ǰ
    ɸ   f   θ   s   š   ç   x   h
    β   v   ð   z   ž   ɣ
    m   n   ñ   ŋ
    w   y
                  l
                  r

_____

Name _____ **Section** _____ **Date** _____

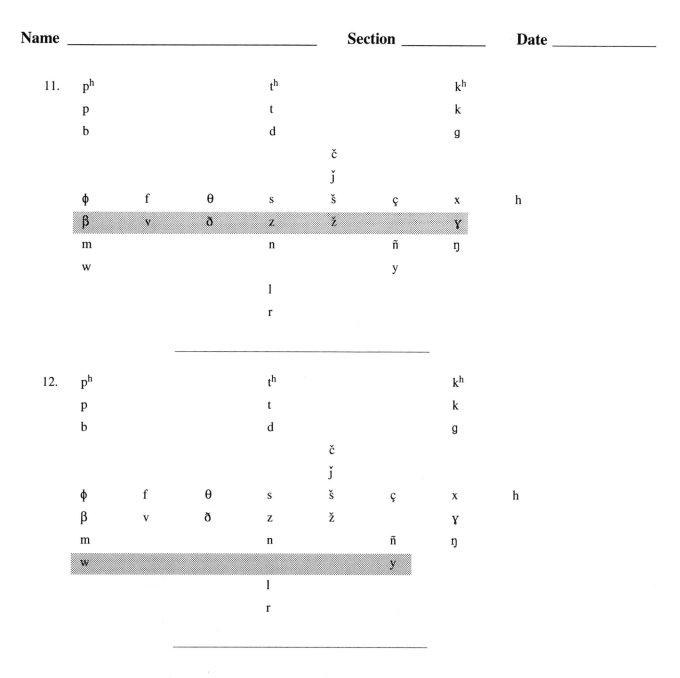

11.

pʰ				tʰ			kʰ	
p				t			k	
b				d			g	
					č			
					ǰ			
ɸ	f	θ	s	š	ç	x	h
β	v	ð	z	ž		ɣ	
m			n		ñ	ŋ	
w					y		
			l				
			r				

_____

12.

pʰ				tʰ			kʰ	
p				t			k	
b				d			g	
					č			
					ǰ			
ɸ	f	θ	s	š	ç	x	h
β	v	ð	z	ž		ɣ	
m			n		ñ	ŋ	
w					y		
			l				
			r				

_____

B. Now do the same for the following vowel classes:

1.

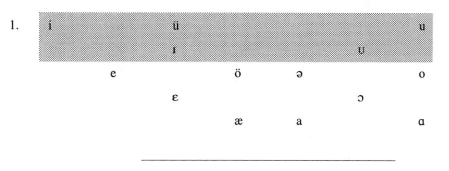

i		ü			u
ı			ʊ		
e	ö	ə		o	
ε			ɔ		
æ	a		ɑ		

_____

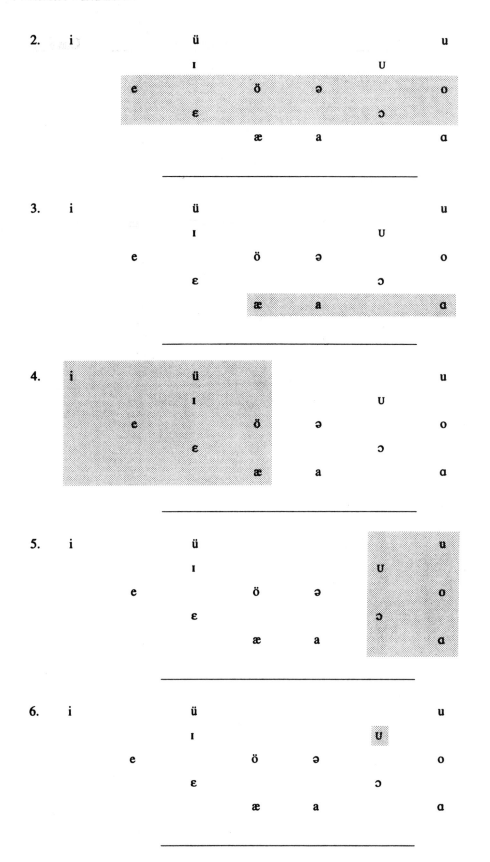

Name _____ **Section** _____ **Date** _____

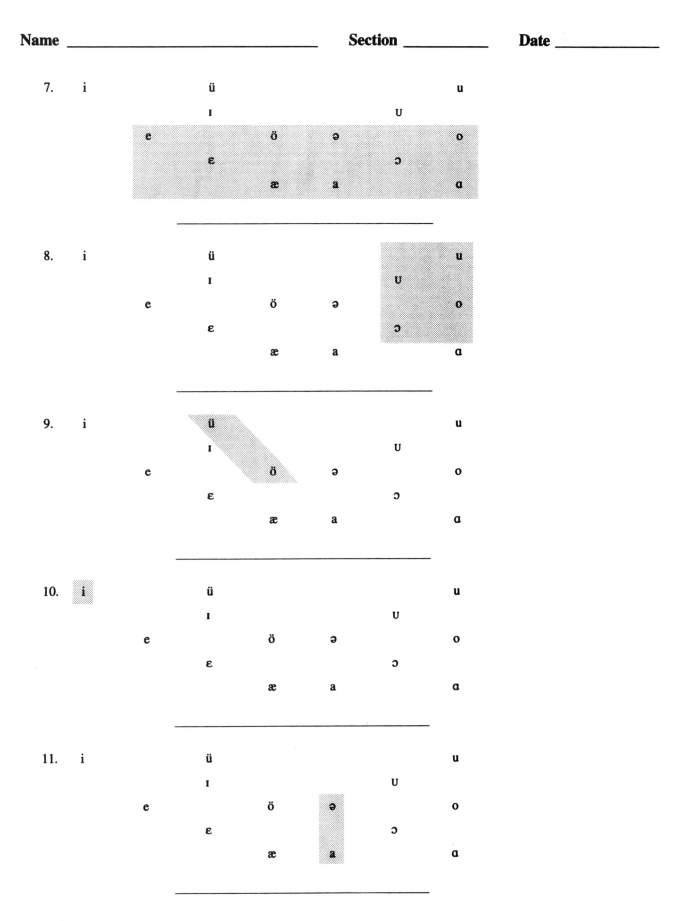

7. i   ü   u

     ɪ   ʊ

   e   ö   ə   o

     ɛ   ɔ

     æ   a   ɑ

_____

8. i   ü   u

     ɪ   ʊ

   e   ö   ə   o

     ɛ   ɔ

     æ   a   ɑ

_____

9. i   ü   u

     ɪ   ʊ

   e   ö   ə   o

     ɛ   ɔ

     æ   a   ɑ

_____

10. i   ü   u

     ɪ   ʊ

   e   ö   ə   o

     ɛ   ɔ

     æ   a   ɑ

_____

11. i   ü   u

     ɪ   ʊ

   e   ö   ə   o

     ɛ   ɔ

     æ   a   ɑ

_____

12.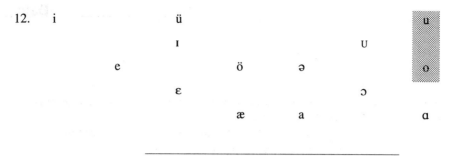

Name _____   **Section** _____   **Date** _____

1.13   EASE OF ARTICULATION EXPERIMENT

A.   Below you will find five sets of nonsense words. Pronounce each set several times at normal conversational speed, noting how each word "feels" in your mouth.

You may find that one word in each set, compared to the other two, seems easier for the vocal apparatus to articulate. Circle whichever words below seem "easier" to you in this sense.

	A	B	C
Set 1:	[wambi]	[wanbi]	[waŋbi]
Set 2:	[plimd]	[plind]	[pliŋd]
Set 3:	[ɛmko]	[ɛŋko]	[ɛnko]
Set 4:	[aŋgosi]	[angosi]	[amgosi]
Set 5:	[sunpi]	[suŋpi]	[sumpi]

B.   Many people find that the "easier" words are 1A, 2B, 3B, 4A and 5C. What is it about the relationship between the nasal and the following stop in these words that makes them easier to articulate than the others?

_____

_____

_____

_____

_____

Name _____   **Section** _____   **Date** _____

1.14   HAWAIIAN CONSONANT AND VOWEL INVENTORY

The Hawaiian language has an unusually small inventory of distinct sounds. You will be able to discover all but one of these by analyzing the Hawaiian words you know. (For most people, these will largely be place names.)

For the purposes of this exercise, you may regard the usual spelling of Hawaiian words as equivalent to a phonetic transcription.

Note: The sound referred to above that is usually not indicated in the spelling is the glottal stop, [?]. This is sometimes notated with a single open quotation mark in the orthography. (You may have noticed such spellings as *Hawai'i* and *Pepe'ekeo*.)

A. Referring to a map or atlas if necessary, list all the sounds of Hawaiian, with an example to justify each one.

_____

_____

_____

_____

_____

_____

_____

B. Now answer these questions:

   1. How many consonants does Hawaiian have?

     _____

   2. How many vowels?

     _____

   3. List the Hawaiian nasals.

     _____

     _____

   4. List the voiceless stops in Hawaiian.

     _____

     _____

5. Stops, affricates and fricatives together are known as *obstruents.* How many voiced obstruents does Hawaiian have?

_____

6. How many fricatives?

_____

7. What are the front vowels in Hawaiian?

_____

8. In contrast, how many consonants and vowels does English have?

_____

_____

Name _____   **Section** _____   **Date** _____

1.15   WICHITA CONSONANT AND VOWEL INVENTORY

Wichita is an American Indian language in the Caddoan family, originally spoken in parts of Texas, Oklahoma and Kansas. Among the world's languages, its inventory of distinctive sounds is quite unusual. (Data adapted from Rood 1975.)

A. The following twelve Wichita words contain all the consonants and vowels found in the language. Enter these consonants and vowels in the appropriate places on the standard charts below—this will give you a graphic picture of the Wichita inventory of distinctive sounds. (*Note:* [ts͡] represents an affricate similar to the *ts* sequence in the English word *cats*. [kʷ] is a labialized voiceless velar stop. [a] is a low central vowel. [:] indicates a long, and [::] an extra-long, vowel. An accent over a vowel indicates one of two distinctive pitches, the other being unmarked.)

1. khat͡s   'white'
2. ksa:rʔa   'bed'
3. ha:t͡sariyarit͡s 'saw'
4. kʔíta:ks   'coyote'
5. thárah   'close'
6. kʷha:t͡s   'red'
7. t͡she:t͡sʔa   'dawn'
8. rhiʔirt͡skha:rʔa 'trousers'
9. kskha:rʔa   'hip joint'
10. t͡skha:rʔa   'night'
11. wa:khat͡siye:s 'calf'
12. isse::wa   'you better go'

Consonants

	labials	alveolars	palatals	velars	glottals
stops:					
affricates:					
fricatives:					
nasals:					
approximants:					

Vowels (Just fill in the basic vowels—disregard length and pitch distinctions.)

	Front	Central	Back
High:			
Mid:			
Low:			

B. Examine the consonant chart you've constructed, and then explain what is so unusual about Wichita's consonant inventory. Your answer should refer to *classes* of sounds, not just to individual segments.

_____

_____

_____

_____

C. Repeat question B for the Wichita vowels: explain what makes this set of vowels highly unusual. As before, you should refer to classes of sounds.

_____

_____

_____

_____

D. As you have seen, Wichita vowels each come in three different degrees of length—short, long, and extra-long—and two different pitch values. Taking length and pitch distinctions into account, how many different CV syllables (syllables consisting of consonants + vowel) can there be in this language? Explain.

_____

_____

_____

_____

_____

_____

Name _____   **Section** _____   **Date** _____

1.16   SOUND SYMBOLISM IN LAKOTA

Lakota belongs to the Western branch of the Siouan family of Native American languages. Today, it is the most widely spoken language in the Siouan group, with several thousand native speakers, including the Oglala Sioux, who reside mainly in South Dakota west of the Missouri River (Murray 1989). You can hear the language spoken in the film *Dances With Wolves*.

In this exercise you will investigate a very interesting kind of iconicity called *sound symbolism* in Lakota. In certain sets of related vocabulary items, the meaning differences represent different points on an increasing scale of intensity, like the English terms *big* and *huge*, or *damp*, *wet* and *soaked*. Unlike English, however, Lakota mirrors these semantic differences in the sounds of the terms themselves through a definite and consistent progression of sound changes.

The data below are given in phonetic transcription. A small raised vowel represents a very short, unstressed vowel that breaks up a consonant cluster by "pre-echoing" the vowel in the following syllable. The mark ˜ above a vowel indicates nasalization. An apostrophe denotes a *glottalized* consonant, produced when air is set in motion by raising the larynx with the glottis closed; a distinct break is heard between such a consonant and the following vowel. Certain required prefixes in the data have been omitted. (Data adapted from Boas and Deloria 1941.)

A.   Examine the sets of Lakota words and glosses below. *Based entirely on the meanings of the words within each set*, rewrite the words in order of "intensity," going from the least to the most intense. (The exact nature of "intensity" will vary from set to set.) In certain cases the words are already in the required order; in other cases you will have to rearrange them.

1.   a.   paža   'it has a thick-skinned blister'

    b.   paza   'it has a thin-skinned blister'

    IN ORDER OF INTENSITY: _____, _____

2.   a.   ptuɣa   'small pieces are cracked off so they fall off'

    b.   ptuza   'it is bent forward'

    c.   ptuža   'small pieces are cracked but not broken off'

    IN ORDER OF INTENSITY: _____, _____, _____

3.   a.   pʰãža   'it is porous and soft'

    b.   pʰãɣa   'it is porous and hard'

    IN ORDER OF INTENSITY: _____, _____

4.   a.   mᶦniɣa   'it is shrunk permanently'

    b.   mᶦniža   'it is curled, contracted or wrinkled but can be smoothed again'

    IN ORDER OF INTENSITY: _____, _____

5.   a.   mᵘnuza   'it gives a crunching sound (said of something easily broken)'

    b.   mᵘnuɣa   'it gives a crunching sound (said of something hard)'

    c.   mᵘnuža   'it gives a crunching sound (said of something of moderate resistance)'

    IN ORDER OF INTENSITY: _____, _____, _____

6. a. šuža   'it is badly bruised'

    b. suza   'it has a slight bruise'

    c. xuɣa   'it is fractured'

    IN ORDER OF INTENSITY: _____, _____, _____

7. a. pʰexniɣa   'it is red hot, quivering with heat'

    b. pʰešniža   'sparks'

    IN ORDER OF INTENSITY: _____, _____

8. a. žata   'it forks into two parts'

    b. ɣata   'it is branching with many angles'

    IN ORDER OF INTENSITY: _____, _____

9. a. izuza   'a smooth whetstone'

    b. iɣuɣa   'rough sandstone'

    IN ORDER OF INTENSITY: _____, _____

10. a. nuɣa   'it is hard and immovable (e.g., gnarl on a tree)'

    b. nuža   'it is semi-hard and movable (e.g., cartilage)'

    c. nuza   'it is soft and movable (e.g., an enlarged gland under the skin)'

    IN ORDER OF INTENSITY: _____, _____, _____

11. a. gᵉleɣa   'striped with wide, strongly contrasting colors'

    b. gᵉleza   'striped with narrow, indistinct lines'

    IN ORDER OF INTENSITY: _____, _____

12. a. kīza   'a single high-pitched tone sounds'

    b. kīža   'several high-pitched tones sound and blend together'

    IN ORDER OF INTENSITY: _____, _____

13. a. k'eɣa   'it is in a scraped condition'

    b. k'eza   'it is in a scratched condition'

    IN ORDER OF INTENSITY: _____, _____

14. a. šli   'semi-liquid matter is being squeezed out'

    b. xli   'it is muddy material'

    c. sli   'a thin liquid (e.g., water) is being squeezed out'

    IN ORDER OF INTENSITY: _____, _____, _____

Name _____   **Section** _____   **Date** _____

15. a. zi   'it is yellow'

  b. ži   'it is tawny'

  c. ɣi   'it is brown'

IN ORDER OF INTENSITY: _____, _____, _____

B. Now compare the words in each intensity-ordered list that you have determined. You should discover that the sounds which change from word to word are always in a definite and consistent order, correlating with the changes from lower to higher intensity in the meanings.

  1. There are two such series of sounds in the data. List both series in order, giving a brief but clear phonetic description of each sound you list.

		Lower I	N	T	E	N	S	I	T	Y	Higher
Series	*Sound:*	_____			_____						_____
I.	*Description:*	_____			_____						_____
		_____			_____						_____
		_____			_____						_____
Series	*Sound:*	_____			_____						_____
II.	*Description:*	_____			_____						_____
		_____			_____						_____
		_____			_____						_____

  2. What is the relationship between Series I and Series II?

_____

_____

  3. Explain how increases in the intensity scale are mirrored in the articulation of these sounds. In other words, how are changes in the meanings of the given words correlated with what's going on in your mouth as you say them?

_____

_____

_____

_____

_____

_____

Name _____   **Section** _____   **Date** _____

1.17   BIBLICAL HEBREW CONSONANT INVENTORY

The following is a phonetic transcription of an Old Testament passage in its original language, Biblical Hebrew (BH). This is the familiar section of *Ecclesiastes* (3:1-8) that begins, "To every thing there is a season..." The first five verses are given below.

Your task is to determine the consonant sounds that occur in BH. Although the passage is brief, all but two of the consonants of BH can be found in it.

You should already be acquainted with most of the notation used in this phonetic transcription. For the symbols that may be new to you, see Appendix B.

Ecclesiastes 3:1-5

1	lakkol zᵊma:n	wᵊ ʕeθ lᵊxɔl ħeɸɛṣ taħaθ haš ša:ma:yim
2	ʕeθ la:lɛðɛθ	wᵊʕeθ la:mu:θ
	ʕeθ la:ṭaʕaθ	wᵊʕeθ laʕᵃqo:r na:ṭu:ᵃʕ
3	ʕeθ lahᵃro:ɣ	wᵊʕeθ lirpo:
	ʕeθ liɸro:ṣ	wᵊʕeθ liβno:θ
4	ʕeθ liβko:θ	wᵊʕeθ liśho:q
	ʕeθ sᵊɸo:ð	wᵊʕeθ rᵊqo:ð
5	ʕeθ lᵊhašli:x ʔᵃβa:ni:m	wᵊʕeθ kᵊno:s ʔᵃβa:ni:m
	ʕeθ laħᵃβoq	wᵊʕeθ lirħoq meħabbeq

A. Enter the BH consonants in their appropriate places on the following consonant chart. The two consonants not found in the data have been entered for you.

	Bilabial	Labio-dental	Inter-dental	Alveolar	Palato-alveolar	Palatal	Velar	Uvular	Pharyngeal	Glottal
Stops voiceless										
voiced				d			g			
Nasals										
Fricatives voiceless										
voiced										
Affricates voiceless										
voiced										
Approximants voiced central										
voiced lateral										

B.   1.   How many phonetic consonants are there in BH?

_____

2.   What BH consonants are not found in English?

_____

_____

3.   What English consonants are not found in BH?

_____

_____

4.   *(Optional)*

Notice that in this corpus, the "common" stops [p], [t], [k], [b], [d], [g] seem to occur relatively rarely. Four of them occur only once each (counting [bb] as one occurrence) and two do not occur at all. Assuming the corpus is representative of the language as a whole, speculate on why this might be so.

_____

_____

_____

_____

C.   Over the millennia, the Hebrew sound system has changed considerably. The following is a transcription of the same passage in modern Israeli Hebrew (IH) pronunciation. Compare this with BH, and make a list of the consonant changes you find. (Example: BH [q] → IH [k].) Try to come up with generalizations whenever possible.

1	lakɔl zᵊman	vᵊʔɛt lᵊxɔl xɛfɛt͡s taxat hašamayim
2	ʔɛt lalɛdɛt	vᵊʔɛt lamut
	ʔɛt lataʔat	vᵊʔɛt laʔakɔR natua
3	ʔɛt lahaRɔg	vᵊʔɛt liRpɔ
	ʔɛt lifRɔt͡s	vᵊʔɛt livnɔt
4	ʔɛt livkɔt	vᵊʔɛt lisxɔk
	ʔɛt sᵊfɔd	vᵊʔɛt Rᵊkɔd
5	ʔɛt lᵊhašlix ʔavanim	vᵊʔɛt kᵊnɔs ʔavanim
	ʔɛt laxavɔk	vᵊʔɛt liRxɔk mɛxabɛk

Note: [t͡s] is a voiceless affricate similar in sound to [ts] in *cats.*
[R] is a uvular approximant similar to "Parisian r."

Name _____   **Section** _____   **Date** _____

_____

_____

_____

_____

_____

_____

_____

_____

_____

_____

_____

_____

_____

_____

_____

_____

_____

_____

_____

_____

_____

_____

_____

_____

_____

_____

_____

_____

Name _____   **Section** _____   **Date** _____

1.18   COMMUNICATING ABOUT PRONUNCIATION

Part of the value of phonetic transcription and related linguistic terminology lies in the fact that these tools help make communication about pronunciation precise, concise and unambiguous.

One place where pronunciation is almost always discussed is at the beginning of language textbooks, phrasebooks and dictionaries. The authors of such works are faced with a dilemma: they need to explain certain matters of pronunciation, but direct demonstration is not a possibility. This is a place where linguistic terminology could make a big difference. In most cases, however, the target audience can't be expected to have a background in linguistics, and terms like "voiced velar fricative" will be mysterious to most readers. Given this predicament, writers have come up with various alternative methods for describing sounds, some more successful than others. In this exercise, you'll see and comment on some of the problems inherent in these alternative descriptions.

A.   Consider the following quotations, all taken from published materials, in which the words "hard" and "soft" are used to explain certain sounds.

1.   From a Welsh textbook:

"c /k/ Always the 'hard' sound of c in 'cap,' never as in 'ace.'"

2.   From a French phrasebook:

"[The sound represented in our transcription as *zh* is] always soft as the *s* in *pleasure.*"

3.   From a Malay textbook:

"The combination 'ng' represents a single sound, the sound of 'ng' in English 'singer,' (NOT hard, as in 'finger')..."

4.   From an Italian-English dictionary:

"*s* when it begins a word and is followed by a vowel or an unvoiced consonant sounds hard as in *essence...*"

5.   From a Turkish-English dictionary:

"*k* with soft vowels is frontal like the *k* in *kill*; with hard vowels it is backward like the *c* and *ck* in *cuckoo* or the two *c*'s in *cocoa...*"

6.   From a Welsh textbook:

"dd /ð/ Used to represent the softer *th* sound as in English 'brea*the*' and '*the*.'"

7.   From an Indonesian textbook:

"The final *h* is soft, but audibly aspirated: *mudah, kalah, bawah* (cf. *muda, kala, bawa*)"

8.   From a Persian textbook:

"d,t—rather softer than in English"

9.   From a Greek phrasebook:

"... this letter, gamma, has two sounds: before a, o, oo, ai, oi it is a guttural 'g' made at the back of the throat. It may be learnt by pronouncing English hard 'g,' as in 'got,' and gradually relaxing the vocal cords; it is a sound which may be held, unlike 'g,' which is momentary."

10. From the tapes for a course in Welsh:

    "*s* is a hard sound, never a *z*."

11. From a Swahili textbook:

    "G is always hard like the *g* in *got*; for the soft *g* in *gin, j* is used."

12. From a Spanish-English dictionary:

    "Between two vowels and when followed by *l* or *r*, [Spanish *b*] has a softer sound, almost like the English *v* but formed by pressing the lips together..."

a. For each example above, list the sounds that the author considers hard and soft. If only one sound is mentioned, take an educated guess as to the other member of the opposition—or put a question mark to indicate that you can't identify the opposing sound.

Example	Hard	Soft
1.	_____	_____
2.	_____	_____
3.	_____	_____
4.	_____	_____
5.	_____	_____
6.	_____	_____
7.	_____	_____
8.	_____	_____
9.	_____	_____
10.	_____	_____
11.	_____	_____
12.	_____	_____

b. Examine the chart you've created, and determine if there is any consistency in the way these authors have used the terms "hard" and "soft." If you find generalizations that hold true for some or all of the examples, state them. Comment on how useful these terms are in identifying sounds.

_____

_____

_____

_____

_____

Name _____   **Section** _____   **Date** _____

B. Sometimes authors compare the sounds they are describing with sounds in particular varieties of English, or in other foreign languages. For each of the examples below, comment on how useful you find the comparison.

13.   From a Portuguese phrasebook:

"*o* is pronounced as in f*oo*d when unstressed, otherwise either as in r*o*ck or as in Scottish l*o*w, usually depending upon the next sound"

_____

_____

_____

14.   From a Dutch phrasebook:

"*g* is pronounced gutturally something like *h* in *hue* (with a little exaggeration)"

_____

_____

_____

15.   From a Maori textbook:

"*Wh.*—Say the English word *what*, then say it without the *t* at the end, and you will have as near as possible the correct sound of *wh*, e.g.:—

Wha-ka-ta-ne   Wha-ka-ki"

_____

_____

_____

16.   From an Icelandic phrasebook:

"*a*—like the same letter in the north of England."

_____

_____

_____

17.   From a Latin-English dictionary:

"*y* is a Greek sound and is pronounced (both short and long) as *u* in French."

_____

_____

_____

18. From a Spanish textbook:

"[Spanish *r*:] Slightly trilled by vibrating the tongue slightly against the hard palate. Like *r* in the English *very*."

(*Note:* Chances are that the *r* in your pronunciation of *very* is not at all what the author has in mind!)

_____

_____

_____

C. For this last group of examples, comment on how effective the description is in offering the reader a clear understanding of the sound being described.

19. From a Yiddish textbook:

"[The letter *samekh*] has the sound of S."

_____

_____

_____

20. From an Indonesian phrasebook:

"*ng* may occur at the beginning, as well as the middle and end of a word. *ng* is always pronounced like the *ng* in si*ng*, never as in fi*ng*er. The sound which comes in the middle of fi*ng*er is spelled and transcribed *ngg*..."

_____

_____

_____

21. From an Indonesian textbook:

"*k* at the beginning of a syllable sounds like English *k* in 'king,' but is pronounced without an 'explosion.'"

_____

_____

_____

22. From a Swahili textbook:

"E is like the *a* in *say*, without the final sound we give it in English by slightly closing the mouth."

_____

_____

_____

Name _____   **Section** _____   **Date** _____

23. From a Spanish textbook:

"[Spanish *g* is pronounced] as *g* in English before *a, o,* and *u* or a consonant, at the beginning of a word, and before *n* and *l*. In all other positions similar to *g* in *big*, but prolonged."

_____

_____

_____

24. From a German textbook:

"*ch* = no English sound. It is nearest to English *k*, which, however, cannot be made into a continuous sound, but comes to an abrupt stop. German *ch*, on the other hand, is produced by contracting the air passages just enough to cause audible friction, but not enough to cause a stop as in *k*. German *ch* can be continued indefinitely as a sound."

_____

_____

_____

C H A P T E R

2

Phonology

2.01   APPLICATION OF A RULE (HYPOTHETICAL DATA)

[handwritten: consonants between vowels.]

A certain language has the following phonological rule: *[handwritten: (voice —all segments that occur into vo___ (between vowels) means between vowels)]*

Voice all segments that occur intervocalically (i.e., between two vowels).

Below are some underlying forms in the language. In each case, provide the form that results when this phonological rule is applied to the given underlying form. In some cases, the surface forms will differ from the underlying forms, and in other cases they will not.

[handwritten right margin: 1. voicing- voice voiceless consonants 2. place of articulation 3. manner of articulation stop stoples affricative]

EXAMPLE: Given underlying forms /bati/ and /zago/:

/bati/ →   [badi]
/zago/ →   [zago]   (no change)

[handwritten: change voiceless to vowels if it is between vowels.]

1. /safi/   →   _savi_   *voiceless to voiced*

2. /saǰi/   →   _same saǰi_

3. /suf/   →   _" suf_

4. /seləmupi/   →   _bi_

5. /strupto/   →   _"_

6. /vraaθinač/ →   _θ > ð_   *voiceless to voiced*

7. /išinumia/   →   _s > z_

8. /firsamili/ →   _≠_

9. /unikæk/   →   _k > g_   *≠ = no change*

10. /ʔayuwinsti/ →   _≠_

11. /pöritipüt/ →   _p > b_

12. /ʊspisədi/   →   _s > z_

Name _____   **Section** _____   **Date** _____

2.02   ARABIC [h] AND [ħ]

throat constriction (like Arabic)

Arabic has two "h"-like sounds, [h] and [ħ]. [h] is the familiar glottal fricative; [ħ] is a pharyngeal frica-tive pronounced with pharyngeal (throat) constriction. The following words very clearly indicate the status of these sounds in the language.

1.	ħuru:b	'wars'	2.	mahdu:d	'destroyed'
3.	tarħi:b	'intimidation'	4.	faħm	'coal'
5.	šabah	'similarity'	6.	maħdu:d	'limited'
7.	habba	'gust, squall'	8.	huru:b	'flight'
9.	šabaħ	'ghost'	10.	ħa:l	'condition'
11.	fahm	'understanding'	12.	tarhi:b	'greeting'
13.	ha:l	'cardamom (spice)'	14.	ħabba	'grain, seed'

A. Consider these 3 statements:

   I.   In Arabic, [h] and [ħ] contrast. *(create new words)*   *minimal pairs = phonemes*

   II.   In Arabic, [h] and [ħ] are in complementary distribution. *do not occur in the same position. They are allophones of /h/*

   III.   In Arabic, [h] and [ħ] are in free variation.

Which of these is correct? (Circle the letter of the correct answer.)

   a. None   b. I only   c. II only   d. III only

   e. I and II   f. I and III   g. II and III   h. I, II, and III

B. Are [h] and [ħ] allophones of the same phoneme in Arabic, or do they represent different phonemes? If the former, state the rule that describes the distribution of allophones. If the latter, justify your answer.

_____

_____

_____

_____

_____

_____

Name _____   **Section** _____   **Date** _____

2.03   TOKYO JAPANESE

Examine the following Japanese words, transcribed phonetically as they are pronounced by some speakers in Tokyo:

1. gakkoo   'school'
2. giri   'obligation'
3. ginza   'Ginza (well-known street)'
4. geta   'wooden clogs'
5. naŋai   'long'
6. amaŋu   'raincoat'
7. daiŋaku   'university'
8. miɲi   'the right side'

A. State the distribution of the sounds [g] and [ŋ]. Does this constitute complementary distribution?

_____

_____

_____

B. What can you say about the phonemic status of [g] and [ŋ] in the Tokyo dialect?

_____

_____

_____

C. Choose an underlying form for each word given above, and provide a rule that will generate all the correct surface forms. If you find there is more than one way of doing this, give the alternative analyses as well.

_____

_____

_____

_____

_____

_____

_____

_____

_____

_____

_____

_____

_____

D. *(Optional)* Here are the same words as they are pronounced by some other Japanese speakers. Compare the two different pronunciations. How does this additional information help you decide which of the alternative analyses you came up with in part C is preferable?

1. gakkoo   'school'
2. giri   'obligation'
3. ginza   'Ginza (well-known street)'
4. geta   'wooden clogs'
5. nagai   'long'
6. amagu   'raincoat'
7. daigaku   'university'
8. migi   'the right side'

_____

_____

_____

_____

_____

_____

Name _____   **Section** _____   **Date** _____

2.04   HINDI [b] AND [bʰ]

Hindi, along with some other languages of the Indian subcontinent, contains a number of *voiced aspirated* sounds, which are much rarer among the world's languages than their unaspirated counterparts. This exercise focuses on Hindi's two voiced bilabial stops, [b] and [bʰ]. The data below will allow you to determine whether these two sounds represent different phonemes in Hindi, or are allophones of the same phoneme.

Examine the data, and then answer the questions that follow. The transcription is phonetic; the tilde mark ˜ over a vowel represents nasalization.

1.	bʰut	'ghost'	2.	bʰi	'also'
3.	bič	'middle'	4.	ǰibʰ	'tongue'
5.	gəmbʰir	'serious'	6.	ʊbalna	'to boil'
7.	bar	'occasion'	8.	abʰari	'grateful'
9.	bʰãǰi	'sister's brother'	10.	bʊzʊrg	'elderly'
11.	ǰəvab	'answer'	12.	dobara	'again'
13.	səbʰi	'all'	14.	bʰar	'burden'
15.	bʰabʰi	'brother's wife'	16.	čabi	'key'
17.	ǰeb	'pocket'	18.	bãka	'crooked'
19.	ləgbʰəg	'approximately'	20.	bɪkna	'to be sold'

A.   Do the sounds [b] and [bʰ] contrast in Hindi, are they in free variation, or are they in complementary distribution? If either contrast or free variation, justify your answer from the data. If complementary distribution, state the distribution of the two sounds.

_____

_____

_____

_____

_____

_____

B.   Do the two sounds in question represent different phonemes in Hindi, or are they allophones of the same phoneme?

_____

_____

_____

Name _____   **Section** _____   **Date** _____

2.05   MODERN ENGLISH [k] AND [kʰ]

Consider the following words with respect to whether the sound represented by <k>, <c>, <ck> or <q> is aspirated or not. Then answer the questions that follow.

A	B	C	D
kinder	skillet	slicker	sequester
cooler	skimmed	wicket	secrete
kangaroo	skewed	docket	include
correct	scope	hacker	incorporate
kosher	squadron	pickle	incurable
kudos	scandal	recondite	recall

A. In column A, do <k> and <c> represent [k] or [kʰ]?

[kʰ]

B. In column B, do <k>, <c> and <q> represent [k] or [kʰ]?

[k]

C. In column C, do <c> and <ck> represent [k] or [kʰ]?

[k]

D. In column D, do <c> and <q> represent [k] or [kʰ]?

[kʰ]

E. Give the distribution of these allophones of /k/ in English.

[k] is found   when following an s and when introducing an unstressed syllable.

[kʰ] is found   at the beginning of words and when introducing a stressed syllable.

Name _____   **Section** _____   **Date** _____

2.06   A PHONOLOGICAL RULE OF OLD ENGLISH

A. Examine the words below, given in both Old English (OE) spelling and phonetic transcription. For the words in column A, <f> represents the sound [f]; for those in column B, it represents [v].

A [f]			B [v]		
fæst	[fæst]	'fast'	wifung	[wiːvuŋg]	'wedlock'
fisc	[fɪš]	'fish'	hlaford	[hlaːvɔrd]	'lord'
fæder	[fædɛr]	'father'	æfre	[ævrɛ]	'ever'
wif	[wiːf]	'woman'	wifel	[wɪvɛl]	'weevil'
ceaf	[čæəf]	'chaff'	cealfian	[čæəlvɪan]	'to calve'
cealf	[čæəlf]	'calf'	ofer	[ɔvɛr]	'over'
æfter	[æftɛr]	'after'	hræfn	[hrævn]	'raven'

1. Identify any minimal pairs among the words above.

    over – ever

    calf – calve

    chaff – calf

2. Determine whether [f] and [v] occur in complementary distribution, and specify the distribution if they do. *where one sound occurs, the other does not occur.*

    [f] and [v] occur in complementary distribution.

3. What can you conclude about the phonemic status of [f] and [v] in OE?

    /f/ has the [f] sound.

    /v/ has the [f] sound too.

4. On the basis of your analysis, give underlying forms for *fisc, ofer* and *wif*, and state a phonological rule that will generate the correct surface forms.

    Rule

    /fɪsk/

    /afər/

    /wɪf/

B.   Now examine the OE words below. For the words in column A, <s> represents the sound [s]; for those in column B, it represents [z].

A [s]			B [z]		
fæst	[fæst]	'fast'	wisa	[wi:za]	'leader'
sæd	[sæd]	'sad'	wesan	[wɛzan]	'to be'
sticca	[stɪkka]	'stick'	risan	[ri:zan]	'to rise'
sendan	[sɛndan]	'send'	ælsyndrig	[ælzündriy]	'separately'
wis	[wi:s]	'wise'	glesan	[gle:zan]	'to gloss'
mos	[mɔs]	'moss'	ceosan	[če:əzan]	'to choose'
spell	[spɛl]	'story'	glisian	[glɪzɪan]	'to glitter'

1.   Identify any minimal pairs among the words above.

wise - rise

2.   Determine whether [s] and [z] occur in complementary distribution, and specify the distribution if they do.

3.   What can you conclude about the phonemic status of [s] and [z] in OE?

4.   On the basis of your analysis, give underlying forms for *fæst, sæd* and *wisa,* and state a phonological rule that will generate the correct surface forms.

/fæst/
/sæd/
/w...

Name _____   **Section** _____   **Date** _____

C. Examine the words below. For the words in column A, both <þ> and <ð> represent the sound [θ]; for those in column B, they represent [ð].

A [θ]			B [ð]		
ðing	[θɪŋg]	'thing'	oðer	[ɔːðɛr]	'other'
bæð	[bæθ]	'bath'	cweðan	[kwɛðan]	'to speak'
wiþ	[wɪθ]	'with'	baþian	[baðɪan]	'to bathe'
þurh	[θʊrx]	'through'	weorðe	[wɛɔrðe]	'worthy'
þridda	[θrɪdda]	'third'	wiþoban	[wɪðɔban]	'collarbone'
ðunor	[θʊnɔr]	'thunder'	mæðel	[mæðel]	'council'
þrotu	[θrɔtʊ]	'throat'	hæþen	[hæːðen]	'heathen'
hæþ	[hæːθ]	'heath'	hæðung	[hæːðʊŋg]	'heating'

1. Identify any minimal pairs among the words above.

    thing — third   leathen — heating

    through — throat

    heath — leather

2. Determine whether [θ] and [ð] occur in complementary distribution, and specify the distribution if they do.

    _____

    _____

    _____

3. What can you conclude about the phonemic status of [θ] and [ð] in OE?

    _____

    _____

    _____

4. On the basis of your analysis, give underlying forms for *bæð, þrotu, weorðe* and *baþian*, and state a phonological rule that will generate the correct surface forms.

    _____

    _____

    _____

D. Examine sections A, B and C above and determine what your three rules have in common. Write a single rule that captures the content of the three separate rules. (Think of the natural classes of sounds represented in the rules you devised.)

_____

_____

_____

_____

_____

Name _____   **Section** _____   **Date** _____

2.07   ITALIAN [s] AND [z]

This problem concerns the sounds [s] and [z] in three regional varieties of Italian. Each of these dialects has both alveolar fricatives among its inventory of phonetic segments. However, the dialects differ with respect to the distributional patterns of these sounds.

In the data below (given in phonetic transcription, *not* necessarily standard Italian spelling!) you will see how certain Italian words are pronounced in the north and south of Italy, as well as in a third area that includes the city of Florence. Examine each dialect in turn to determine whether in that dialect [s] and [z] are allophones of a single phoneme or members of two different phonemes. If the former, describe the distribution of allophones; then give the underlying form and state the phonological rule that yields the correct surface forms. If the latter, justify your answer.

	NORTHERN	FLORENTINE	SOUTHERN	
1.	sugo	sugo	sugo	'juice'
2.	kaze	kase	kase	'houses'
3.	znɛllo	znɛllo	znɛllo	'slender'
4.	fuzo	fuzo	fuso	'melted'
5.	pasta	pasta	pasta	'pasta'
6.	zdentato	zdentato	zdentato	'toothless'
7.	korsa	korsa	korsa	'race'
8.	skuzi	skuzi	skusi	'excuse me'
9.	rizo	riso	riso	'rice'
10.	meze	mese	mese	'month'
11.	zbruffone	zbruffone	zbruffone	'braggart'
12.	fuzo	fuso	fuso	'spindle'
13.	pensare	pensare	pensare	'to think'
14.	zvenire	zvenire	zvenire	'to faint'
15.	zraǰonare	zraǰonare	zraǰonare	'to talk nonsense'
16.	dispare	dispare	dispare	'uneven'
17.	sadizmo	sadizmo	sadizmo	'sadism'
18.	autopsia	autopsia	autopsia	'autopsy'
19.	dizdire	dizdire	dizdire	'to cancel'
20.	sfortuna	sfortuna	sfortuna	'bad luck'
21.	falso	falso	falso	'false'
22.	illuzione	illuzione	illusione	'illusion'

NORTHERN DIALECT:

_____

_____

_____

_____

_____

_____

_____

FLORENTINE DIALECT:

_____

_____

_____

_____

_____

_____

_____

SOUTHERN DIALECT:

_____

_____

_____

_____

_____

_____

_____

Name _____   **Section** _____   **Date** _____

2.08   JAPANESE [h], [ɸ], [ç]

The following three sounds exist phonetically in Japanese: [h], [ɸ], [ç]. ([ɸ] is a voiceless bilabial frica-tive; it is usually romanized in transliteration as f. [ç] is a voiceless palatal fricative. Note also that [ɯ] is a high, back, unrounded vowel.) Examine the data below, given in phonetic transcription, and then determine which of these three possibilities is the case for Japanese:

  i.   The three sounds are allophones of a single phoneme.

 ii.   Two of the three sounds are allophones of one phoneme, while the third belongs to another phoneme.

iii.   The three sounds represent three different phonemes.

Justify your answer. If you find that some or all of these sounds belong to the same phoneme, give the rule or rules determining the distribution of allophones. If you find that some or all of these sounds contrast, prove it.

1.	çito	'person'
2.	haha	'mother'
3.	çiɸɯ	'skin'
4.	asaçi	'morning sun'
5.	heta	'awkward, unskillful'
6.	ɸɯne	'ship'
7.	hon	'book'
8.	haši	'chopsticks'
9.	hohei	'infantryman'
10.	ɸɯhenɸɯto	'neutrality'

_____

_____

_____

_____

_____

_____

_____

_____

_____

_____

Name _____   **Section** _____   **Date** _____

2.09 [t], [ṭ], AND [θ] IN BIBLICAL HEBREW AND STANDARD ARABIC

Biblical Hebrew (BH) and Standard Arabic (SA) both contain the sounds [t], [ṭ], and [θ]. (For information on the velarized or "emphatic" stop [ṭ] and other sounds you may be unfamiliar with, see Appendix B.)

A.   Examine the following BH words:

1.	ṭεrεm	'not yet'	2.	tᵊxelεθ	'violet-blue'
3.	tu:r	'seek out'	4.	šεlεṭ	'shield'
5.	haššabba:θ	'the Sabbath'	6.	la:θu:r	'to seek out'
7.	ma:ṭa:r	'rain'	8.	wayyešt	'and he drank'
9.	lišḥoṭ	'to slay'	10.	ma:θay	'when'
11.	pa:θaḥti:	'I opened'	12.	ṭu:r	'row'
13.	ru:θ	'Ruth'	14.	u:θᵊxelεθ	'and violet-blue'
15.	ṭabbaʕaθ	'ring'	16.	liɸtoᵃḥ	'to open'

On the basis of these data, determine whether BH [t], [ṭ], and [θ] are different phonemes, or whether two or three of them are allophones of a single phoneme. If the former, justify your answer. If the latter, state the rule that describes the distribution of each allophone.

_____

_____

_____

_____

_____

_____

_____

_____

_____

B.   Now consider the following SA words:

1.	ṭu:b	'bricks'	2.	baḥθ	'discussion'
3.	θawb	'garment'	4.	θalaba	'he slandered'
5.	ʔassabt	'the Sabbath'	6.	baḥt	'pure'
7.	maṭar	'rain'	8.	qaḥṭ	'drought'
9.	ṭalaba	'he searched'	10.	mata:	'when'
11.	tu:b	'repent'	12.	maṭlab	'quest'
13.	ʔaθar	'effect'	14.	šabaθ	'spider'
15.	taθbi:t	'strengthening'	16.	muṭaṭallaba:θ	'requirements'

Analyze these data just as you analyzed the BH data—that is, determine whether SA [t], [ṭ] and [θ] are different phonemes, or whether two or three of them are allophones of a single phoneme. If the former, justify your answer. If the latter, state the rule that describes the distribution of each allophone.

_____

_____

_____

_____

_____

_____

_____

_____

_____

C.   As you've seen, on the phonetic level BH and SA both contain the sounds [t], [ṭ] and [θ]. Are these languages also the same on the *phonological* level with respect to these three sounds? That is, do the sounds have the same phonological status in the sound patterns of BH and SA? Explain.

_____

_____

_____

_____

_____

Name _____ **Section** _____ **Date** _____

2.10   A PHONOLOGICAL RULE OF RUSSIAN

In the data below you will find several examples of a certain class of Russian noun. Each example is given in two different forms, the nominative singular and the genitive plural. Your task is to isolate all the morphemes present in the data in their *unique underlying forms*, and to posit a general phonological rule that will account for all the surface forms.

Examine the following data, given in broad phonetic transcription. Then answer the questions that follow.

Note: Certain aspects of the surface phonetics—e.g., palatalization before front vowels, stress and vowel reduction—have not been indicated. [ɯ] is a high, back, unrounded vowel.

Nom. Sg.		Gen. Pl.	
1a. reka	'river'	1b. rek	'of the rivers'
2a. kniga	'book'	2b. knik	'of the books'
3a. rɯba	'fish'	3b. rɯp	'of the fish'
4a. rana	'wound'	4b. ran	'of the wounds'
5a. rabota	'work'	5b. rabot	'of the works'
6a. moda	'fashion'	6b. mot	'of the fashions'
7a. opira	'opera'	7b. opir	'of the operas'
8a. rosa	'dew'	8b. ros	'of the dews'
9a. repa	'turnip'	9b. rep	'of the turnips'
10a. duša	'spirit'	10b. duš	'of the spirits'
11a. platforma	'platform'	11b. platform	'of the platforms'
12a. loža	'boxseat'	12b. loš	'of the boxseats'

1. Give a single, unique underlying form for each morpheme present in the data.

_____

_____

_____

_____

_____

_____

2. Propose a phonological rule that will account for all the surface forms. Your rule should be as general as possible.

_____

_____

_____

_____

3. Show the derivation of 'book' and 'of the books':

'book'

Underlying form: /   /

Application of P-rule:

Surface form: [   ]

'of the books'

Underlying form: /   /

Application of P-rule:

Surface form: [   ]

Name _____   **Section** _____   **Date** _____

2.11   STRESS IN ICELANDIC, SWAHILI, MODERN GREEK, AND STANDARD ARABIC

In some languages, stress is *phonemic* or *distinctive*—i.e., the placement of stress in a word is not generally predictable, and can therefore be used to distinguish words that would otherwise be identical. In other languages, stress is *predictable*—i.e., the placement of stress in a word is determined by phonological rules, and is therefore not capable of distinguishing words. (In still other languages, stress is extremely weak or non-existent; French is an example of such a language.)

Examine the Icelandic, Swahili, Modern Greek, and Standard Arabic words given below. The main stress in each word has been indicated by ´. For each language, determine whether stress is distinctive or predictable. If the former, justify your answer. If the latter, state the rule or rules that determine the placement of stress in a word.

A.   Icelandic

The data are given in standard Icelandic orthography. <þ> = [θ], <j> = [y], <ð> = [ð], <æ> = [æ]. Although some of the words below have secondary stress, only the main stress has been indicated and is relevant to the problem.

1. éftir — 'after'
2. dískur — 'plate'
3. svéfnherbergi — 'bedroom'
4. drótning — 'queen'
5. vérzlunarviðskifti — 'commerce'
6. élska — '(I) love'
7. kǽrleikur — 'love (n.)'
8. skípbrotsmaður — 'shipwrecked man'
9. kénnari — 'teacher'
10. éftirlæti — 'favorite'
11. þéssvegna — 'therefore'
12. jókulbunga — 'rounded summit of a glacier'
13. élskuðum — '(we) loved'

In this language, stress is: [   ] distinctive

[   ] predictable

EXPLANATION:

_____

_____

_____

_____

_____

_____

B. Swahili

Data are given in standard Swahili orthography, which has been influenced by English spelling. Thus, <sh> = [š], <ch> = [č]. In most other respects, the orthography is phonetic. Note that <ng> = [ng], not [ŋ]. (The latter is written <ng'>.)

As in the Icelandic data, only the main stress has been indicated. Note that in these examples, word-initial <m> before a consonant represents a syllable by itself. Thus, *mbu* has two syllables.

1.	watóto	'children'
2.	símba	'lion'
3.	ḿto	'river'
4.	Kiswahíli	'Swahili language'
5.	Kiingeréza	'English language'
6.	ḿbu	'mosquito'
7.	walijitazáma	'they looked at themselves'
8.	nimesikía	'I hear'
9.	kilichotutósha	'which was enough for us'
10.	mchúngwa	'orange tree'
11.	amekwénda	'he has gone'
12.	amekwendápi	'where has he gone?'
13.	zitakazowaharibía	'which will ruin for them'

In this language, stress is: [   ] distinctive

[   ] predicatable

EXPLANATION:

_____

_____

_____

_____

_____

_____

C. Modern Greek

Data are given in phonetic transcription.

1.	ánθropos	'man'
2.	staθmós	'station'
3.	xóros	'spare room'
4.	kinimatóɣrafos	'movie theater'
5.	ðrómos	'road'
6.	viós	'property'
7.	εŋgonós	'grandson'

Name _____   **Section** _____   **Date** _____

8.   éðafos   'soil, earth'
9.   víos   'life'
10. aðɛrfós   'brother'
11. naós   'temple'
12. karkínos   'cancer'
13. xorós   'dance, ball'

In this language, stress is: [   ] distinctive
                                      [   ] predictable

EXPLANATION:

_____

_____

_____

_____

_____

D. Standard Arabic

Data are given in transcription. For a description of some of the phonetic symbols used, see Appendix B.

1.   mádrasatun   'a school'
2.   muqá:tilun   'a fighter'
3.   wáladun   'a boy'
4.   ʔawlá:dun   'boys'
5.   ǰadá:wilu   'streams'
6.   karí:mun   'generous'
7.   ʕá:limun   'learned, erudite'
8.   šáǰaratun   'a tree'
9.   ʔáswadu   'black'
10. ʔaswadá:ni   'two black men'
11. šaríbtum   'you (m. pl.) drank'
12. ǰadí:dun   'new'
13. ʔaǰáddu   'newer'
14. ḍarabtúnna   'you (f. pl.) struck'
15. katábna: 'we wrote'
16. katábtuma: 'you two wrote'
17. talá:miðatun   'a student'

18.   mašɣú:lun   'busy (m. sg.)'
19.   mašɣu:lá:tun   'busy (f. pl.)'
20.   tarǰamtumú:ha: 'you (m. pl.) translated them'

In this language, stress is: [   ] distinctive

                              [   ] predictable

EXPLANATION:

_____

_____

_____

_____

_____

_____

Name _____   **Section** _____   **Date** _____

2.12   ENGLISH DISCUSSION QUESTION

You are teaching English in a foreign country. Your students are having some pronunciation problems. They can't distinguish between [i] and [ɪ], or between [pʰ] and [p]. Since your time is limited, you want to give your priority to the more serious problem.

You have decided on this philosophy with respect to teaching pronunciation: It is not so important to try to make students sound exactly like native speakers, but it *is* important for their speech to be clear and completely comprehensible, so that they will not be misunderstood.

Which of the two problems mentioned above would you expect to be the more serious? Why? Make sure you include examples to support your statements and justify your choice. You may want to mention the terms *contrast* and *complementary distribution* in your discussion.

Since it is most important that the students have clear and comprehensible speech, it is more important that they are able to distinguish between the [i] and [ɪ] than the [pʰ] and [p].

Ex. If attempting to say the word bead [bid] results in a pronunciation [bɪd] bid, the meaning is completely different. A pronunciation [pɪt] pit instead of [pʰɪt] pit does not change the meaning of the word.

Name _____ **Section** _____ **Date** _____

2.13 CUBAN SPANISH AND "R-LESS" ENGLISH

In this problem you will take a look at two different phonological processes, one in Cuban Spanish and the other in certain types of English, which share an interesting similarity.

A. *Cuban Spanish*

The data below, given in phonetic transcription, provide pairs of Spanish words in two alternate pronunciations. Column 1 gives a standard pronunciation in many parts of the Spanish-speaking world; column 2 gives the corresponding pronunciation in one variety of Cuban Spanish.

Assuming that the forms in column 1 represent the underlying forms for those in column 2, state a phonological rule that accounts for the Cuban pronunciations. Carefully and explicitly state the environment in which the rule operates.

	1		2	
1a.	eso	1b.	eso	'that'
2a.	esta	2b.	ehta	'this'
3a.	sabroso	3b.	sabroso	'delicious'
4a.	dos latinos	4b.	doh latinoh	'two Latins'
5a.	buskar	5b.	buhkar	'to look for'
6a.	ospital	6b.	ohpital	'hospital'
7a.	asistentes	7b.	asihtenteh	'assistants'
8a.	mostasa	8b.	mohtasa	'mustard'
9a.	eski	9b.	ehki	'ski'
10a.	kurso	10b.	kurso	'course'

RULE:

_____

_____

_____

B. *"R-Less" English*

Standard British, Australian and New Zealand English, along with several varieties of regional American English, are referred to as "r-less" dialects, since in these types of English *r* is dropped in certain linguistic environments.

In the following list of words, the underlined *r*'s are the ones that may drop in the "r-less" dialects. First transcribe the words in phonetic notation; then state the rule that determines which *r*'s are lost.

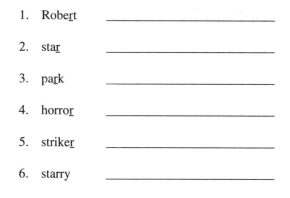

1. Robe<u>r</u>t   _____

2. sta<u>r</u>   _____

3. pa<u>r</u>k   _____

4. horro<u>r</u>   _____

5. strike<u>r</u>   _____

6. starry   _____

7. harder   _____

8. clear   _____

9. clearer   _____

10. bare   _____

11. care   _____

12. cared   _____

13. caring   _____

14. caretaker   _____

15. tear   _____ _____

16. tore   _____

17. pour   _____

18. poured   _____

RULE:

_____

_____

_____

C. What do the rules you discovered for Cuban Spanish and "r-less" English have in common?

_____

_____

_____

_____

Name _____   **Section** _____   **Date** _____

2.14   CONSTRAINTS ON INITIAL CONSONANT CLUSTERS IN ENGLISH

Syllables in English can begin with up to three consonants. Your task is to discover the phonotactic constraints that specify which initial sequences of consonants are possible. In other words, what are the rules that allow *play* but not *pnay, stray* but not *stpay*, etc.?

The rules you come up with should be as general as possible. For example, it is quite true that English syllables can begin with p + r, but a list of specific cases of this sort is not what you're after as a final result. The p + r case is part of a more general pattern, which is what you are to discover.

You may find it helpful to discuss the 1-consonant, 2-consonant, and 3-consonant cases separately. (In the 1-consonant case, determine if there are any English consonants that cannot begin a syllable. Hint: There is one!)

Finally, consider some foreign terms which have become part of the English vocabulary of some speakers: *shtick, shnook, knish, shlemiel*. Do these recent imports obey the phonotactic constraints you have proposed? Explain.

Name _____   **Section** _____   **Date** _____

2.15   JAPANESE VS. ENGLISH SYLLABLE STRUCTURE

Syllable structure is generally thought of in terms of permissible sequences of consonants and vowels. Thus, CVC represents a syllable of the pattern consonant-vowel-consonant; this is a very common pattern for English (*hat, shack, thought,* etc.), but other languages—Hawaiian is an example—may totally disallow this kind of syllable.

This problem contrasts Japanese and English syllable structure. You will be able to come up with the English data on your own. For the Japanese examples, use the phonetically transcribed words in the following representative list, which have been divided into syllables for you. (Note: [ɯ] is a high, back, unrounded vowel.)

1.	a na ta	'you'
2.	to mo da či	'friend'
3.	o too to	'younger brother'
4.	ɯn čin	'fare'
5.	da i ga kɯ	'university'
6.	hak ki ri	'clearly'
7.	oo kii	'big'
8.	ha ǰi me ma ši te	'How do you do?'
9.	den wa	'telephone'
10.	ke i san ki	'calculator'
11.	an ra kɯ	'comfort'
12.	gyɯt to	'tight'
13.	kyoo kɯn	'instruction'
14.	mya kɯ	'pulse'
15.	ryok kɯ	'tree planting'
16.	i ǰip pa ri	'obstinacy'
17.	kyo šin	'open mind'

A. Fill in the spaces below with two Japanese and two English examples for each of the syllable types given. For your Japanese examples, write the Japanese word and underline the syllable; for your English examples, write the word in ordinary spelling and in phonetic transcription, and underline the syllable in the transcription.

EXAMPLE:

	Japanese	English
CV	an<u>a</u>ta	to [tʰu]

	Japanese	English
1. *CV*	_____	_____
	_____	_____

Japanese	English

2. *V*

_____   _____

_____   _____

3. *VC*

_____   _____

_____   _____

4. *CVC*

_____   _____

_____   _____

5. *CVV*

_____   _____

_____   _____

6. *CCV*

_____   _____

_____   _____

7. *CCVC*

_____   _____

_____   _____

8. *VCC*

_____   _____

_____   _____

9. *CVCC*

_____   _____

_____   _____

10. *CCVCC*

_____   _____

_____   _____

11. *CCCVC*

_____   _____

_____   _____

12. *CVCCC*

_____   _____

_____   _____

13. *CCVCCC*

_____   _____

_____   _____

14. *CCCVCCCC* _____   _____
(One example is enough!)

Name _____   **Section** _____   **Date** _____

B.   Now answer these questions:

1.   Which language has the wider variety of possible syllable types?

_____

2.   Assuming the given data are fairly representative of the language as a whole, which syllable type predominates in Japanese?

_____

3.   What can you say about the kinds of *consonant clusters* (sequences of two more consonants) that may begin a syllable in Japanese? Does this hold true for English as well?

_____

_____

_____

4.   What can you say about the kinds of consonant clusters (sequences of two or more consonants) that may end a syllable in Japanese? Is this also true for English?

_____

_____

_____

Name _____   **Section** _____   **Date** _____

2.16   MANDARIN SYLLABLE STRUCTURE

Syllable structure in Mandarin Chinese is traditionally analyzed in terms of *initials* (onsets) and *finals* (rhymes). The 22 initials[1] exhaust the possibilities for the start of a syllable, while the 37 finals give all the possible continuations.

If all the initials and finals could combine with each other freely, there would be $22 \times 37 = 814$ possible syllables, ignoring tonal differences. In fact, however, only a little over 400 of these exist. This is because there are constraints that limit the free combination of initials and finals.

A.   Here are the fricative initials or onsets of Mandarin:

[f], [s], [ṣ], [ç], [x]

Recall that [ç] is a voiceless palatal, as in German *ich*. [x] is a voiceless velar, which often tends towards [h]. [ṣ] is similar to [š], but retroflexed, i.e., articulated with the tip of the tongue curled back towards the hard palate.

Consider the following 8 finals or rhymes:

[u], [in], [ou], [aŋ], [ü], [iaŋ], [ei], [üe]

If these rhymes could combine freely with the fricative onsets, how many syllables (ignoring tone) could be constructed from them?

_____

B.   The following words will show you which combinations of these onsets and rhymes actually exist. (Tones are indicated, but are not relevant for this problem.) The list is exhaustive, in that if a particular combination of the given onsets and rhymes isn't present, it doesn't exist in Mandarin. (Mandarin has an abundance of homonyms; the glosses indicate only one of a sometimes very large number of possible meanings for each word.)

1.	ṣàŋ	'up'	2.	xēi	'black'
3.	fú	'clothes'	4.	çǘe	'study'
5.	ṣéi	'who?'	6.	fǒu	'deny'
7.	çiǎŋ	'think'	8.	sù	'tell'
9.	sāŋ	'funeral'	10.	xáŋ	'line'
11.	çü	'empty'	12.	xǔ	'tiger'
13.	xòu	'rear'	14.	fēi	'fly'
15.	fáŋ	'house'	16.	sōu	'search'
17.	çīn	'new'	18.	ṣǒu	'hand'
19.	ṣū	'book'			

The grid on the next page will help you see the patterns in the data. The boxes of the grid represent all the logically possible combinations of onsets and rhymes. Referring to the data, check the boxes that represent actually occurring syllables in Mandarin.

_____

[1]Twenty-one single consonants plus the "zero" initial (absence of a consonant).

	in	iaŋ	ü	üe	u	ei	ou	aŋ
f								
s								
ʂ								
ç								
x								

Now state the generalization that captures which of the given onsets combine with which rhymes.

_____

_____

_____

_____

C. There is one potential syllable whose absence will not be accounted for by the general rule you formulated in part B. Which syllable is this? What are some possible reasons for its non-existence?

_____

_____

_____

Name _____   **Section** _____   **Date** _____

2.17   MANDARIN TONE CHANGE OF *pù* AND *ī*

Mandarin Chinese has four distinctive tones:

1st tone: High level	**EXAMPLE:**	fāŋ	'square'
2nd tone: Rising		fáŋ	'house'
3rd tone: Low falling-rising		făŋ	'copy'
4th tone: Falling		fàŋ	'release'

Although tone is an intrinsic part of a Mandarin syllable, some tones change depending on their environment.

A. Consider the following data involving the words for 'one' and 'no, not.' In isolation, these are respectively [ī] and [pù].

1a.	xăo	'good'		1b.	pù xăo	'not good'
2a.	gāo	'tall'		2b.	pù gāo	'not tall'
3a.	nién	'year'		3b.	ì nién	'one year'
4a.	twèi	'correct'		4b.	pú twèi	'not correct'
5a.	tă	'hit'		5b.	pù tă	'not hit'
6a.	mièn	'side'		6b.	í mièn	'one side'
7a.	tʰài	'too'		7b.	pú tʰài	'not too'
8a.	tà	'big'		8b.	pú tà	'not big'
9a.	tʰiēn	'day'		9b.	ì tʰiēn	'one day'
10a.	lái	'come'		10b.	pù lái	'not come'
11a.	pʰà	'fear'		11b.	pú pʰà	'not fear'
12a.	tiĕn	'dot, bit'		12b.	ì tiĕn	'one bit'

State the rules that determine the tones of 'not' and 'one' in Mandarin.

_____

_____

_____

_____

B. The word for 'type, kind' is [yàŋ]. The expression for 'not the same' is literally 'not one kind.' How do you say 'not the same' in Mandarin? Explain how you determined the tones.

_____

_____

_____

_____

Name _____   **Section** _____   **Date** _____

2.18   TONES IN AKAN

Akan, also known as Twi, belongs to the Kwa branch of the Niger-Congo family of languages. It is spoken by about five to eight million people, mainly in Ghana. Like almost all the languages south of the Sahara, Akan is a tone language. Recall that a tone language is one in which pitch is used along with consonants and vowels to distinguish syllables, and hence words.

Unlike the Chinese languages, in which the tones can involve a *change* of pitch on a single syllable, the tones of Akan are all level, differing among themselves only in relative pitch. There are three such tones, which are indicated in the data below by diacritics written over the segment that bears the tone:

á   high tone

à̍   mid tone

à   low tone

The following data, given in phonetic transcription, provide a number of two-syllable words exhibiting different tonal patterns. The list is exhaustive with respect to these patterns, in the sense that all the permissible combinations of tones in two-syllable words are illustrated. Examine the data carefully, and then answer the questions that follow. (Data adapted from Redden, Owusu *et al.*, 1963.)

1. kírà   'to leave'
2. pàpà   'a palm-leaf fan'
3. bùà   'to help'
4. kírà̍   'soul'
5. kásà̍   'a language'
6. pápá   'good'
7. fùǽ   'single, one'
8. kàsà   'to speak'
9. sèè   'to use up'
10. pàpá   'father'
11. pépà   'paper'
12. séė̍   'as, like'
13. bípɔ́   'mountain, hilltop'
14. fùæ̀   'to hold, seize'
15. fìtá   'to fan a fire'
16. káà   'automobile'
17. sísí   'a bear'
18. kɔ́tà   'quart'
19. kàá   'ring, bracelet'
20. bùá   'to tell a lie'

A.   Determine which of the following statements is true with respect to *high tone* and *low tone* in Akan. Circle the letter of the correct statement, and then give the evidence that allows you to draw your conclusion: if (a), prove it; if (b), state the complementary distribution; if (c) or (d), explain.

(a)   These two tones contrast.

(b)   These two tones are in complementary distribution.

(c)   No conclusion can be drawn from the data.

(d)   Other (state): _____

_____

Evidence or explanation:

_____

_____

_____

B.   Repeat part A for *low tone* and *mid tone*.

(a)   These two tones contrast.

(b)   These two tones are in complementary distribution.

(c)   No conclusion can be drawn from the data.

(d)   Other (state): _____

_____

Evidence or explanation:

_____

_____

_____

C.   Repeat part A for *high tone* and *mid tone*.

(a)   These two tones contrast.

(b)   These two tones are in complementary distribution.

(c)   No conclusion can be drawn from the data.

(d)   Other (state): _____

_____

Evidence or explanation:

_____

_____

_____

D.   In general, given three distinct tones—call them H, M and L for short—how many logical or mathematical possibilities are there for different sequences of two tones (e.g., HH, HM, etc.)?

_____

Name _____   **Section** _____   **Date** _____

List all these logical possibilities:

_____

_____

_____

E. Now go back to the Akan data and determine which of the logical possibilities that you listed in part D actually exist in the language. (It may help to write the tone sequence of each Akan word next to it, using H, M and L.)

FOR EXAMPLE:

                pápá   HH

Circle the actually occurring tonal sequences on your list.

F. State a rule or generalization that characterizes all the "good" sequences. Your rule must correctly predict precisely which logically possible sequences of tones can and cannot exist in two-syllable words in Akan.

_____

_____

_____

Name _____   Section _____   Date _____

2.19   VOICELESS VOWELS IN JAPANESE

There is a phonological rule in Japanese that *devoices* certain vowels, with an effect something like a whispered vowel. Whether or not this devoicing takes place depends on several factors, including the rate and style of speech: the faster and more casual the speech, the more devoicing.

The data below, given in phonetic transcription, illustrate this phenomenon. Some of the symbols used deserve special comment. [ɯ] represents a high, back, unrounded vowel; [ɸ] is a voiceless bilabial fricative; [ç] is a voiceless palatal fricative, similar to the first sound of the English word *hue*. If a vowel has a small circle beneath it, it is "eligible" for devoicing, in the sense that it will be devoiced in at least some styles of speech; vowels without this symbol are never devoiced. The apostrophe indicates the position of the Japanese pitch accent[1].

Analyze these data to discover the rule or rules that determine which vowels are eligible for devoicing. Your goal is to come up with a brief paragraph that will describe in general terms—as far as can be determined from the data—the exact conditions under which devoicing can take place. The following questions should guide your analysis:

1. Do all Japanese vowels participate in the process or only certain ones? If the latter, what if anything sets these vowels apart from the others?

2. Does the process depend on the neighboring sounds? If so, how?

3. Does it depend on position in the word (initial, medial, final)?

4. Is the accent involved? If so, what effect does it have on whether or not devoicing can take place?

Make sure that your analysis correctly accounts for all the data presented. (Data adapted from Jorden 1963.)

1.	hatake	'dry field'	2.	sɯ̥kiyaki̥	'sliced beef dish'
3.	sošite	'and then'	4.	mɯ̥ra'saki̥	'purple'
5.	watarɯ	'go across'	6.	watasɯ̥	'hand over'
7.	t͡sɯ̥ki'	'moon'	8.	t͡sɯ̥'kɯ̥	'arrive'
9.	sašimi'	'raw fish dish'	10.	mo'šimoši̥	'hello (on telephone)'
11.	çi̥to'ri	'one person'	12.	çi̥to't͡sɯ̥	'one unit'
13.	sɯ̥ko'ši̥	'a small quantity'	14.	bo'kɯ̥tači̥	'we'
15.	ɸɯ̥kɯ'	'clothing'	16.	kimoči̥	'mood'
17.	ha'ši	'chopsticks'	18.	gakɯ̥sei	'student'
19.	haši'	'bridge'	20.	ɸɯ̥'kɯ	'blow'
21.	sɯgi'rɯ	'exceed'	22.	šinbɯn	'newspaper'
23.	k̥itto	'certainly'	24.	kɯ̥ši'	'a comb'
25.	sɯ̥ki'	'pleasing'	26.	watakɯ̥ši̥	'I'
27.	sɯ̥ši'	'sushi'	28.	sɯmi'	'ink stick'
29.	çi̥kima'ši̥ta	'pulled'	30.	čiči'	'father'
31.	iči'	'one'	32.	ɯsagi	'rabbit'
33.	kɯ̥t͡sɯ̥'ši̥ta	'socks'	34.	çi̥ka'ši̥t͡sɯ̥	'basement'
35.	kabɯki̥	'kabuki (theater)'	36.	ne'kɯ̥tai	'necktie'
37.	çikatet͡sɯ̥	'subway'	38.	sɯ̥pɯ'ɯn	'spoon'
39.	kakika'ta	'style of writing'	40.	ito'ko	'cousin'

[1]The nature of the pitch accent, while not relevant to this problem, is quite interesting. The accent indicates the location of a high–low pitch transition: the syllable or part of a syllable preceding the accent is at a high pitch, and is immediately followed by a fall in pitch. When the accent occurs after the last syllable, the pitch fall is "potential," and is only manifested when certain particles are attached to the word. Note that it is perfectly possible for a multi-syllabic word not to have a pitch accent. (See Shibatani 1990:177ff.)

Name _____   **Section** _____   **Date** _____

2.20   VOWEL HARMONY IN TURKISH

Turkish vowels enter into a process known as *vowel harmony*, a type of assimilation in which vowels within a word tend to share some of the same characteristics. It has been described as "basically a stringing together of vowels of similar quality, so that there is a sound harmony extending over the whole word." (Rona 1989) In this exercise you will become familiar with the Turkish vowel system, and explore some aspects of the vowel harmony that operates within Turkish words.

The data are given in standard Turkish orthography, which is quite close to a phonetic transcription. Here are some differences you should be aware of:

<c>	=	[ǰ]
<ç>	=	[č]
<ş>	=	[š]

Most importantly for this problem, the undotted i, <ı>, represents a vowel similar to [u] except that it is *non-round*; such a vowel is also found in Russian and Japanese. Two different phonetic symbols for this vowel are [ɨ] and [ɯ].

A.   Turkish has a particularly symmetric vowel system. You will be able to identify the Turkish vowels by examining the brief passage below, which contains them all. (Data and translation Rona 1989, from a passage on visiting mosques in Turkey.)

Kadınların başlarını örtmeleri lazımdır. Yanınızda bir eşarp ya da başınızı örtecek bir şey olmayabilir. O takdirde oradaki bir görevliden bir başörtüsü isteyebilirsiniz, ve camiden çıkarken bunu geri verirsiniz.

'Women must cover their heads. It is possible you may not have with you a scarf or something else to cover your head. In that case, you'll be able to ask for a headscarf from one of the officials there, and when you go out of the mosque you'll give it back.'

1.   List the eight vowels of Turkish:

    _____

2.   The symmetry of this vowel system becomes apparent when the vowels are analyzed according to the following criteria:

    HEIGHT: High or non-high
    BACKNESS: Back or non-back (i.e., front)
    ROUNDNESS: Round or non-round

Describe each of the Turkish vowels in terms of these criteria. (One vowel has been done for you as an example.)

    a.   ___i___   high, non-back, non-round _____

    b.   _____   _____

    c.   _____   _____

    d.   _____   _____

e.   _____   _____

f.   _____   _____

g.   _____   _____

h.   _____   _____

3.   Now present the same information in a different form. Using the chart below (an example of a *distinctive feature matrix*), write the vowels in the left-hand column and then enter a plus or minus in each blank according to whether the value of the feature is positive or negative for the vowel in question.

Vowel	High	Back	Round
i	+	–	–

4.   As an aid to visualizing the symmetry of the Turkish vowel system, assign each vowel to the appropriate vertex of this cube:

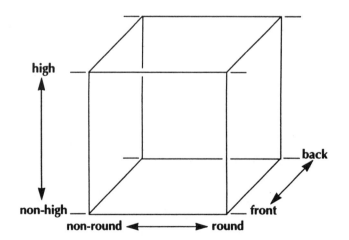

Name _____   **Section** _____   **Date** _____

5. List all the Turkish vowels that are:

    a.   non-round: _____

    b.   front and round: _____

    c.   high and back: _____

    d.   back: _____

    e.   non-high, back and non-round: _____

B.   Having identified the vowels and their features, you are now ready to analyze some examples of vowel harmony.

    The data below show certain Turkish nouns with and without the suffix meaning 'in,' an example of what we may call a Class I suffix. Examine the data, and then answer the questions that follow. (Note: Turkish has no definite article; although the word 'the' appears in the glosses, it is not reflected anywhere in the Turkish.)

1a. ev	'house'		1b. evde	'in the house'
2a. kutu	'box'		2b. kutuda	'in the box'
3a. köy	'village'		3b. köyde	'in the village'
4a. oda	'room'		4b. odada	'in the room'
5a. deniz	'sea'		5b. denizde	'in the sea'
6a. halı	'carpet'		6b. halıda	'in the carpet'
7a. gül	'rose'		7b. gülde	'in the rose'
8a. kol	'arm'		8b. kolda	'in the arm'

1. What are the possible forms of the suffix for 'in'?

    _____

2. Referring to the vowel analysis you did in part A, fill in the blanks below to characterize precisely the two different vowels that can appear in this suffix:

    These are exactly the vowels that are both _____ and _____

3. How do these vowels *differ*?

    _____

4. The next step is to determine when each variant of the suffix is used. The key is to look at the vowel in the syllable immediately preceding it.

    For each variant of the suffix, determine all the vowels that are possible in the preceding syllable. Then, looking at each set of vowels you've listed, characterize them precisely, again referring to your previous analysis:

    The variant _____ can follow the vowels_____; these are exactly

    the vowels that are _____.

The variant _____ can follow the vowels_____; these are exactly

the vowels that are _____.

5. What is the connection between each suffix variant and the vowels that it can follow?

_____

_____

6. Now state the generalization for Class I suffixes by filling in the blanks below:

There are _____ possible vowels that can appear in a Class I suffix, namely

_____; these vowels are characterized by the fact that they are

_____ and _____. The vowel in the suffix is chosen

so as to agree in _____ with the vowel of the immediately preceding syllable.

C. In the data below you will find all the variants of the Turkish suffix meaning 'with'—an example of what we may call a Class II suffix—along with a representative sampling of their distribution.

Examine the data carefully, and then analyze the distribution of the variants as you did for the Class I suffix in the previous section. You should proceed along the lines of the six-step process above, ending up with a generalization for Class II suffixes comparable to the one you formulated for Class I.

1a. balık	'fish'	1b. balıklı	'with fish'
2a. biber	'pepper'	2b. biberli	'with pepper'
3a. süt	'milk'	3b. sütlü	'with milk'
4a. limon	'lemon'	4b. limonlu	'with lemon'
5a. tuz	'salt'	5b. tuzlu	'with salt'
6a. peynir	'cheese'	6b. peynirli	'with cheese'
7a. ordövr	'hors d'oeuvres'	7b. ordövrlü	'with hors d'oeuvres'
8a. çikolata	'chocolate'	8b. çikolatalı	'with chocolate'

_____

_____

_____

_____

_____

_____

_____

_____

Name _____   **Section** _____   **Date** _____

_____

_____

_____

_____

_____

_____

_____

_____

_____

_____

_____

_____

D. The first column below lists eight Turkish verbs. Fill in the blanks in the other two columns by adding on the appropriate forms of the infinitive suffix *-mek* (Class I) in column 2, and the past tense suffix *-di* (Class II) in column 3.

1. gel   'come'   ___gelmek___   'to come'   ___geldi___   'came'

2. çevir   'dial'   _____   'to dial'   _____   'dialed'

3. gör   'see'   _____   'to see'   _____   'saw'

4. yüz   'swim'   _____   'to swim'   _____   'swam'

5. kal   'stay'   _____   'to stay'   _____   'stayed'

6. ısır   'bite'   _____   'to bite'   _____   'bit'

7. koy   'put'   _____   'to put'   _____   'put'

8. oku   'read'   _____   'to read'   _____   'read'

CHAPTER

3

Morphology

3.01   SPANISH VS. HEBREW GENDER AND NUMBER

A. Examine the following Spanish data, given in phonetic transcription. Then identify all the morphemes that are present, and state the meaning or function of each.

amigo	'male friend'	amigos	'male friends'
amiga	'female friend'	amigas	'female friends'
mučačo	'boy'	mučačos	'boys'
mučača	'girl'	mučačas	'girls'

_____

_____

_____

_____

B. Do the same for the following Modern Hebrew data.

xavɛr	'male friend'	xavɛrim	'male friends'
xavɛra	'female friend'	xavɛrɔt	'female friends'
talmid	'male student'	talmidim	'male students'
talmida	'female student'	talmidɔt	'female students'

_____

_____

_____

_____

C. Based on what you have discovered, explain how Spanish and Hebrew differ in the way they mark gender and number.

_____

_____

_____

Name _____   **Section** _____   **Date** _____

3.02   MALAY/INDONESIAN MORPHEME IDENTIFICATION

Malay (known in Malaysia as Bahasa Malaysia, 'the Malaysian language') and Indonesian (known in Indonesia as Bahasa Indonesia) are essentially the same language, differing only slightly more than do British and American English. Malay/Indonesian (MI) is among the top ten languages in the world in terms of numbers of speakers.

Examine the following MI sentences, given in phonetic transcription. One possible translation has been given for each.

1.	ini kuda	'This is a horse.'
2.	ini ali	'This is Ali.'
3.	ali bagus	'Ali is good.'
4.	ali mənǰual kuda itu	'Ali sells that horse.'
5.	kuda ali bagus	'Ali's horse is good.'
6.	ǰualan ini bagus	'This merchandise is good.'
7.	kuda ini diǰual oleh ali	'This horse is sold by Ali.'
8.	ali pənǰual kain	'Ali is a cloth seller.'

A.   List all the *morphemes* in the data, giving their meanings or explaining their uses in each case.

_____

_____

_____

_____

_____

_____

B.   Identify one *inflectional* and two *derivational* morphemes in the data.

_____

_____

C.   Based on the above data, are these statements true or false?

1.	Every MI sentence must have a verb.	[ ] T	[ ] F
2.	There is no possessive morpheme in MI.	[ ] T	[ ] F
3.	There is no indefinite article in MI.	[ ] T	[ ] F

D.   Translate into English:

kuda bagus ini kuda ali

_____

E.   Translate into MI:

1.   Ali's merchandise is cloth.

_____

2.   This is a good horse.

_____

3.   This horse is good.

_____

F.   If məndidik means 'educate,' what is the probable meaning of:

1.   pəndidik

_____

2.   didikan

_____

Name _____   **Section** _____   **Date** _____

3.03   ENGLISH MORPHOLOGY

[handwritten: noun, adj. verb = open, adpositions/pronouns = closed]

A.   For each italicized word in the passage below, identify its lexical category and specify whether it is a member of an open or a closed class. Then list the morphemes that make up the word and, in the columns to the right, indicate for each constituent morpheme whether it is a stem (Stem), prefix (Pre), or suffix (Suf); a bound (Bound) or free (Free) form; and, for prefixes and suffixes, whether they are inflectional (Inflec) or derivational (Deriv) morphemes.

Even the *skeptical* historian develops a humble respect for religion, since he sees it functioning, and *seemingly indispensable,* in every land and age. To the *unhappy,* the suffering, the bereaved, the old, it has brought super-natural comforts valued by millions of souls as more precious than any *natural* aid. It has helped parents and teachers to discipline the young. It has conferred meaning and dignity upon the *lowliest existence,* and through its sacraments has made for *stability* by transforming human convenants into solemn *relationships* with God. It has kept the poor (said Napoleon) from murdering the rich. For since the natural *inequality* of men dooms many of us to poverty or defeat, some supernatural hope may be the sole alternative to despair. [From *The Lessons of History* by Will and Ariel Durant (New York: Simon and Schuster, 1968)]

[handwritten right margin: (cat/cats), collect/collected]

[handwritten: Inflection morpheme - alters form of word without changing meaning or lexical category]

EXAMPLE: NATURAL

Lexical category __Adjective__   Open/Closed __Open__

Morphemes	Stem/Pre/Suf	Bound/Free	Inflec/Deriv
nature	Stem	Free *(can stand alone)*	
-al	Suf	Bound	Deriv

[handwritten: derivational morphemes - can produce new words 1) change meaning (true - untrue); change lexical category true (adj)/truly (adverb).   function only as parts of words]

1.   SKEPTICAL

Lexical category __adj.__   Open/Closed __Open__

Morphemes	Stem/Pre/Suf	Bound/Free	Inflec/Deriv
skeptic	Stem	Free	
al	Suf.	Bound	Der.

2.   SEEMINGLY

Lexical category __adv.__   Open/Closed __Open__

Morphemes	Stem/Pre/Suf	Bound/Free	Inflec/Deriv
Seem	Stem	Free	
ing	suf	Bound	Der.
ly	suf	Bound	Der.

3. INDISPENSABLE

Lexical category __adj.__   Open/Closed __open__

Morphemes	Stem/Pre/Suf	Bound/Free	Inflec/Deriv
dispense	stem	free	
in	pre		deriv.
able	suf	bound	deriv.

4. UNHAPPY

Lexical category __adj.__   Open/Closed __open__

Morphemes	Stem/Pre/Suf	Bound/Free	Inflec/Deriv
happy	stem	free	
un	pre	bound	deriv.

5. LOWLIEST

Lexical category __adv.__   Open/Closed _____

Morphemes	Stem/Pre/Suf	Bound/Free	Inflec/Deriv
low	stem	free	
li	suf	bound	Inflec.
est	suf	bound	Inflec.

6. EXISTENCE

Lexical category __noun__   Open/Closed __open__

Morphemes	Stem/Pre/Suf	Bound/Free	Inflec/Deriv
exist	stem	free	
ence	suf	bound	deriv.

Name _____   **Section** _____   **Date** _____

7. STABILITY

Lexical category __noun__   Open/Closed __open__

Morphemes	Stem/Pre/Suf	Bound/Free	Inflec/Deriv
(stabile) stable	stem	free	
ity	suf.	bound	deriv.

8. RELATIONSHIPS

Lexical category __noun__   Open/Closed __open__

Morphemes	Stem/Pre/Suf	Bound/Free	Inflec/Deriv
relation	stem	free	
ships	suf.		inflec

9. INEQUALITY

Lexical category __noun__   Open/Closed __open__

Morphemes	Stem/Pre/Suf	Bound/Free	Inflec/Deriv
equal	stem	free	
in	pre		deriv.
ity	suf	bound	inflec

B.   Now do the same for the following three words not found in the passage:

1. ENCODER

Lexical category _____noun_____   Open/Closed _____open_____

Morphemes	Stem/Pre/Suf	Bound/Free	Inflec/Deriv
code	stem	free	
en	pre	bound	deriv.
er	suf.	bound	deriv.

2. UNHERALDED

Lexical category _____adj._____   Open/Closed _____open_____

Morphemes	Stem/Pre/Suf	Bound/Free	Inflec/Deriv
herald	stem	free	
un	pre.	bound	deriv.
ed	suf.	bound	inflec.

3. SKATEBOARDING

Lexical category _____noun_____   Open/Closed _____open_____

Morphemes	Stem/Pre/Suf	Bound/Free	Inflec/Deriv
skate	stem	free	
board	stem	free	
ing	suf.	bound	inflec.

Name _____   **Section** _____   **Date** _____

C. Identify and list eleven monomorphemic words in the passage, including four monosyllabic ones, four disyllabic ones, and three consisting of more than two syllables. An example of each is given:

Monosyllabic	Disyllabic	Multisyllabic
EXAMPLE: young	humble	poverty
land	respect	religion
age	precious	dignity
hope	solemn	natural
poor	human	discipline

D. List all monosyllabic words in the passage with more than one morpheme:

develops	men	conferred
every	dooms	sacraments
sees	murdering	supernatural
functioning	meaning	transforming

Name _____   Section _____   Date _____

3.04   CONSTITUENCY AND WORD-FORMATION RULES IN ENGLISH

For each word below, identify its root; then give the sequence of additions for each word in the left column, the morphological rule by which the addition was made in the middle column, and the bracketing for the word in the right column.

pg. 83 in book

EXAMPLE: UNENLIGHTENED

Stem	Rule	Bracketing
light	root	[light]
light + en	adj + en → verb	[[light] en]
en + lighten	en + verb → verb	[en [[light] en]]
enlighten + ed	verb + ed → adj	[[en [[light] en]] ed]
un + enlightened	un + adj → adj	[un [[en [[light] en]] ed]]

1.   REAPPEARANCE

stay in lexical category as long as you can.

Stem	Rule	Bracketing
1. appear	root verb	[appear]
3. appear + ance	verb + ance → noun	[appear]ance]
2. re + appearance	re + noun → noun	[re [appear] ance]
re appear		[re [appear]]
		[re [appear]] ance]

2.   UNTOUCHABLE

Stem	Rule	Bracketing
touch	root	[touch]
touch + able	verb + able → adj.	[[touch] able]
un + touchable	un + adj → adj.	[un [[touch] able]]

3. OWNERSHIP

Stem	Rule	Bracketing
own	root	[own]
own + er	verb + er → noun	[own] er]
owner + ship	noun + ship → noun	[[own] er] ship]

4. UNTROUBLED

Stem	Rule	Bracketing
trouble	root	[trouble]
troubl + ed	verb + ed → adj.	[[trouble] ed]
un + troubled	un + adj → adj.	[un [[trouble] ed]]

5. UNLIKELIHOOD

Stem	Rule	Bracketing
like	root	[like]
like + li	adv. + li → adj.	[[like] li]
likeli + hood	adj. + hood → noun	[[[like] li] hood]
un + likelihood	un + noun → noun	[un [[[like] li] hood]]
likely	root	[likely]
un + likely	un + adj → adj	[un [likely]]
unlikely + hood	un + adj → ~~to~~ noun	[[un [likely]] hood]

Name _____   **Section** _____   **Date** _____

6. INSENSITIVITY

Stem	Rule	Bracketing
sensitive	root	[sensitive]
sensitiv+ity	adj. + ity→ noun	[[sensitiv]ity]
in+sensitivity	in + noun→ adj.	[in[[sensitiv]ity]]

7. REINFORCEMENTS

Stem	Rule	Bracketing
(en) force	root	[force]
in+ force	in + verb→ verb	[in [force]]
inforce+ ment	verb+ ment→ noun	[in [force]ment]
re+ inforcement	re+noun→ noun	[re[in[force]ment]]

8. DISENCHANTMENT

Stem	Rule	Bracketing
chant	root	[chant]
enchant	en+ noun→ verb	[en[chant]]
enchant + ment	verb+ment→noun	[[enchant]ment]
dis+ enchantment	dis+noun→noun	[dis [[enchant]ment]]

chant	root	[chant]
en+ chant	en + noun → verb	[en [chant]]
dis +enchant	dis + verb → verb	[dis [en[chant]]]
disenchant+ ment	verb+ ment → noun	[[dis [en [chant]]]ment]

9. UNSHOCKABILITY

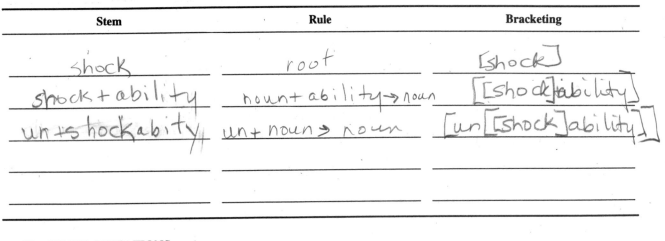

Stem	Rule	Bracketing
shock	root	[shock]
shock + ability	noun + ability → noun	[[shock]ability]
un + shockabity	un + noun → noun	[un[[shock]ability]]

10. RECOLONIZATIONS

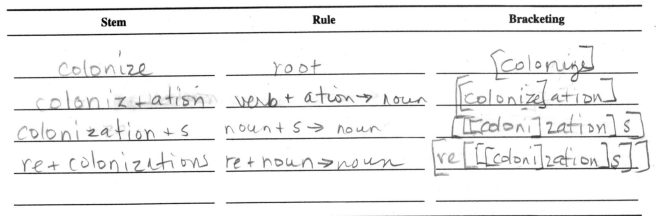

Stem	Rule	Bracketing
colonize	root	[colonize]
coloniz + ation	verb + ation → noun	[[colonize]ation]
colonization + s	noun + s → noun	[[coloni]zation]s]
re + colonizations	re + noun → noun	[re[[[coloni]zation]s]]

Name _____   **Section** _____   **Date** _____

3.05   PERSIAN MORPHEME IDENTIFICATION 1

Here are some data in Modern Colloquial Persian, given in phonetic transcription:

1.	mæn mixunæm	'I am reading.'
2.	šoma ketab mixunid	'You are reading a book.'
3.	šoma ketabro næxundid	'You didn't read the book.'
4.	mæn ketab nemixunæm	'I am not reading a book.'
5.	mæn næxundæmeš	'I didn't read it.'
6.	šoma xundideš	'Did you read it?'
7.	šoma xundideš	'You read it.' (past tense)

A. Isolate and identify *all* the morphemes present in the data, and state the meaning of each one. Point out any instances of two or more allomorphs belonging to a single morpheme.

_____

_____

_____

_____

_____

B. Translate into Persian: 'You aren't reading it.'

_____

C. How do you suppose yes-no questions are formed in Colloquial Persian? (A yes-no question is one to which the answer is either yes or no.)

_____

_____

_____

D. Consider the following additional data: (As usual, * indicates that something is ungrammatical.)

8.	*mæn šoma mibinæm	'I see you.'
9.	mæn šomaro mibinæm	'I see you.'

How will you have to revise your original analysis, if at all, to account for these new data? Explain.

_____

_____

_____

E.   To express a "past progressive" verb ('was reading,' 'were eating,' etc.), the two morphemes you isolated above that relate to tense or aspect are used *together*.

Translate into Persian: 'I wasn't reading the book.'

Name _____   **Section** _____   **Date** _____

3.06   LAKOTA VERBS

Examine the following inflected forms for several verbs in the Native American language Lakota. (For some general information on this language as well as an explanation of some of the phonetic symbols used in the transcription, see the introduction to Problem 1.16.) By comparing the given forms, you will be able to identify the morphemes present and state their meanings or functions.

A. Identify the morphemes present in the data given below. You should be able to isolate the stems of the verbs as well as several agreement markers. Indicate which such markers are prefixed to the stems in this data, and which are suffixed. In one case, you should also indicate the semantic effect of using two of the markers in combination.

Note that two abbreviations have been used in the glosses:

we_1 = you (sg.) and I

we_2 = she/he and I, or several of us (more than two)

1. wahi — 'I arrive'
2. čĩ — 'she/he wants'
3. ũk'upi — 'we_2 give to him/her'
4. ʔũpi — 'they are'
5. gⁱli — 'she/he arrives here'
6. yačĩpi — 'you (pl.) want'
7. wak'u — 'I give to him/her'
8. ũpsičapi — 'we_2 jump'
9. škatapi — 'they play'
10. ũhi — 'we_1 arrive'
11. yaʔũ — 'you (sg.) are'
12. yapsičapi — 'you (pl.) jump'
13. ũškata — 'we_1 play'
14. yagⁱli — 'you (sg.) arrive here'

Verb Stems   **Agreement Markers**

_____

_____

_____

_____

_____

_____

_____

B. Now, using the morphemes you have identified, give the complete paradigm of the verb <u>t</u>^hi 'to live or dwell':

_____   'I dwell'

_____   'you (sg.) dwell'

_____   'he/she dwells'

_____   'you (sg.) and I dwell'

_____   'she/he and I/several of us dwell'

_____   'you (pl.) dwell'

_____   'they dwell'

Name _____   **Section** _____   **Date** _____

3.07   LATIN DECLENSIONS

Latin, the ancestor of the modern Romance languages, is a language in which nouns change their form according to their grammatical role in the sentence. In this problem you will examine some different forms, or *cases*, of certain Latin nouns.

Examine the Latin sentences given below in standard orthography, and answer the questions that follow.

Note: Since Latin has distinctive vowel length, long vowels are sometimes represented with a macron (‾), even though the Romans themselves did not do this. You need not try to account for any changes in vowel length in your solution to this problem.

1. Senātor gladiātor erat.   'The senator was a gladiator.'
2. Crātēr senātōris est.   'It is the senator's bowl.'
3. Structor senātōrem aspexit.   'The carpenter looked at the senator.'
4. Senātōrem aspexit structor.   'The carpenter looked at the senator.'
5. Senātor aspexit structōrem.   'The senator looked at the carpenter.'
6. Structōrem senātor aspexit.   'The senator looked at the carpenter.'
7. Senātor sorōrem gladiātōris aspexit.   'The senator looked at the gladiator's sister.'
8. Structor crātērem senātōrī dedit.   'The carpenter gave the bowl to the senator.'
9. Gladiātōrī crātērem dedit senātor.   'The senator gave the bowl to the gladiator.'

A. List the nouns in the data, and divide them into their component morphemes. Then state the meaning or function of each of these morphemes.

senātor
gladiātor
crātēr
senātōris
senātōrem
structor
senātor
structōrem
sorōrem
gladiātōris
crātērem
gladiātōrī

B. Examine carefully sentences 3 through 6. Compared to English, is word order in Latin more or less important in determining the meaning of a sentence? Justify your answer.

In Latin, word order is less important in determining the meaning of a sentence because the endings on nouns are changed based on their grammatical role in the sentence, not on word order.

C. Translate into English:

Gladiātōrī structōrem senātor commendāvit. [commendāvit = 'recommended']

The senator recommended the carpenter to the gladiator.

D. Translate into Latin:

The gladiator gave the carpenter's bowl to the senator's sister.

Gladiator crater structoris senatoris sororem dedit.

Name _____ **Section** _____ **Date** _____

3.08   PERSIAN MORPHEME IDENTIFICATION 2

Below you will find a number of sentences in Modern Formal Persian. The sentences have been translated, but individual words and morphemes have not been identified. Examine the data carefully, comparing the different sentences and their translations, and then answer the questions that follow.

1.	šoma koǰa budid	'Where were you?'
2.	mæn bæd næbudæm	'I wasn't bad.'
3.	mæn emruz ketab mixanæm	'I am reading a book today.'
4.	an zæn bæd bud	'That woman was bad.'
5.	mæn ketabra mixanæm	'I am reading the book.'
6.	mærd ketabra xand	'The man read the book.'
7.	ketab xub bud	'The book was good.'
8.	aya šoma ketab mixanid	'Are you reading a book?'
9.	in mærd xub bud	'This man was good.'
10.	zæne mæn ketabra anǰa nemixanæd	'My wife doesn't read the book there.'
11.	mæn diruz ketab næxandæm	'I didn't read a book yesterday.'
12.	šoma ketabra inǰa xandid	'You read (PAST) the book there.'
13.	aya šoma ketabe mærdra mibinid	'Do you see the man's book?'
14.	aya in zæn šomara mibinæd	'Does this woman see you?'
15.	mæn ura nædidæm	'I didn't see him.'
16.	u zænra did	'She saw the woman.'
17.	nanra nædaræm	'I don't have the bread.'
18.	zænra did	'He saw the woman.'

Note: One possible translation has been given for each sentence. There may be other possible translations as well.

A. Isolate and identify all the morphemes that are present in the data, *stating the meaning or function* of each one. In giving your answers, group the morphemes into categories (nouns, verb roots, verb suffixes, etc.).

_____

_____

_____

_____

_____

_____

_____

_____

_____

_____

_____

_____

_____

_____

_____

_____

_____

_____

B.　What are the two allomorphs of the negative morpheme?

_____

C.　What is unusual about the way Persian expresses the verb 'see'?

_____

_____

_____

D.　The verb 'have' is somewhat irregular in many languages. How about Persian? Explain.

_____

_____

_____

E.　Translate into English:

　　　mæn ketabe zæne šomara nædidæm

_____

F.　Translate into Persian:

　　　Do you have her bread?

_____

Name _____   **Section** _____   **Date** _____

3.09   A NEGATIVE PREFIX IN ENGLISH

A. Consider the following English words, each of which includes a prefix spelled *in-* or *im-*:

insurmountable	indefinable	inexhaustible
inanimate	impartial	involuntary
indignity	inexplicable	inoperable
insufferable	indecisive	impossible
inordinate	inappropriate	independent
imbalance	inexpressible	infamous
ineligible	impractical	inutile
inarticulate	invalid	inalienable

What determines for each of the adjectives or noun roots whether the negative prefix is *im-* or *in-*?

im- is used when followed by a "b" or "p"

_____

_____

B. Now consider the following words:

incomplete	inconclusive	incorrigible
incoherent	incommodious	inconsiderate
incomprehensible	ingratitude	inconvenient
incompetence	inconsistency	incurable

What two different pronunciations of the negative prefix occur in these words? What accounts for the variant pronunciations?

_____

_____

_____

C. Next to each of the words below, write its negative form:

legible   *illegible*   legitimate   *illegitimate*

literate   *illiterate*   logical   *illogical*

legal   *illegal*

D. There is another set of words which, like those in C above, require a special form of the negative prefix. Give some members of this set along with their negative forms.

disappoint

disagree

disappear

disallow

E. Now summarize your findings: What generalizations can be made about the distribution of the allomorphs of this negative prefix?

il- before words beginning with an "l"

dis- before some words beginning with an "a"

Name _____   **Section** _____   **Date** _____

3.10   THE DEFINITE ARTICLE IN ARABIC

A.   Examine the following list of nouns in Standard Arabic. The first column gives the form without the definite article, while the second column gives the form with the definite article. Then posit an underlying form for the definite article in Arabic. (Note: [q] is a voiceless uvular stop. The vowel transcribed as [a] has some phonetic variation which has not been indicated.)

1.	?ab	?al?ab	'father'
2.	ba:b	?alba:b	'door'
3.	xari:f	?alxari:f	'autumn'
4.	fa:ris	?alfa:ris	'knight'
5.	qabr	?alqabr	'tomb'
6.	kalb	?alkalb	'dog'
7.	madrasa	?almadrasa	'school'
8.	hila:l	?alhila:l	'crescent'
9.	wa:ǰib	?alwa:ǰib	'duty'
10.	?ax	?al?ax	'brother'
11.	bint	?albint	'girl'
12.	funduq	?alfunduq	'hotel'
13.	qism	?alqism	'part'
14.	kita:b	?alkita:b	'book'
15.	maǰd	?almaǰd	'glory'
16.	walad	?alwalad	'boy'

UNDERLYING FORM OF DEFINITE ARTICLE: _____

B.   Now examine the following additional data. Notice that in these cases, the definite article is pronounced differently.

Formulate a rule that determines how the article is actually pronounced. Your goal is not to come up with a large number of different rules for specific cases, but rather to find one *general* rule that will work in every case.

17.	tarbiya	?attarbiya	'education'
18.	da:r	?adda:r	'house'
19.	ra:kib	?arra:kib	'rider'
20.	zayt	?azzayt	'oil'
21.	sala:m	?assala:m	'peace'
22.	šaǰara	?aššaǰara	'tree'
23.	nati:ǰa	?annati:ǰa	'result'
24.	ta?rix	?atta?rix	'history'
25.	dars	?addars	'lesson'
26.	raǰul	?arraǰul	'man'
27.	zava:ǰ	?azzava:ǰ	'marriage'
28.	sinn	?assinn	'tooth'
29.	šama:l	?aššama:l	'north'
30.	nabi	?annabi	'prophet'

_____

_____

_____

_____

Name _____   **Section** _____   **Date** _____

3.11   A DERIVED VERB STEM IN ARABIC

As in other Semitic languages, most verb forms in Arabic and their corresponding nominals are derived from a sequence of three root consonants or "radicals," to which are added various affixes. The three consonants embody a basic semantic notion, which is modified, refined and extended by the affixes.

For example, the consonants ħ-k-m relate to the idea of judging or ruling. These consonants, of course, are unpronounceable by themselves. However, with the insertion of vowels in various patterns, the addition of certain prefixes, infixes and suffixes, and the lengthening of certain consonants and vowels, a wide range of Arabic words is produced with meanings related in various ways to judging or ruling. Here is a partial list of words derivable from the root ħ-k-m in this way:

Verbs:

ħakama	'pass judgment, govern, rule, dominate'
ħukima	'be judged, receive judgment'
ħa:kkama	'appoint as judge or ruler'
ħakama	'prosecute, bring to trial'
ʔaħkama	'do expertly, be proficient in, master'
taħakkama	'pass arbitrary judgment, be in control'
taħa:kama	'appeal for a legal decision, be heard (in court)'
ʔiħtakama	'have one's own way, proceed at will, reign, hold sway'
ʔistaħkama	'be strong, firm, deep-seated, ingrained'

Nouns and adjectives:

ħukm	'judgment, legal decision' (pl.: ʔaħkam)
ħukmi:	'legal'
ħakam	'arbitrator, umpire, referee'
ħikma	'wisdom'
ħaki:m	'wise man, sage, physician'
ħuku:ma	'government'
ħuku:mi:	'governmental, official'
ʔaħkam	'wiser'
maħkama	'court'
taħki:m	'arbitration'
muħa:kama	'trial'
ʔiħka:m	'perfection in performance'
taħakkum	'despotism, domination'
ħa:kim	'judge, ruler'

There are ten common patterns or stems for verbs in Arabic. Stem I is the basic, simplest pattern. This problem concerns Stem II, the second of these verbal patterns.

Each pair of words below consists of the Stem I form of the verb along with the Stem II form. Compare the forms and meanings carefully, paying particular attention to the meaning relationship between Stems I and II. Then answer the questions that follow.

Note: Arabic verbs are listed in dictionaries under their simplest forms, namely the third person singular masculine (Semitic verbs have gender!) of the perfect, Stem I. These are the "citation" forms—the forms people give when they wish to talk about the item in question. In English, we speak of the verb 'to write,' the citation form being the infinitive; Arabic speakers talk about the verb *kataba*, which means 'he wrote.' The words below are accordingly given in their third-person citation forms but glossed as English infinitives. Many of these verbs have a wide range of meanings, often including metaphorical ones; the glosses below most clearly point to the systematic relationship between the two stems.

If you are unfamiliar with any of the phonetic symbols used in the transcription, see Appendix B.

1. I: nazala   'to descend, go or come down'
   II: nazzala   'to lower, let down'

2. I: baraza   'to come out, appear'
   II: barraza   'to bring out, expose, show'

3. I: baṭala   'to become null, void, invalid'
   II: baṭṭala   'to nullify, neutralize, invalidate'

4. I: nafaḍa   'to shake, shake off, shake out'
   II: naffaḍa   'to shake violently'

5. I: xasira   'to go astray'
   II: xassara   'to corrupt'

6. I: šarada   'to run away, flee, escape'
   II: šarrada   'to frighten or chase away'

7. I: θabata   'to stand firm, be fixed or stationary'
   II: θabbata   'to fasten, make fast, stabilize'

8. I: ħasuna   'to be handsome, beautiful, proper'
   II: ħassana   'to beautify, embellish, improve'

9. I: qatala   'to kill, slay'
   II: qattala   'to massacre, cause carnage'

10. I: xalada   'to be immortal, eternal, everlasting'
    II: xallada   'to perpetuate, immortalize'

11. I: wasixa   'to be or become dirty'
    II: wassaxa   'to dirty, sully, soil'

12. I: raɣiba   'to desire, wish, crave'
    II: raɣɣaba   'to awaken a desire, excite interest'

13. I: kasara   'to break, shatter, break open'
    II: kassara   'to break into pieces, fragmentize, smash'

Name _____   **Section** _____   **Date** _____

14. I: sakana   'to be tranquil; to calm down, abate, subside'

    II: sakkana   'to calm, placate, soothe'

15. I: ṭaraḥa   'to throw away, discard'

    II: ṭarraḥa   'to throw far away'

16. I: ʕalima   'to know, be informed'

    II: ʕallama   'to teach, instruct'

17. I: hataka   'to tear or rip apart'

    II: hattaka   'to tear to shreds, rip to pieces'

18. I: qaruba   'to be near, to approach'

    II: qarraba   'to bring into proximity'

19. I: labisa   'to put on, wear'

    II: labbasa   'to clothe, garb, attire'

20. I: matuna   'to be firm, strong, solid'

    II: mattana   'to strengthen, fortify'

A. If we call the three root consonants in each example above C_1, C_2 and C_3, what is the pattern or patterns for the Stem I verbs?

_____

_____

B. What is the pattern or patterns for the Stem II verbs?

_____

_____

C. You will have noticed that the meanings of the Stem II forms are related in systematic ways to those of the corresponding Stem I forms. There are two basic semantic relationships between the two stems apparent in these data. One holds for the majority of examples, but a second, different relationship is evident as well.

    Explain what these two relationships are; in the case of the "minority" relationship, include the numbers of the examples in the data that give evidence for it.

_____

_____

_____

_____

_____

_____

_____

_____

_____

_____

D. Consider the following two verbs:

    I: raǰaʕa   'to return'

    II: raǰǰaʕa   'to return'

    Notice that they have been glossed identically. Are these words exceptions to the generalizations you found in C above, or do they fit into the pattern? Explain.

_____

_____

_____

Name _____   Section _____   Date _____

3.12   RULE ORDERING

In some linguistic theories, phonological rules must be applied to underlying forms in a definite order. Varying this order may affect the phonetic manifestation of the word, i.e., its ultimate pronunciation.

In one such theory, phonological rules apply to underlying forms in the following way:

Once the complete underlying form has been determined, the list of rules is gone through one by one. Assuming these rules are all *obligatory* and not optional, each rule in its turn MUST apply whenever it CAN. If the rule CANNOT apply, it is simply skipped over, and the next rule in the list applies. It is NOT possible to return to a rule that has already been passed over in the sequence.

Here are some morphemes of Communico, a newly-discovered language, given in their underlying forms:

Nouns		Noun prefixes	
/il/	'water snake'	/pom/	'my'
/papi/	'flower'	/n/	'your'
/gælo/	'grape'	/ka/	'his'
		/g/	'her'

Here are some obligatory phonological rules of Communico:

NASAL ASSIMILATION: A nasal consonant assimilates in place of articulation to an immediately following stop.

VOWEL DROP: A vowel is deleted if it immediately precedes another vowel.

***i*-INSERTION:** The vowel *i* is inserted between two consonants at the beginning of a word.

PALATALIZATION: *k* becomes *č*, and *g* becomes *ǰ*, when immediately preceding a *high front* vowel.

A.   For the Valley Dialect of Communico, the rules apply *in the order given above.*

Give the underlying forms for 'my grape,' 'his water snake,' 'your flower' and 'her flower,' and show how the rules apply in each case to yield the pronunciations in the Valley Dialect.

	'my grape'	'his water snake'	'your flower'	'her flower'
Underlying Forms:	/	/ /	/ /	/ / /
Rules				
	_____	_____	_____	_____
	_____	_____	_____	_____
	_____	_____	_____	_____
	_____	_____	_____	_____
Surface Forms:	[ ]	[ ]	[ ]	[ ]

B. In the River Dialect of Communico, the underlying forms and rules are the same, but the rules apply in a different order, namely:

** *i*-INSERTION**
** PALATALIZATION**
** VOWEL DROP**
** NASAL ASSIMILATION**

Determine how the words for the four phrases given in A sound in the River Dialect.

	'my grape'	'his water snake'	'your flower'	'her flower'
Underlying Forms:	/	/ /	/ /	/ / /
Rules				
Surface Forms:	[ ]	[ ]	[ ]	[ ]

C. The Mountain Dialect orders the rules in still another way:

** NASAL ASSIMILATION**
** *i*-INSERTION**
** PALATALIZATION**
** VOWEL DROP**

Go through the derivations a third time to determine how the four words are pronounced in the Mountain Dialect.

	'my grape'	'his water snake'	'your flower'	'her flower'
Underlying Forms:	/	/ /	/ /	/ / /
Rules				
Surface Forms:	[ ]	[ ]	[ ]	[ ]

Name _____ **Section** _____ **Date** _____

3.13   MALAY/INDONESIAN MORPHOPHONEMICS

A.   Examine the following Malay/Indonesian words. The first column gives a number of verbs in their root forms and the second gives the forms with a prefix attached. This prefix has a number of different allomorphs. (The forms in the second column have been glossed in only one of several possible ways.)

1a.	bawa	'bring'		1b.	məmbawa	'bringing'
2a.	dapat	'get'		2b.	məndapat	'getting'
3a.	gaŋgu	'bother'		3b.	məŋgaŋgu	'bothering'
4a.	doroŋ	'push'		4b.	məndoroŋ	'pushing'
5a.	ambil	'take'		5b.	məŋambil	'taking'
6a.	bwat	'do'		6b.	məmbwat	'doing'
7a.	hilaŋ	'disappear'		7b.	məŋhilaŋ	'disappearing'
8a.	učap	'say'		8b.	məŋučap	'saying'

List the different allomorphs of the prefix that are found among these data. Then propose a single, unique underlying form for the prefix, and state the rule or rules that will account for the appearance of the various allomorphs. Your rule(s) should be as general as possible.

ALLOMORPHS: _____

UNDERLYING FORM: _____

RULE:

_____

_____

B.   Now consider the following additional data:

9a.	tari	'dance'		9b.	mənari	'dancing'
10a.	pandaŋ	'gaze'		10b.	məmandaŋ	'gazing'
11a.	tulis	'write'		11b.	mənulis	'writing'
12a.	kandoŋ	'contain'		12b.	məŋandoŋ	'containing'
13a.	pəgaŋ	'hold'		13b.	məməgaŋ	'holding'
14a.	kata	'say'		14b.	məŋata	'saying'
15a.	pakay	'wear'		15b.	məmakay	'wearing'
16a.	tərima	'receive'		16b.	mənərima	'receiving'

Propose an additional rule that will correctly account for the forms in the second column.

_____

_____

_____

C.   The rules you proposed in parts A and B must be applied in a certain order. What is this order?

_____

_____

Show how the words for 'taking,' 'pushing' and 'gazing' are derived.

	'taking'		'pushing'		'gazing'	
Underlying Forms:	/	/ /		/ /		/
Rules						
_____	_____	_____	_____			
_____	_____	_____	_____			
Surface Forms:	[	] [		] [		]

Name _____   **Section** _____   **Date** _____

3.14   MORPHOPHONEMICS OF CERTAIN ARTICLES AND PRONOUNS IN MODERN GREEK (OR: THE GIRL OR THE SAILOR)

Modern Greek has considerable inflectional morphology. The data below concern a subset of the Modern Greek articles and pronouns, both of which categories are inflected for gender, number and case.

Nouns, pronouns and adjectives in Modern Greek fall into one of three genders, traditionally referred to as masculine, feminine and neuter. The data presented here are restricted to masculine and neuter genders. Note that the word for 'man' is, appropriately enough, masculine.

A. Examine the following sentences in Modern Greek. (The data are given in transcription; stress is indicated.)

1. (a) o ándras íne εðó   'The man is here.'
   (b) vlέpo ton ándra   'I see the man.'
   (c) ton vlέpo   'I see him.'

2. (a) to krasí ine εðó   'The wine is here.'
   (b) pínumε to krasí   'We drink the wine.'
   (c) to pínumε   'We drink it.'

3. (a) o kafέs íne εðo   'The coffee is here.'
   (b) píno toŋ gafé   'I drink the coffee.'
   (c) tom bíno   'I drink it.'

4. (a) o tíxos íne εðo   'The wall is here.'
   (b) vlέpumε ton díxo   'We see the wall.'
   (c) ton vlέpumε   'We see it.'

5. (a) to pεðí íne εðó   'The child is here.'
   (b) ksέro to pεðí   'I know the child.'
   (c) to ksέro   'I know him/her.'

6. (a) o kírios íne εðó   'The gentleman is here.'
   (b) ksέrumε toŋ gírio   'We know the gentleman.'
   (c) toŋ gzέrumε   'We know him.'

7. (a) to pεrioðikó íne εðó   'The magazine is here.'
   (b) έxumε to pεrioðikó   'We have the magazine.'
   (c) to έxumε   'We have it.'

8. (a) o páɣos íne εðó   'The ice is here.'
   (b) έxo tom báɣo   'I have the ice.'
   (c) ton έxo   'I have it.'

1. Isolate all the morphemes present in the data, giving each one in its underlying form. For the articles and pronouns, you may want to present your solutions in a chart like the following:

	Masc.	Neuter
Subj.	_____	_____
Obj.	_____	_____

_____

_____

_____

_____

_____

_____

_____

_____

_____

_____

_____

_____

_____

_____

_____

_____

_____

_____

_____

_____

_____

_____

Name _____   **Section** _____   **Date** _____

2. State the rule or rules that will derive the surface forms from the underlying forms. For 'I have the ice,' give the underlying form, and show how your rule or rules apply to yield the surface form.

RULE(S):

_____

_____

_____

_____

	'I have the ice.'

Underlying Form: /   /

Rules

_____   _____

_____   _____

Surface Form: [   ]

B. Some of the (b) and (c) sentences in the data have alternate forms in spoken Greek. These are given below.

3. (b′) píno to gafé
    (c′) to bíno

4. (b′) vlépumɛ to díxo
    (c′) to vlépumɛ

6. (b′) ksérumɛ to gírio
    (c′) to gzérumɛ

8. (b′) éxo to báɣo

What additional rule is needed to account for these spoken variants? How must this rule be ordered with respect to the rule(s) you formulated in part A? Justify your answers.

_____

_____

_____

_____

_____

C. You overhear a conversation in an Athenian taverna concerning a sailor and a girl. The noise level is such that you can't follow the conversation completely. However, you clearly hear someone saying that he knows the individual under discussion. What you hear is:

to gzéro

Is the speaker saying that he is acquainted with the sailor (o náftis) or the girl (to korítsi)? How do you know?

_____

_____

_____

Name _____   Section _____   Date _____

3.15   THE DEFINITE ARTICLE IN WELSH

A.   Examine the data below, given in both standard Welsh orthography and phonetic transcription. Then answer the questions that follow.

1a.	y tŷ	[ə ti]	'the house'
2a.	y gwaith	[ə gwaiθ]	'the workplace'
3a.	yr ysgol	[ər əskol]	'the school'
4a.	y car	[ə kar]	'the car'
5a.	yr adeilad	[ər adeilad]	'the building'
6a.	yr eglwys	[ər egluis]	'the church'

1b.	yn y tŷ	[ən ə ti]	'in the house'
2b.	yn y gwaith	[ən ə gwaiθ]	'in the workplace'
3b.	yn yr ysgol	[ən ər əskol]	'in the school'
4b.	yn y car	[ən ə kar]	'in the car'
5b.	yn yr adeilad	[ən ər adeilad]	'in the building'
6b.	yn yr eglwys	[ən ər egluis]	'in the church'

1c.	i'r tŷ	[ir ti]	'to the house'
2c.	i'r gwaith	[ir gwaiθ]	'to the workplace'
3c.	i'r ysgol	[ir əskol]	'to the school'
4c.	i'r car	[ir kar]	'to the car'
5c.	i'r adeilad	[ir adeilad]	'to the building'
6c.	i'r eglwys	[ir egluis]	'to the church'

1d.	o'r tŷ	[or ti]	'from the house'
2d.	o'r gwaith	[or gwaiθ]	'from the workplace'
3d.	o'r ysgol	[or əskol]	'from the school'
4d.	o'r car	[or kar]	'from the car'
5d.	o'r adeilad	[or adeilad]	'from the building'
6d.	o'r eglwys	[or egluis]	'from the church'

1.   What are the allomorphs of the definite article in Welsh?

_____

_____

2. What is the distribution of these allomorphs—i.e., what determines when each one is used? (Make sure your statements determine unambiguously which form of the word is to be used in any situation!)

_____

_____

_____

_____

B. In part A, you came up with a descriptive, distributional analysis of the data. In this part, you'll do a generative analysis of the same data.

1. Find a unique underlying form for the definite article from which all the allomorphs can be derived.

_____

2. Propose one or more phonological rules which will allow the surface forms to be derived. If there is more than one rule, do they have to be ordered with respect to each other? Explain.

_____

_____

_____

_____

_____

3. Show the derivation of 'in the house,' 'in the school,' 'from the house,' and 'from the school' by filling in the chart below. (Use phonetic transcription.)

	'in the house'		'in the school'
Underlying Forms:	/	/ /	/
Phonological Rules			
	_____	_____	_____
	_____	_____	_____
	_____	_____	_____
Surface Forms:	[ ]	[	]

Name _____   **Section** _____   **Date** _____

	'from the house'	'from the school'
Underlying Forms:	/	/ /	/

Phonological Rules

_____ _____ _____

_____ _____ _____

_____ _____ _____

Surface Forms: [   ] [   ]

C. Translate into Welsh: 'The car is in the house.' (Give your answer in standard Welsh spelling.)

Note: Welsh is a *verb-initial* language, with basic word order VERB—SUBJECT—OBJECT—EVERYTHING ELSE. 'is' = mae [mae].

_____

_____

Name _____   **Section** _____   **Date** _____

3.16   ENGLISH PAST-TENSE PRODUCTIVITY EXPERIMENT

A.   Consider the following pairs of English verbs:

A		B	
live	d	give	gave
fake	d	take	took
like	d	strike	struck
leak	ed	speak	spoke
side	d	ride	rode
link	ed	think	thought
sin	ned	spin	spun

1.   How do the A-verbs form their past tense?

   by adding d , ed

2.   How do the B-verbs form their past tense?

   the form of the word is changed

B.   Here are some brand new, just-coined English verbs, with definitions and examples:

a.   bive   [bɪv]   'gulp down'

   Why do you always bive your food?

b.   vake   'have someone vacation'

   I think I'm going to vake my mother in Tahoe this year.

c.   slike   'attend only the last half of a class, lecture, concert, etc.'

   You shouldn't slike math so often.

d.   deak   'have a strong feeling of distaste or revulsion'

   I deak whenever I hear him sing.

e.   mide   'pour honey over'

   He usually mides his pancakes.

f.   strink   'drive a vehicle within the speed limit'

   You'd better start strinking—here comes the Highway Patrol!

g.   lin   'stare with narrowed, accusing eyes'

   Don't you lin at me like that!

You are going to conduct some linguistic research, and you will need to find an informant to help you. Your informant may be anyone at all—a family member, friend, person you meet on the street—just so long as she or he is:

(i)   at least six years of age;

(ii) a native speaker of English;

(iii) a "civilian"—i.e., not a linguistics student, language major, etc.

Your job is to elicit the past tense forms of the "new" verbs from your informant.

The way *not* to do this is to say something like, "Here's a new verb—*bive*. It means 'gulp down.' What's the past tense?" Rather, you want to elicit the desired forms as *naturally* as possible. Besides, you can't expect your informant necessarily to know the meaning of 'verb' or 'past tense.' So you will want to proceed along the following lines:

1. Teach your informant to play a language game with you. You will ask a question, and he/she will respond with a "long" answer.

    EXAMPLE: You say, "Did you eat lunch at noon?"
    Informant replies, "Yes, I ate lunch at noon."

    Try your informant out on a few random verbs, such as *eat, take, walk, go, hit, beg*. Make sure things are proceeding smoothly before going on to the next step. (You will probably want to work with a prepared "script" rather than trying to come up with your questions extemporaneously.)

2. Now teach your informant each "new" verb in turn. Give the meaning, plus an example of its use. When you are satisfied he/she has grasped the idea, try the question-answer game as in part 1.

    EXAMPLE: You say, "Did you bive your dinner last night?"
    Informant replies, "Yes, I _____ my dinner last night."

    Remember—we are interested in *speech*. The entire experiment is to be conducted orally. Do not let your informant see anything written, and do *not* spell the words—just pronounce them. You may ask your informant to repeat the answer or say it slowly, but you may not ask him/her to spell anything.

    Record all the past tense forms you get below.

Verb	Past Tense Form Elicited	
bive	_____	
vake	_____	
slike	_____	
deak	_____	
mide	_____	
strink	_____	
lin	_____	

Name _____   **Section** _____   **Date** _____

3. (a)   Summarize the results of your experiment.

_____

_____

_____

_____

_____

_____

_____

(b)   A *productive* process in a language is one that is "alive," in the sense that it can be applied to new forms entering the language. Considering the results of your experiment, comment on the productivity of the two kinds of past tense formation in English, "A-type" and "B-type."

_____

_____

_____

_____

_____

(c)   It has been proposed that the *strong* ("B-type") verbs in English form a closed set—there are a fixed number of them, and there will never be any more. Is this prediction borne out by your experiment? Explain.

_____

_____

_____

Name _____ Section _____ Date _____

CHAPTER

4

Syntax

4.01 ENGLISH CONSTITUENT STRUCTURE

Here is the first sentence of Lincoln's Gettysburg Address[1]. Several of its word sequences are isolated below. Determine whether each of these is or is not a constituent of the sentence; if it is, indicate what kind.

Fourscore and seven years ago, our forefathers brought forth on this continent a new nation, conceived in liberty and dedicated to the proposition that all men are created equal.

EXAMPLES: and seven   Not a constituent
a new nation   Constituent: NP

1. our forefathers
   [ ] Not a constituent   [✓] Constituent: ___NP___

2. forth on this
   [✓] Not a constituent   [ ] Constituent: _____

3. on this continent
   [✓] Not a constituent   [✓] Constituent: ___PP___

4. on this continent a new nation
   [✓] Not a constituent   [ ] Constituent: _____

5. all men
   [ ] Not a constituent   [✓] Constituent: ___NP___

6. men are created
   [✓] Not a constituent   [ ] Constituent: _____

[1]Delivered in 1863, Lincoln's great speech long preceded current sensitivities to sexist language.

7. are created equal
    [   ] Not a constituent   [✓] Constituent: ___VP_____

8. all men are created equal
    [   ] Not a constituent   [✓] Constituent: ___Sentence_____

9. proposition
    [   ] Not a constituent   [✓] Constituent: ___NP_____

10. the proposition that all men are created equal
    [   ] Not a constituent   [✓] Constituent: ___NP_____

11. to the proposition that all men are created equal
    [   ] Not a constituent   [✓] Constituent: ___PP_____

12. a new nation, conceived in liberty and dedicated to the proposition that all men are created equal
    [   ] Not a constituent   [✓] Constituent: ___NP_____

13. brought forth on this continent a new nation, conceived in liberty and dedicated to the proposition that all men are created equal
    [   ] Not a constituent   [✓] Constituent: ___VP_____

14. years ago, our forefathers brought forth
    [✓] Not a constituent   [   ] Constituent: _____

15. Fourscore and seven years ago, our forefathers brought forth on this continent a new nation, conceived in liberty and dedicated to the proposition that all men are created equal.
    [   ] Not a constituent   [✓] Constituent: ___Sentence_____

16. a new nation, conceived in liberty
    [✓] Not a constituent   [   ] Constituent: _____

17. dedicated to the proposition
    [✓] Not a constituent   [   ] Constituent: _____

Name _____   **Section** _____   **Date** _____

4.02   TREE DIAGRAMS FOR ENGLISH SENTENCES

Below you will find a number of tree diagrams, ranging from simple to fairly complex. These are basically "empty" trees that will each fit a large number of different sentences.

For each example, provide a sentence that fits the structure. Write the lexical items where they belong in the tree, and write the whole sentence below the tree in the space provided.

Note: Triangles have been used when the details of a particular structure are not required. Although in some theories of syntax the AUX node is always present, for simplicity AUX has not been consistently indicated in the diagrams. The same is true for the COMP node relating to the matrix sentence.

EXAMPLE:

Given

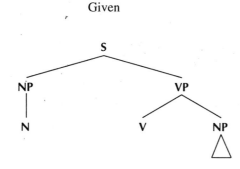

One possible answer

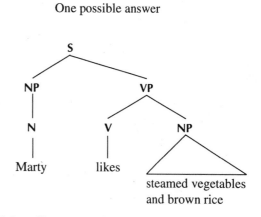

Marty likes steamed vegetables and brown rice.

1.

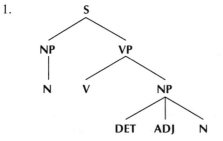

_____

_____

2.

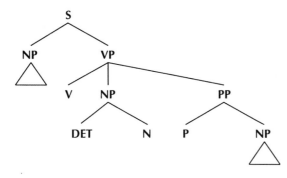

_____

_____

3.

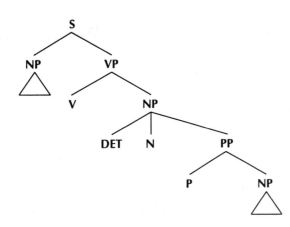

_____

_____

4.

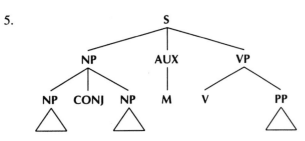

_____

_____

5.

_____

_____

6.

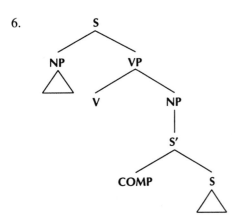

_____

_____

Name _____   **Section** _____   **Date** _____

7.

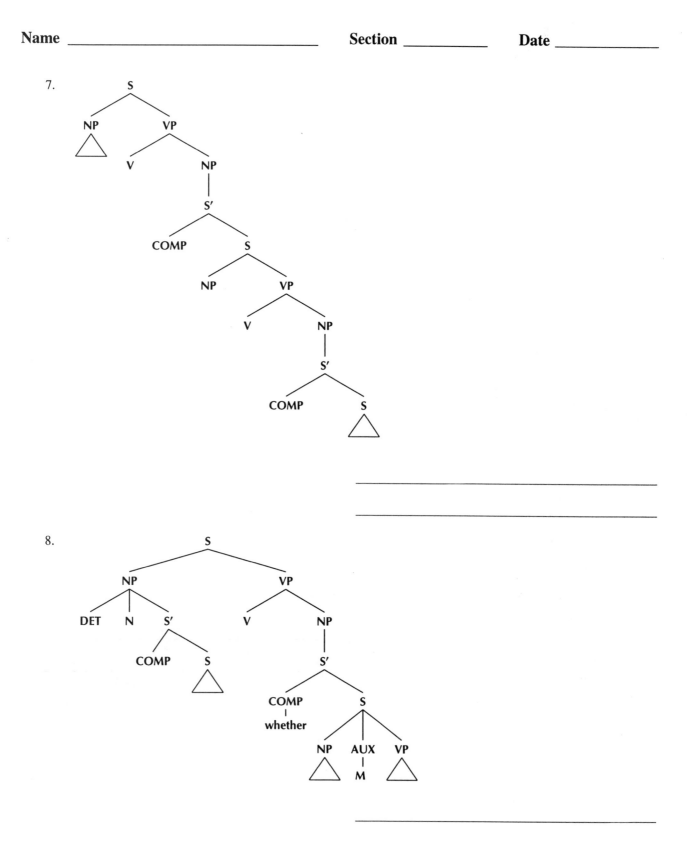

_____

_____

8.

_____

_____

9.

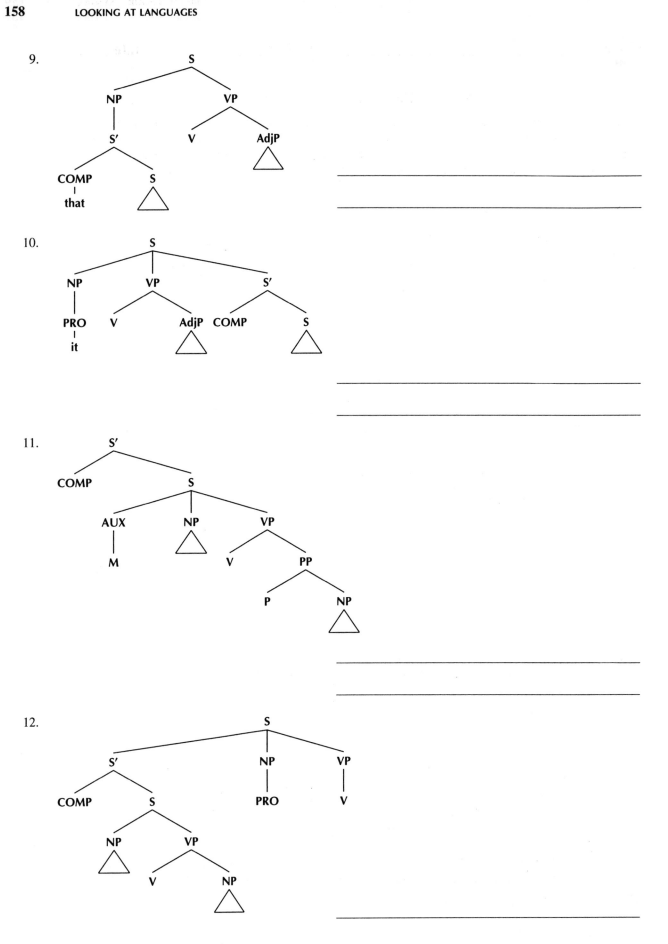

10.

11.

12.

Name _____   **Section** _____   **Date** _____

4.03   STRUCTURAL AMBIGUITY IN ENGLISH

Sentences can be ambiguous for many different reasons. The type of sentence ambiguity we are concerned with here is known as *structural ambiguity*. Sentences that are structurally ambiguous have two or more different interpretations, not because of any ambiguous words or morphemes they contain, but rather because their words or morphemes can be organized in *different constituent structures*, resulting in different meanings.

A.   The following sentence is structurally ambiguous:
   I hate *raw fish and onions.*

1. Give an unambiguous paraphrase of the sentence if the italicized part has the following structure:

raw   fish   and   onions

PARAPHRASE: _____

2. Now give a second paraphrase if the italicized part has *this* structure:

raw   fish   and   onions

PARAPHRASE: _____

B.   Consider this structurally ambiguous sentence found on a restaurant menu:

   The price includes *soup or salad and french fries.*

You should have no trouble finding two different interpretations of this sentence. For each interpretation, draw a tree diagram as in A of the italicized constituent (you needn't label the nodes) and give an unambiguous paraphrase.

Interpretation 1

PARAPHRASE: _____

Interpretation 2

PARAPHRASE: _____

Name _____   Section _____   Date _____

4.04   ENGLISH PASSIVES

Underline each passive-voice verb and bracket the underlying (deep) subject of the passive-voice clause; if the underlying subject does not appear in the surface structure of the passive sentence, write NA for "No Agent" after the sentence. (Data taken from the *Los Angeles Times*.)

EXAMPLE: The museum is directed by [Fernando Trevino Lozano].

EXAMPLE: I was told that my mental circuitry was all twisted.   NA

A.   He was once prescribed lithium to combat manic-depressive tendencies.

B.   Slash was so unruly that he was kicked out of three high schools.

C.   Rose was raised in such a strict family environment that for years he couldn't even listen to rock 'n' roll on the radio.

D.   The CD is being played at a volume that would bring complaints if Guns N' Roses had not taken over the whole floor.

E.   The song was widely attacked by critics and others who objected to the use of certain slur words to refer to blacks and homosexuals.

F.   Across the Channel, the Jeu de Paume has been refurbished as a showcase for contemporary art.

G.   Almost everything about the Museo de Arte Contemporaneo and its inaugural exhibition has been done on a grand and sumptuous scale.

H.   Half the structure is devoted to 14 galleries, which yield more exhibition space than will be found in the Anderson Building.

I.   MARCO is clearly designed to impress—and it does.

J.   Salinas' rise to political power has been tied to his vigorous championship of privatization in the Mexican economy.

K.   MARCO was organized and has been funded by an unusual partnership of private and government leaders.

L.   Galan's highly decorated paintings are often populated by porcelain-skinned, doll-like heads.

M.   He was paid $100 every two weeks to attend dance and theater classes at the Inner City Cultural Center.

N.   He recalls being questioned about why people of color were not at the forefront of the National Endowment for the Arts protests.

O.   But there's this other viewpoint, my idea, which is that before you can be censored, you have to be heard.

P.   It is the subject matter, not the person, that is being censored.

Name _____   **Section** _____   **Date** _____

4.05   ENGLISH RELATIVE CLAUSES

For each of the following sentences:

a.   Bracket the relative clause.

b.   Insert a caret (∧) in the gap where the relative pronoun originated.

c.   Underscore the head noun of the noun phrase to which the relative clause is attached.

d.   Above each relative pronoun indicate its grammatical relation in its clause: SUB = subject; DO = direct object; IO = indirect object; OBL = oblique (e.g., object of preposition); PO = possessor. Insert any relative pronouns that are omitted.

(Data taken from the *Los Angeles Times*.)

                                                              OBL

EXAMPLE: This is the <u>teacher</u> [that I told you about ∧].

                                            SUB

EXAMPLE: Those <u>fans</u> [who ∧ braved the weather] paid a price.

1.   The new law has been cheered by developers and officials who have inundated prospective immigrants with investment options.

2.   Armed Croatians and Serbians confront each other in Serbian enclaves of the Krajina, which has resisted Croatia's secession.

3.   Activist Mike Hernandez is taking an "up-close and personal" approach that he hopes will help him win the council seat.

4.   Pugnacious people on both sides use tax-deductible donations to carry on a fight that is really about values.

5.   The environmental experts who conducted the study found that about one-third of the dangerous wastes are properly disposed of.

6.   Without the benefits that free trade can provide, Mexico will never have enough money to clean up its environment.

7.   Salinas must show good faith by using the limited resources that he has at hand to crack down now on polluters in Mexico.

8.   Otherwise, environmental issues will continue to undermine the free-trade pact he so badly wants.

9. Axl Rose made news by decrying the forces that he believes can rob young people of their individuality and aspirations.

10. Rose—who is the hottest lightning rod for controversy in rock since Sinead O'Connor—suggested that many young people are like prisoners.

11. There's a Latino community, and then there's a Latino gay community, which is really invisible.

12. If they didn't have my older brother, who's a sports jock, it would have been more of a problem.

13. The postgame dramatics were as good as the game, which gave the Dodgers their second victory in three days.

14. The Angels, who collected only five hits against a rookie pitcher who was winless in his previous 10 starts, are in a slump.

15. Baker-Finch, whose 64 wiped out the Royal Birkdale course record, is a co-leader with O'Meara of the 120th British Open.

16. Born prematurely on a train and named after the doctor who was able to help, Rodney Cline Carew visited the Hall of Fame in May.

17. As the season went along and I saw the guys they were bringing off the bench, I asked myself what went wrong.

18. Tehran police have vowed to shut down any foreign company whose female staff members flout Iran's strict Islamic dress code.

19. This is my first trip to this land to which all our hearts are bound forever.

20. Every indication I see is that he is pulling out.

Name _____   **Section** _____   **Date** _____

4.06   ENGLISH QUESTION FORMATION WITH MODALS

English has several types of auxiliary verbs, one of which is the set of *modals (will, would, shall, should, can, could, may, might* and *must)*. Each of the sentences below contains a modal verb:

1. Harriet will slice the brie.
2. Their uncle can tell them the answer.
3. Kittens should be fed seventeen times a day.
4. All employees in the accounting department must submit their timesheets to Carol in triplicate.
5. You could at least help me with the dishes once in a while.

A. For each of the above sentences, form the associated Yes–No question.

1. _____

2. _____

3. _____

4. _____

   _____

5. _____

   _____

B. Consider the following formulation of the rule of Yes-No Question Formation with modal verbs, a sub-part of a more inclusive rule:

> R1:   To form a Yes-No question for a sentence that contains a modal verb, move the modal to the front of the sentence.

Will R1 accurately generate the Yes–No questions you wrote in part A? (If the rule fails in any way with respect to these sentences, explain how.)

_____

_____

_____

_____

C. Now apply R1 to the following sentences, and write down exactly what the results are in each case. If by any chance a result of applying the rule is ungrammatical, write the correct Yes-No question as well. If you find any cases where it is difficult to know how to apply the rule, explain what the problem is.

1. Anyone who can count to ten will know the answer.

_____

_____

_____

2. The guy you should talk to is out sick today.

_____

_____

_____

3. We shall give the $50,000 to a charitable organization that will use it to help the homeless.

_____

_____

_____

_____

4. Norbert seems to think that people will be living on the moon in thirty years.

_____

_____

_____

_____

5. The question of how state governments can simultaneously address the concerns of developers and environmentalists will be taken up at the next session.

_____

_____

_____

_____

D. If you found that R1 is inadequate in any way, explain and illustrate exactly how it can be modified to avoid incorrect answers in all the above cases.

_____

_____

_____

Name _____   **Section** _____   **Date** _____

4.07   CONSTRAINTS ON WH-QUESTIONS IN ENGLISH

The formation of WH-questions can be thought of as a way of "questioning" various constituents of a sentence. For example, consider:

John devoured several durians in Kota Bharu.
 a   b

Each of the underlined constituents can be questioned by:

(1)   substituting the appropriate WH-expression (who, what, where, etc.);

(2)   moving that WH-expression to the front of the sentence;

(3)   making the necessary word order and verb adjustments.

Thus, to question constituent *a*, we get

Who devoured several durians in Kota Bharu?

and no further adjustments are necessary. To question constituent *b*, we get the following sequence of stages:

John devoured what in Kota Bharu? (an *echo question*)

What John devoured in Kota Bharu?

What did John devour in Kota Bharu?

A large variety of constituents can be questioned in this way. Sometimes, however, the process unexpectedly yields an ungrammatical sentence. This is because there are constraints on the constituents that can be moved by the WH-process.

For the following sentences, form WH-questions by "questioning" each of the indicated constituents as above. You needn't show the intermediate stages in your derivations—just give the final results. "Star" any sentences you derive that are ungrammatical.

1.   Jerome emptied the liquid into a beaker.
     A   —B—   —C—

     A: _____

     B: _____

     C: _____

2.   This problem was first solved by Einstein.
     ——D——   E

     D: _____

     E: _____

3. John and Mary like onions and garlic.
      F   G   I   J
  —— H ——   —— K ——

F: _____

G: _____

H: _____

I: _____

J: _____

K: _____

4. He$_i$ said Hermione kissed him$_i$. (The subscripts indicate coreference.)
   L   M   N

L: _____

M: _____

N: _____

5. Jacqui has no idea how this computer works.
   O   —— P ——

O: _____

P: _____

6. Mary felt Barbara wanted Herman to ask Carol to fire Timothy.
   Q   R   S   T   U

Q: _____

R: _____

S: _____

T: _____

U: _____

7. The man who gave the diamond ring to Eddie's mother crashed his truck into a brick wall.
  —— V —— —— W —— —Y— —Z—
  ———————— X ————————

V: _____

W: _____

X: _____

Y: _____

Z: _____

Name _____   **Section** _____   **Date** _____

8. Raymond believes Charlotte likes Benny.
     AA   BB   CC

     AA: _____

     BB: _____

     CC: _____

9. Raymond believes that Charlotte likes Benny.
     DD   EE   FF

     DD: _____

     EE: _____

     FF: _____

10. Raymond believes the claim that Charlotte likes Benny.
      GG   HH   II

      GG: _____

      HH: _____

      II: _____

Name _____   **Section** _____   **Date** _____

4.08   FRENCH INTERROGATIVES

A. French has several ways of forming interrogative sentences. Examine the data below, given in standard French orthography, and then answer the questions that follow.

1. (a) Vous êtes Monsieur Renoir.

        You are

        'You are Monsieur Renoir.'

   (b) Etes-vous Monsieur Renoir?

        are   you

        'Are you Monsieur Renoir?'

   (c) Est-ce que vous êtes Monsieur Renoir?

        is   it that you are

        'Are you Monsieur Renoir?'

2. (a) Vous aimez ces   croissants.

        you like   these croissants

        'You like these croissants.'

   (b) Aimez-vous ces   croissants?

        like   you these croissants

        'Do you like these croissants?'

   (c) Est-ce que vous aimez ces   croissants?

        is   it that you   like   these croissants

        'Do you like these croissants?'

   (d) Pourquoi aimez-vous ces   croissants?

        why   like   you   these croissants

        'Why do you like these croissants?'

   (e) Pourquoi est-ce que vous aimez ces   croissants?

        why   is   it that you   like   these croissants

        'Why do you like these croissants?'

3. (a) Ils   mangent du   gâteau tous les jours.

        they eat   some cake   all   the days

        'They eat cake every day.'

   (b) Mangent-ils du   gâteau tous les jours?

        eat   they some cake   all   the days

        'Do they eat cake every day?'

   (c) Est-ce qu'ils   mangent du   gâteau tous les jours?

        is   it that-they eat   some cake   all   the days

        'Do they eat cake every day?'

(d) Quand mangent-ils du   gâteau?

when eat   they some cake

'When do they eat cake?'

(e) Quand est-ce qu'ils   mangent du   gâteau?

when is it that-they eat   some cake

'When do they eat cake?'

4. (a) Vous voyez un pigeon sur le   toit.

you   see   a pigeon on the roof

'You see a pigeon on the roof.'

(b) Voyez-vous un pigeon sur le   toit?

see   you a pigeon on the roof

'Do you see a pigeon on the roof?'

(c) Est-ce que vous voyez un pigeon sur le   toit?

is   it that you   see   a pigeon on the roof

'Do you see a pigeon on the roof?'

(d) Que voyez-vous sur le   toit?

what see   you on the roof

'What do you see on the roof?'

(e) Qu'est-ce que vous voyez sur le   toit?

what-is it that you see   on the roof

'What do you see on the roof?'

(f) Où   voyez-vous un pigeon?

where see   you a pigeon

'Where do you see a pigeon?'

(g) Où   est-ce que vous voyez un pigeon?

where is it that you   see   a   pigeon

'Where do you see a pigeon?'

1. Judging from the data above, what are two ways of constructing Yes-No questions in French when the subject is a pronoun? Be as precise as you can.

_____

_____

_____

_____

_____

Name _____   **Section** _____   **Date** _____

2. Repeat question 1 for the type of WH-questions found in the data.

_____

_____

_____

B. Questions in colloquial French sometimes take a different form. Examine these very informal equivalents of the more formal French interrogatives already given, and then answer the questions that follow.

1. (d) Vous êtes Monsieur Renoir?
   You are
   'Are you Monsieur Renoir?'

2. (f) Vous aimez ces croissants?
   you   like   these croissants
   'Do you like these croissants?'

   (g) Pourquoi vous aimez ces croissants?
   why   you   like   these croissants
   'Why do you like these croissants?'

3. (f) Ils mangent du   gâteau tous les jours?
   they eat   some cake   all   the days
   'Do they eat cake every day?'

   (g) Quand ils mangent du   gâteau?
   when they eat   some cake
   'When do they eat cake?'

4. (h) Vous voyez un pigeon sur le toit?
   you see   a pigeon on the roof
   'Do you see a pigeon on the roof?'

   (i) Vous voyez quoi sur le toit?
   you see   what on the roof
   'What do you see on the roof?'

   (j) Où   vous voyez un pigeon?
   where you see   a pigeon
   'Where do you see a pigeon?'

1. Explain exactly what the differences are between the more formal and the more colloquial rules of question formation.

_____

_____

_____

_____

_____

_____

_____

_____

_____

_____

2. Change to informal colloquial French:

   Est-ce que vous voulez aller avec moi?

   is   it that you   want   to-go with me

   'Do you want to go with me?'

   _____

3. Change to formal French:

   Ils   boivent quoi?

   they drink   what

   'What are they drinking?'

   _____

Name _____   **Section** _____   **Date** _____

4.09   ANALYSIS OF A JAPANESE SIMPLE SENTENCE

A.   Consider the following representative Japanese sentence:

Biru ga Michiko ni kamera o yatta.

'Bill gave Michiko a camera.'

1. Judging from this sentence, what is the normal word order for subject, object and verb in Japanese? (Circle the correct answer.)

OSV   OVS   SOV   SVO   VOS   VSO

2. Japanese has particles that indicate subject, direct object and indirect object. What is their position relative to their associated NP?

_____

_____

B.   Draw a tree diagram for this sentence, and alongside it list the phrase structure rules implied by your diagram.

Note: Assume that a noun plus a particle forms an NP.

Name _____   **Section** _____   **Date** _____

4.10   BRANCHING STRUCTURES IN SPANISH, JAPANESE, AND ENGLISH

In this exercise, you will diagram some multiply-embedded NPs in two languages, Spanish and Japanese, which consistently use different syntactic constructions for such phrases. Then you will examine a corresponding phrase in English, which makes use of both types of syntactic devices.

A.   Spanish

Glossary:

el amigo	'the (male) friend'
el coche	'the car'
el maestro	'the (male) teacher'
la puerta	'the door'
de	'of'

Note: de + el is converted into *del* by a phonological rule.

For a phrase like 'Naomi's friend,' Spanish uses a word order corresponding to 'the friend of Naomi':

el amigo de Naomi

This phrase has the following structure, where the node labels correspond to the English categories you are already familiar with:

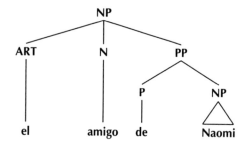

(The triangle symbol is used here in the usual way: to represent a node whose internal structure is irrelevant, and therefore not indicated.)

1.   Translate into Spanish:

Naomi's friend's teacher _____

Now draw a labeled tree diagram for this phrase.

2.   Now do the same for:

Naomi's friend's teacher's car

_____

3.   Finally, do the same for:

the door of Naomi's friend's teacher's car

_____

Choose one: A structure such as this is referred to as:

[   ] left-branching   [   ] right-branching

Name _____   **Section** _____   **Date** _____

B. *Japanese*

Glossary: doa   'door'
              kuruma   'car'
              sensei   'teacher'
              tomodachi   'friend'

Note: There is no definite article in Japanese.

For a phrase like 'Naomi's friend,' Japanese uses a word order similar to English:

Naomi no tomodachi

Here, the postposition *no* corresponds to the *'s* in English. This phrase has the following structure, where the node labels correspond to the English categories you are already familiar with, except that PP here means Postpositional Phrase, and P means Postposition:

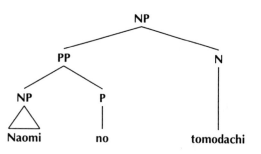

1. Translate into Japanese:

    Naomi's friend's teacher _____

    Now draw a labeled tree diagram for this phrase.

2. Now do the same for:

    Naomi's friend's teacher's car

    _____

3. Finally, do the same for:

    the door of Naomi's friend's teacher's car

    _____

Choose one: A structure such as this is referred to as:

[   ] left-branching   [   ] right-branching

Name _____   **Section** _____   **Date** _____

C. *English*

English, as already noted, makes use of both the Spanish- and Japanese-style constructions you have previously analyzed.

Assume a phrase like *John's house* has the following structure:

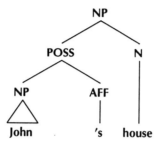

Here, AFF stands for Affix, and POSS for Possessive.

A phrase like *the cover of the book* has this structure:

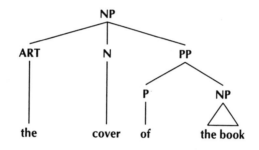

Draw a labeled tree diagram for the following English phrase:

   the outside of the door of Lisa's mother's house

Name _____   **Section** _____   **Date** _____

4.11   WORD ORDER IN TURKISH

A.   Examine the following Turkish sentences, given in standard Turkish orthography. Then answer the questions below. (*Note:* i and ı are different vowels: i is the common high front unrounded vowel, while ı is the less common high *back un*rounded vowel.) As usual, an asterisk indicates ungrammaticality.

1.	Et aldım.	'I bought meat.'
2.	Et aldı.	'He bought meat.'
3.	Mektup yazdım.	'I wrote a letter.'
4.	Mektup yazdı.	'He wrote a letter.'
5.	Mektubu yazdım.	'I wrote the letter.'
6.	Eti aldı.	'He bought the meat.'
7.	Et pahalı.	'Meat is expensive.'
8.	Et pahalı.	'The meat is expensive.'
9.	*Eti pahalı.	'The meat is expensive.'
10.	Mektup güzel.	'The letter is beautiful.'

1.   On the basis of the above data, do objects in Turkish come before or after the verb?

   _____

2.   What is the difference in grammatical relation between *et/eti* and between *mektup/mektubu*?

   _____

   _____

3.   What, besides grammatical relation, determines the choice between the pairs of words in question 2?

   _____

   _____

   _____

B.   Now consider the following additional data:

11.	Kasaptan et aldım.	'I bought meat from the butcher.'
12.	*Et kasaptan aldım.	'I bought meat from the butcher.'
13.	Kıza mektup yazdım.	'I wrote a letter to the girl.'
14.	*Mektup kıza yazdım.	'I wrote a letter to the girl.'
15.	Kasaptan eti aldım.	'I bought the meat from the butcher.'
16.	Eti kasaptan aldım.	'I bought the meat from the butcher.'
17.	Kıza mektubu yazdım.	'I wrote the letter to the girl.'
18.	Mektubu kıza yazdım.	'I wrote the letter to the girl.'

On basis of these sentences, what is the rule in Turkish regarding the proximity of direct objects to their verbs?

(*Note:* Turkish uses suffixes and postpositions where English uses prepositions. For example: kıza 'to the girl,' kızdan 'from the girl,' etc.)

_____

_____

_____

Name _____   **Section** _____   **Date** _____

4.12   WORD ORDER IN YIDDISH

Yiddish, like its sister language Modern German, is descended from Middle High German, spoken during the Middle Ages.

The data below, given in phonetic transcription, consist of a Yiddish sentence in twelve different versions, distinguished only by the word order. These all have basically the same meaning, although the pragmatics (how they are used in context) may vary. Ungrammatical variants are starred. The last four items are questions related to the original sentence.

Although there is quite a bit of word order flexibility exhibited in these data, you will be able to discover one overriding principle of Yiddish word order that will account for all the grammaticality judgments below. What is this principle? (Data adapted from Uriel Weinreich, *College Yiddish.*)

1. yɪdn rɛdn   yɪdɪš   haynt ɪn a sax lɛndɛr.

   Jews speak Yiddish today in many countries

   'Jews speak Yiddish today in many countries.'

2. haynt rɛdn yɪdn yɪdɪš ɪn a sax lɛndɛr.

3. *ɪn a sax lɛndɛr haynt rɛdn yɪdn yɪdɪš.

4. yɪdɪš rɛdn yɪdn haynt ɪn a sax lɛndɛr.

5. *ɪn a sax lɛndɛr haynt yɪdn rɛdn yɪdɪš.

6. ɪn a sax lɛndɛr rɛdn yɪdn yɪdɪš haynt.

7. *ɪn a sax lɛndɛr yɪdn rɛdn haynt yɪdɪš.

8. yɪdn rɛdn haynt yɪdɪš ɪn a sax lɛndɛr.

9. *rɛdn yɪdn yɪdɪš haynt ɪn a sax lɛndɛr.

10. yɪdɪš rɛdn haynt ɪn a sax lɛndɛr yɪdn.

11. yɪdɪš rɛdn haynt yɪdn ɪn a sax lɛndɛr.

12. *haynt yɪdn rɛdn yɪdɪš ɪn a sax lɛndɛr.

13. t͡si rɛdn yɪdn yɪdɪš haynt ɪn a sax lɛndɛr?

    'Do Jews speak Yiddish in many countries today?'

14. *t͡si yɪdn rɛdn yɪdɪš haynt ɪn a sax lɛndɛr?

    'Do Jews speak Yiddish in many countries today?'

15. vu rɛdn yɪdn yɪdɪš haynt?

    'Where do Jews speak Yiddish today?'

16. vɔs rɛdn yɪdn haynt ɪn a sax lɛndɛr?

    'What do Jews speak today in many countries?

_____

_____

_____

Name _____   **Section** _____   **Date** _____

4.13   CASE MARKING AND RELATIVE CLAUSES IN GERMAN

A. Examine the following sentences, given in standard German orthography. Then identify the *subject* and *object* forms (often referred to as *nominative* and *accusative cases*) of 'the man,' 'the woman,' 'the child' and 'the dog.' What is the normal order of subject, object and verb in main sentences such as these?

1.	Der Mann liebt den Hund.	'The man loves the dog.'
2.	Der Hund liebt den Mann.	'The dog loves the man.'
3.	Der Mann liebt die Frau.	'The man loves the woman.'
4.	Das Kind liebt den Mann.	'The child loves the man.'
5.	Der Hund liebt das Kind.	'The dog loves the child.'
6.	Die Frau liebt den Hund.	'The woman loves the dog.'

	'the man'	'the woman'	'the child'	'the dog'
Subject Form:	_____	_____	_____	_____
Object Form:	_____	_____	_____	_____

WORD ORDER: _____

B. Now examine the following sentences, and determine the normal order of subject, object and verb in subordinate (embedded) clauses.

7.	*Ich weiss, dass der Mann liebt den Hund.	'I know that the man loves the dog.'
8.	Ich weiss, dass der Mann den Hund liebt.	'I know that the man loves the dog.'
9.	*Ich weiss nicht, ob der Hund liebt das Kind.	'I don't know whether the dog loves the child.'
10.	Ich weiss nicht, ob der Hund das Kind liebt.	'I don't know whether the dog loves the child.'

WORD ORDER: _____

C. A *relative clause* is an embedded sentence that modifies a noun. The noun being modified is called the *head*; if the noun phrase that contains it is NP_i, then the embedded sentence must also contain this same NP_i; the two noun phrases are *coreferential*.

A large number of German relative clauses can be derived by the following rules:

(1) The relative clause comes after the head.

(2) Since they are embedded sentences, relative clauses follow subordinate-clause word order.

(3) Two transformations apply in the following order to yield the correct surface structure:

ATTRACTION: The coreferential NP inside the relative clause is moved to the front of the clause, adjacent to the head.

NOUN DROP: The coreferential *noun* within the relative clause is dropped; the article that is retained functions as a relative pronoun.

EXAMPLE: To derive the German for 'the man who(m) the dog loves':
We start with the NP 'the man' followed by the modifying sentence containing the coreferential NP:

the man [the dog loves the man]

Remembering to use subordinate clause word order, the German for this is:

der Mann [der Hund den Mann liebt]

Now we apply the two transformations:

ATTRACTION gives: der Mann [den Mann der Hund liebt]

NOUN DROP gives: der Mann [den der Hund liebt]

We now have the correct surface form:

der Mann den der Hund liebt.

Translate each of the following phrases into German by going through a derivation like the one in the example. You can assume that the head in each case is a subject.

1. the man who loves the dog

    START WITH: _____

    ATTRACTION:_____

    NOUN DROP: _____

    SURFACE FORM: _____

2. the dog that loves the man

    START WITH: _____

    ATTRACTION:_____

    NOUN DROP: _____

    SURFACE FORM: _____

3. the dog that the man loves

    START WITH: _____

    ATTRACTION:_____

    NOUN DROP: _____

    SURFACE FORM: _____

4. the man who loves the woman

    START WITH: _____

    ATTRACTION:_____

    NOUN DROP: _____

    SURFACE FORM: _____

Name _____   **Section** _____   **Date** _____

5.   the man who(m) the woman loves

   START WITH: _____

   ATTRACTION:_____

   NOUN DROP: _____

   SURFACE FORM: _____

6.   the woman who loves the man

   START WITH: _____

   ATTRACTION:_____

   NOUN DROP: _____

   SURFACE FORM: _____

7.   the woman who(m) the man loves

   START WITH: _____

   ATTRACTION:_____

   NOUN DROP: _____

   SURFACE FORM: _____

8.   the woman who loves the child

   START WITH: _____

   ATTRACTION:_____

   NOUN DROP: _____

   SURFACE FORM: _____

9.   the woman who(m) the child loves

   START WITH: _____

   ATTRACTION:_____

   NOUN DROP: _____

   SURFACE FORM: _____

D.   If you did the derivations in C correctly, you will have noticed that German can run into a problem with relative clauses.

1.   Identify the problem. Specifically, which pair of English phrases in part C does German have trouble with? What exactly is the problem? Why does German run into this difficulty?

_____

_____

_____

_____

_____

_____

2.   German speakers have not been observed to have any more trouble understanding each other than English speakers do. Speculate on how speakers of German get around the problem you identified above.

_____

_____

_____

_____

_____

_____

_____

Name _____   **Section** _____   **Date** _____

4.14   ARTICLES, DEMONSTRATIVES, AND POSSESSIVES IN ENGLISH, ITALIAN, AND MODERN GREEK

Every language contains the syntactic category NP with N as its head, but the distribution of the other elements found in noun phrases varies among languages. In this exercise you will examine some simple noun phrases containing articles, demonstratives and possessives in three languages, and you will determine how the phrase structure rules that rewrite NP in these languages differ.

A.   *English*

Consider the following simple phrase structure (PS) grammar that generates certain definite NPs in English.

$$NP \rightarrow DET\ N$$

$$Det \rightarrow \left\{ \begin{array}{c} ART \\ DEM \\ POS \end{array} \right\}$$

N: {house, car, ...}

ART: {the}

DEM: {this, that, ...}

POS: {my, your, his, ...}

(Here, DET, ART, DEM and POS stand respectively for the lexical categories Determiner, Article, Demonstrative and Possessive.)

1.   Utilizing the PS grammar above, draw labeled tree diagrams for the following English NPs:

   the house

   my house

   this house

2.   Consider the following ungrammatical phrases in English:

   *the my house

   *the this house

   *this my house

Will the given PS grammar generate any of these phrases? Justify your answer.

_____

_____

_____

B. *Italian*

Here are some grammatical and ungrammatical definite NPs in Italian:

la casa	'the house'
la mia casa	'my house'
questa casa	'this house'
*mia casa	
*la questa casa	

1. Using the same categories found in the English PS grammar in part A, write a comparable phrase structure grammar that will generate all of the grammatical phrases above and none of the ungrammatical ones. (*Hint:* You will have to make a distinction between obligatory and optional elements in one of your rules. Note that the parenthesis notation for optional elements: A → B (C) collapses the two rules A → B and A → B C.)

_____

_____

_____

_____

_____

_____

2. Now draw a labeled tree diagram for *la mia casa* that makes use of your phrase structure rules.

Name _____ **Section** _____ **Date** _____

C. *Modern Greek*

Examine these grammatical and ungrammatical definite NPs in Modern Greek, and answer the questions that follow:

to spiti	'the house'
to spiti mu	'my house'
afto to spiti	'this house'
afto to spiti mu	'my house'
*spiti mu	
*afto spiti	

1. Do the same for these Modern Greek data as you did for the Italian data above, i.e., write a phrase structure grammar that will generate all of the grammatical phrases and none of the ungrammatical ones. (*Hint:* Not all of the categories used in the English and Italian sections may be appropriate here!)

_____

_____

_____

_____

_____

_____

_____

2. Draw a labeled tree diagram for *afto to spiti mu* that makes use of your phrase structure rules.

Name _____   **Section** _____   **Date** _____

4.15   ASPECTS OF KLINGON

Examine the following sentences in the Klingon language, devised for the *Star Trek*® feature films and the *Star Trek: The Next Generation*® television series by linguist Marc Okrand. Then answer the questions that follow.

Note: The data are adapted from Okrand's *Klingon Dictionary,* which contains the only grammatical sketch of the language so far available to non-Klingons, and are given in the transcription used in that work. The symbols employed have their usual phonetic values, but note the following:

gh	=	[ɣ]
S	=	a voiceless fricative halfway between [s] and [š]
H	=	[x]
j	=	[ǰ]
I	=	[ɪ]
tlh	=	apparently a *t* with an aspirated lateral release, equal to Aztec *tl*.
'	=	[ʔ]

1. puq legh yaS   'The officer sees the child.'
2. yaS legh puq   'The child sees the officer.'
3. puq vIlegh jIH   'I see the child.'
4. jIH mulegh puq   'The child sees me.'
5. puq vIlegh   'I see the child.'
6. mulegh puq   'The child sees me.'
7. puq lulegh yaSpu'   'The officers see the child.'
8. Salegh   'I see you (pl.).'
9. tlhIH Salegh   'I see you (pl.).'
10. Salegh jIH   'I see you (pl.).'
11. relegh   'We see you (pl.).'
12. relegh maH   'We see you (pl.).'
13. yaSpu' legh puq   'The child sees the officers.'
14. jIH tulegh tlhIH   'You (pl.) see me.'
15. nulegh yaSpu'   'The officers see us.'
16. maH nulegh   'They see us.'

A. Isolate all the morphemes present in the data, giving the meaning or function of each.

_____

_____

_____

_____

_____

_____

_____

_____

B.   What is the basic sequencing of subject, object and verb in Klingon? Name any Earth languages you are familiar with that employ this particular sequencing as a basic word order. How common is this basic word order among the languages of Earth?

_____

_____

_____

C.   Judging from the data, what elements of a Klingon sentence are optional? Are these same elements optional in English? If not, what is it about Klingon grammar that allows the omission of these elements? Explain.

_____

_____

_____

_____

_____

_____

_____

_____

D.   Translate into English:

tlhIH relegh

_____

E.   Translate into Klingon:

'The children see the officer.'

_____

Name _____   **Section** _____   **Date** _____

4.16   CHINESE NOUN MODIFIERS AND RELATIVE CLAUSES

In the first part of this problem, you will examine some simple noun modifiers in Mandarin Chinese. Then you will look at noun modifiers which are themselves clauses. The data are transcribed in the Pinyin system (see Appendix A).

A. Examine the following data and then answer the questions that follow.

1. wǒ de shū
   I   book
   'my book'

2. tāmen de péngyou
   they   friend
   'their friend'

3. shūfu   de yìzi
   comfortable   chair
   'comfortable chair'

4. piàoliang de nǚpéngyou
   pretty   female friend
   'pretty girlfriend'

5. là   de cài
   spicy   food
   'spicy food'

6. lǎoshī   de qìchē
   teacher   car
   'teacher's car'

7. piányi de jiājù
   cheap   furniture
   'cheap furniture'

8. lǎoshī de piányi de qìchē
   teacher   cheap   car
   'the teacher's cheap car'

1. Which is the order of elements in Chinese?
   [   ] modifier + noun   [   ] noun + modifier

2. Explain the function of *de* as it appears in these data.

_____

_____

_____

_____

B. Now examine these sentences and phrases, and answer the questions that follow:

1. (a) Lǎoshī chī píngguǒ.

      teacher eat apple

      'The teacher eats apples.'

    (b) chī píngguǒ de lǎoshī

      'the teacher who eats apples'

    (c) lǎoshī chī de píngguǒ

      'the apples that the teacher eats'

2. (a) Jīnglǐ   mài zìxíngchē.

      manager sell bicycle

      'The manager sells bicycles.'

    (b) mài zìxíngchē de jīnglǐ

      'the manager who sells bicycles'

    (c) jīnglǐ mài de zìxíngchē

      'the bicycles that the manager sells'

3. (a) Háizi hē   jiǔ.

      child drink wine

      'The child drinks wine.'

    (b) hē jiǔ de háizi

      'the child who drinks wine'

    (c) háizi hē de jiǔ

      'the wine that the child drinks'

1. Do Chinese relative clauses precede or follow their heads? Taking a relative clause to be a modifier of its head noun, is this pattern consistent or inconsistent with the result you determined in part A for simple noun modifiers?

_____

2. The derivation of Chinese relative clauses such as the ones illustrated above becomes transparent if *the underlying form of the relative clause is taken to be a full sentence.* (In a comparable analysis for English, for example, the underlying form of *books that children read* is taken to be

      books$_i$ [children read books$_i$]

in which the two occurrences of *books* are coreferential, as indicated by the identical subscripts.)

Name _____   **Section** _____   **Date** _____

(a) Under such an analysis, give the underlying form of 'the child who drinks wine.' What is the grammatical relation of the coreferential NP within the relative clause?

_____

_____

(b) What is the underlying form of 'the wine that the child drinks'? What is the grammatical relation of the coreferential NP within the relative clause?

_____

_____

(c) Show how the underlying forms you posited in parts (a) and (b) above yield the correct surface forms. You will have to come up with one or more transformations that apply consecutively to the underlying forms to give the surface forms. If you do this correctly, you will find that *exactly the same transformations can be used to arrive at the correct surface forms in both cases.*

_____

_____

_____

_____

_____

_____

_____

_____

*(d) (Optional) Compare and contrast the Chinese relative clause strategy you have just analyzed with the corresponding strategy in English. What are the similarities and differences between the two strategies? (You can take as your English data the glosses of the Chinese relative clauses. Be sure to address the differences between *who* and *that*.)

_____

_____

_____

_____

_____

_____

Name _____   **Section** _____   **Date** _____

4.17   OBJECTS AND POSSESSION IN MODERN HEBREW

In this exercise you will discover how Modern Hebrew (MH) marks certain objects, and how it forms possessive constructions. Along the way you will discover other facts about the language as well.

A.   Examine the sentences below, and then answer the questions that follow. The data are given in phonetic transcription; stress is on the last syllable except where marked otherwise.

Abbreviations: m. = masculine, f. = feminine.

1.	hamɔre ɔhɛv yᵊladim	'The teacher likes children.'
2.	hamɔre ɔhɛv ɛt hayᵊladim	'The teacher likes the children.'
3.	hayᵊladim ɔhavim ɛt hamɔre	'The children like the teacher.'
4.	hayᵊladim ɔhavim sᵊfarim	'The children like books.'
5.	hayᵊladim ɔhavim ɛt hasᵊfarim	'The children like the books.'
6.	yᵊladim ɔhavim sᵊfarim	'Children like books.'
7.	hamɔra rɔtsa séfer	'The teacher (f.) wants a book.'
8.	hamɔra rɔtsa ɛt hasᵊfarim	'The teacher (f.) wants the books.'
9.	hamɔre rɔtse séfer tɔv	'The teacher (m.) wants a good book.'
10.	hayᵊladim rɔtsim sᵊfarim tɔvim	'The children want good books.'
11.	hamɔrim ɔhavim ɛt hayélɛd	'The teachers (m.) like the boy.'
12.	hamɔrɔt ɔhavɔt sᵊfarim	'The teachers (f.) like books.'
13.	ani ɔhɛv ɛt hamɔra	'I like the teacher (f.).'
14.	anáxnu ɔhavim yᵊladim tɔvim	'We like good children.'
15.	anáxnu ɔhavim ɛt hayᵊladim hatɔvim	'We like the good children.'

1.   What is the basic word order in MH for subject, object and verb?

_____

2.   What are the definite and indefinite articles in MH? How, if at all, do they change their form depending on the word they modify?

_____

_____

_____

3.   Judging from the sentences above, what kind of agreement, if any, is there between a present-tense verb and its subject? Between a present-tense verb and its object?

_____

_____

_____

_____

4. Explain fully the use of *et* in these sentences. Your explanation must account for why *et* appears in certain sentences but not in others.

_____

_____

_____

_____

B. Now examine this next set of sentences, all of which contain pronominal objects, and answer the questions below.

1. hamɔrɛ ɔhɛv ɔti   'The teacher (m.) likes me.'
2. hu ɔhɛv ɔti   'He likes me.'
3. hayélɛd ɔhɛv ɔtɔ   'The boy likes him.'
4. ani ɔhɛv ɔta   'I like her.'
5. hayᵊladim ɔhavim ɔtánu   'The children like us.'
6. hɛm ɔhavim ɔta   'They (m.) like her.'
7. hi ɔhévɛt ɔtánu   'She likes us.'
8. anáxnu ɔhavim ɔtɔ   'We like him.'

1. Isolate the object pronouns present in the data and divide them into their component morphemes, giving the meaning or function of each.

_____

_____

_____

_____

_____

2. Do you have to modify your previous analysis of *et* to explain these new data? If so, how?

_____

_____

_____

C. Next, examine these sentences which contain indirect objects, and answer the questions that follow.

1. hu nɔtɛn ɛt haséfɛr lᵊdavid   'He gives the book to David.'
2. hu nɔtɛn lɔ ɛt haséfɛr   'He gives him the book.'
3. ani nɔtɛn la séfɛr   'I give her a book.'
4. hamɔrɛ nɔtɛn lánu sᵊfarim   'The teacher (m.) gives us books.'

Name _____   **Section** _____   **Date** _____

5. hamɔrɛ nɔtɛn ɔtɔ lᵊraxɛl   'The teacher (m.) gives it to Rachel.'
6. raxɛl nɔténɛt li ɛt hasᵊfarim   'Rachel gives the books to me.'
7. anáxnu nɔtnim la sᵊfarim tɔvim   'We give her good books.'
8. hi nɔténɛt ɛt hasᵊfarim layᵊladim   'She gives the books to the children.'

1. What is the function of *lᵊ*?

    _____

    _____

2. As you did for the direct object pronouns in part B, isolate the indirect object pronouns present in these data and divide them into their component morphemes, giving the meaning or function of each. What similarities do you observe between the two types of pronouns you analyzed?

    _____

    _____

    _____

    _____

    _____

    _____

3. Explain the appearance of *la-* in the last word of sentence 8.

    _____

    _____

D. Now examine this next set of sentences. (As usual, the * indicates something ungrammatical.)

1.   haséfɛr al hašulxan   'The book is on the table.'
2.   hamɔrim bᵊyisraɛl   'The teachers (m.) are in Israel.'
3.   yɛš séfɛr al hašulxan   'There is a book on the table.'
4.   yɛš sᵊfarim al hašulxan   'There are books on the table.'
5.   yɛš mɔrim tɔvim bᵊyisraɛl   'There are good teachers in Israel.'
6.   yɛš li séfɛr   'I have a book.'
7.   yɛš li sᵊfarim   'I have books.'
8.   yɛš li haséfɛr   'I have the book.'
9.   yɛš lánu mɔrim tɔvim   'We have good teachers.'
10. yɛš la šulxan   'She has a table.'
11. yɛš lɔ šney yᵊladim   'He has two children.'
12. *yɛš li ɛt haséfɛr   'I have the book.'

1. How is the present tense of the verb 'to be' expressed in MH?

_____

_____

2. Does MH have a verb corresponding to *have* in English? If so, what is it? If not, how is the idea of possession expressed?

_____

_____

_____

_____

3. Sentence 12 is, according to one authority, an example of a famous and very common grammatical error in MH. Why is it ungrammatical, and what do you suppose is the reason that this error is so widespread?

_____

_____

_____

_____

E. Finally, examine the following phrases carefully, and answer the questions at the end.

1. mɔre šeɔhɛv yᵊladim   'a teacher who like children'
2. hayᵊladim šeɔhavim sᵊfarim   'the children who like books'
3. haséfer šeani rɔt͡sɛ   'the book that I want'
4. hamɔrim šeraxɛl ɔhévɛt   'the teachers (m.) that Rachel likes'
5. haséfer šeli   'my book'
6. hasᵊfarim šeli   'my books'
7. hamɔra šelɔ   'his teacher (f.)'
8. hamɔrɛ šelánu   'our teacher (m.)'
9. hayᵊladim šela   'her children'
10. hasᵊfarim hatɔvim šelɔ   'his good books'

1. What is the function of *šɛ* - in these phrases?

_____

_____

_____

Name _____   **Section** _____   **Date** _____

2. Separate the words in the phrase *haséfɛr šɛli* into their component morphemes and give the meaning or function of each one.

_____

_____

_____

3. Translate into MH:

   (a) The teacher (f.) likes her good students.

       ('student' = talmid)

_____

   (b) The teacher (m.) has a small house in Tel Aviv.

       ('small' = katan; 'house' = báyit; 'Tel Aviv' = tɛl aviv)

_____

C H A P T E R

5

Semantics and Pragmatics

5.01   ENGLISH LEXICAL SEMANTICS

Lexical items can be compared along several dimensions. Two such dimensions are *sound* and *meaning*, which form the basis for such concepts as homonymy and synonymy. To these we can add *look*, referring to the way the word appears orthographically—its spelling, capitalization, abbreviations, etc.

The following chart gives all the mathematical possibilities for comparing pairs of words along the three dimensions of sound, look and meaning. (Since these dimensions are binary—that is, each can have only two values, same or different—there are $2 \times 2 \times 2$ or 8 possible combinations.) Filling in the *Examples* column in the chart will help you review and organize some basic concepts in the area of lexical semantics.

A. Provide two examples for each of the eight categories in the chart below. An example consists of a pair of English words that fits the description of the category.

In the chart, S = Same, D = Different.

EXAMPLE: Category 7 asks for a pair of words that sound the same and look the same but have different meanings—that is, words that are spelled and pronounced identically but mean different things. A standard example is *bank* 'financial institution' and *bank* 'land along the edge of a river.'

Category	Sound	Look	Meaning	Examples		
1	D	D	D	a. _____	and	_____
				b. _____	and	_____
2	D	D	S	a. _____	and	_____
				b. _____	and	_____

3   D   S   D   a. _____ and _____

    b. _____ and _____

4   D   S   S   a. _____ and _____

    b. _____ and _____

5   S   D   D   a. _____ and _____

    b. _____ and _____

6   S   D   S   a. _____ and _____

    b. _____ and _____

7   S   S   D   a. _____ and _____

    b. _____ and _____

8   S   S   S   _____ and _____

B. Now answer the following questions:

1. Which category or categories represent(s) *synonymy?*

   _____

2. Which category or categories represent(s) *homonymy?*

   _____

3. Which category or categories represent(s) *alternate pronunciations of the same word?*

   _____

4. Which category or categories represent(s) *alternate spellings of the same word?*

   _____

Name _____ **Section** _____ **Date** _____

5.02 REFERENTIAL, SOCIAL, AND AFFECTIVE MEANING

Referential meaning refers to the object, notion, or state of affairs described by a word or sentence. *Social* meaning is the dimension of meaning that conveys information about the social characteristics of speakers and situations. *Affective* meaning is the emotional connotation attached to words and utterances—the dimension of meaning that yields information about the speaker's feelings, attitudes, and opinions.

After each utterance pair below, provide a *Yes* or *No* decision three times to indicate whether the utterances have the same (1) referential, (2) social and (3) affective meaning. Then explain the differences that you have indicated by any *No* decisions. Some utterance pairs may differ on more than one dimension of meaning.

EXAMPLE: a.   She's not my friend now.
   b.   She ain't my friend now.
   "Y, N, Y. *a* and *b* differ in social meaning in that *ain't* is frequently used by speakers of nonstandard English and by many other speakers in informal situations or to indicate emphasis."

1.   a.   She don't want no more.

   b.   She doesn't want any more.

   _____

   _____

   _____

2.   a.   She said that she will select whichever one she wishes.

   b.   She said she'll pick the one she wants.

   _____

   _____

   _____

3.   a.   If the governor doesn't sign the bill ...

   b.   If that sonofabitch doesn't put his John Hancock on that bill ...

   _____

   _____

   _____

4.   a.   Me and him was friends in the Army.

   b.   He and I were friends in the Army.

   _____

   _____

   _____

5. a. Is there a Miss Smith in this office?

    b. Is it a Miss Smith in this office?

    _____

    _____

    _____

6. a. May I use your washroom?

    b. Where's the john?

    _____

    _____

    _____

7. a. My uncle often goes to the races.

    b. My aunt never squanders her money gambling.

    _____

    _____

    _____

8. a. The first American president chopped down a cherry tree.

    b. George Washington did not chop down a cherry tree.

    _____

    _____

    _____

9. a. Take the elevator to the first floor and find the exit.

    b. Take the lift to the ground floor and find the way out.

    _____

    _____

    _____

10. a. Let's go to the flicks together, but it'll be Dutch treat.

    b. Let's go to the movies together, but let's pay our own way.

    _____

    _____

    _____

Name _____   **Section** _____   **Date** _____

5.03   TRUE SYNONYMY AND THE RARITY THEREOF

We can say two words are strictly synonymous if, in *any* utterance in which one of them occurs, the other can be substituted with no change in referential, social or affective meaning. True synonyms, so defined, are rare.

The following pairs of words are often thought of as synonymous. There are contexts, however, in which only one of them is appropriate. For each pair of words, give (i) a sentence where the words may be used interchangeably, and (ii) a sentence where substituting one for the other results in strangeness or a change of meaning. Explain the difference.

EXAMPLE: large, big
(i) a. This plate is much too large to use for dessert.
    b. This plate is much too big to use for dessert.

(ii) a. This is Henry, my big brother.
     b. This is Henry, my large borther.

In *a*, "big brother" means elder brother. In *b*, "large brother" cannot mean elder brother; it may be a way of saying that Henry is obese.

1. small, little

(i) a. _____

    b. _____

(ii) a. _____

    b. _____

Explanation: _____

_____

_____

_____

2. nice, pleasant

(i) a. _____

    b. _____

(ii) a. _____

    b. _____

Explanation: _____

_____

_____

_____

3. inexpensive, cheap

   (i)   a. _____

         b. _____

   (ii) a. _____

         b. _____

   Explanation: _____

   _____

   _____

   _____

4. keep, retain

   (i)   a. _____

         b. _____

   (ii) a. _____

         b. _____

   Explanation: _____

   _____

   _____

   _____

5. correct, right

   (i)   a. _____

         b. _____

   (ii) a. _____

         b. _____

   Explanation: _____

   _____

   _____

   _____

Name _____   **Section** _____   **Date** _____

6. interfere, meddle

   (i) a. _____

        b. _____

   (ii) a. _____

        b. _____

   Explanation: _____

   _____

   _____

   _____

   _____

7. difficult, hard

   (i) a. _____

        b. _____

   (ii) a. _____

        b. _____

   Explanation: _____

   _____

   _____

   _____

   _____

8. annoy, irritate

   (i) a. _____

        b. _____

   (ii) a. _____

        b. _____

   Explanation: _____

   _____

   _____

   _____

9. street, road

    (i)   a. _____

          b. _____

    (ii) a. _____

          b. _____

    Explanation: _____

    _____

    _____

    _____

10. capital, upper-case

    (i)   a. _____

          b. _____

    (ii) a. _____

          b. _____

    Explanation: _____

    _____

    _____

    _____

Name _____   **Section** _____   **Date** _____

5.04   DEICTIC EXPRESSIONS

Deixis is the marking of the orientation or position of people, objects and events with respect to certain points of reference. A characteristic of deictic expressions is that they become vague or difficult to interpret if the needed point of reference is missing.

Briefly explain what makes each of the underlined words in the following utterances (reported in the *Los Angeles Times*) a deictic expression:

EXAMPLE: I will be here tomorrow.
The referent of I depends on who is speaking.
The referent of here depends on the place of utterance.
The referent of tomorrow depends on the time of utterance.

1. I think the people of this city have won.

    _____

    _____

2. We are in a position now where serious division can be healed.

    _____

    _____

3. We thought it was appropriate at this moment to just have it among us.

    _____

    _____

4. He has promised to retire by the end of this year.

    _____

    _____

5. If he was concerned about how Friday's events would fly with his constituents, he wasn't showing it.

    _____

    _____

6. "I really feel good about this place," he said.

    _____

    _____

7. <u>Last night</u> he gave his approval for an orderly process of change.

    _____

    _____

8. Within the <u>next few months</u>, the voters will express their views.

    _____

    _____

9. The result came <u>yesterday</u> when the chief of police indicated that he would retire at the end of <u>this year</u>.

    _____

    _____

10. We can <u>immediately</u> begin to work changes in the city charter.

    _____

    _____

Name _____   Section _____ Date _____

5.05   SENTENTIAL IMPLICATURE

The sentences below are taken, sometimes adapted, from the *Los Angeles Times*. For each of the sentences, provide another sentence that the first implies.

EXAMPLE: The proposed rules would make it even more difficult for most foreign performers to get visas.
IMPLIES: The existing rules already make it difficult to get visas.

1. Arts groups said Thursday that controversy over the rules is certain to intensify.
   IMPLIES:

   _____

   _____

2. Shakespeare Festival/LA has been awarded a $20,000 grant, the largest of 13 awarded in the arts funding program.
   IMPLIES:

   _____

   _____

3. In lieu of admission, theatergoers are asked to bring canned food, which will be donated to the Salvation Army.
   IMPLIES:

   _____

   _____

4. It is Singleton's gift to make us empathize with their hopelessness.
   IMPLIES:

   _____

   _____

5. Unfortunately, the other two entrees were inedible.
   IMPLIES:

   _____

   _____

6. Perlman has now fulfilled the promise of his early virtuosity.
   IMPLIES:

   _____

   _____

7. At least four aircraft chose inappropriate fly-by times during the evening.
    IMPLIES:

    _____

    _____

8. Surprisingly, attendance at this concert reached only 9,124.
    IMPLIES:

    _____

    _____

9. She responded by suing two of the eight musicians for slander.
    IMPLIES:

    _____

    _____

10. Like most arts organizations, this one does not earn enough to support itself.
    IMPLIES:

    _____

    _____

Name _____   Section _____   Date _____

5.06   DEFINITENESS, REFERENTIALITY, AND SPECIFICITY

A noun phrase is *definite* if the addressee is assumed to be able to identify its referent. Otherwise it is *indefinite*. A noun phrase is *referential* when it refers to a particular entity. Otherwise it is *non-referential*. A noun phrase is *general* if it refers to a category. If it refers to a particular member of a category, it is *specific*.

Determine whether each of the underlined phrases below is definite or indefinite, referential or non-referential, and generic or specific.

1. There was <u>a rather large possum</u> outside the door, eating the cat food. The cat saw it and stayed a
    A

    few yards away, but <u>the possum</u> seemed oblivious to her presence.
    B

    A: [ ] Definite   [ ] Referential   [ ] Generic

    [ ] Indefinite   [ ] Non-referential   [ ] Specific

    B: [ ] Definite   [ ] Referential   [ ] Generic

    [ ] Indefinite   [ ] Non-referential   [ ] Specific

2. <u>The unicorn</u> is <u>a mythical beast</u>.
    A   **B**

    A: [ ] Definite   [ ] Referential   [ ] Generic

    [ ] Indefinite   [ ] Non-referential   [ ] Specific

    B: [ ] Definite   [ ] Referential   [ ] Generic

    [ ] Indefinite   [ ] Non-referential   [ ] Specific

3. Have you seen <u>a little white kitten with grey and orange spots</u>? <u>She</u> must have gotten out about fif-
    A   **B**

    teen minutes ago.

    A: [ ] Definite   [ ] Referential   [ ] Generic

    [ ] Indefinite   [ ] Non-referential   [ ] Specific

    B: [ ] Definite   [ ] Referential   [ ] Generic

    [ ] Indefinite   [ ] Non-referential   [ ] Specific

4. Hello, Crown Books? I'm looking for <u>a book on referentiality in Lithuanian</u>. Do you have anything
    A

    like that? [PAUSE] Young man, I just bought <u>a book on definiteness in Hungarian</u> from you last
    B

    week, so you could at least take a look!

    A: [ ] Definite   [ ] Referential   [ ] Generic

    [ ] Indefinite   [ ] Non-referential   [ ] Specific

    B: [ ] Definite   [ ] Referential   [ ] Generic

    [ ] Indefinite   [ ] Non-referential   [ ] Specific

5. I've traveled far and wide in my quest for <u>the perfect cheeseburger</u>.
                                                              A

    A: [ ] Definite   [ ] Referential   [ ] Generic
        [ ] Indefinite   [ ] Non-referential   [ ] Specific

6. X. I'm <u>a highly experienced automotive engineer</u>.
                          A

    Y. Unfortunately there's no job here for <u>a highly experienced automotive engineer</u>.
                                                                              A

    A: [ ] Definite   [ ] Referential   [ ] Generic
        [ ] Indefinite   [ ] Non-referential   [ ] Specific

    B: [ ] Definite   [ ] Referential   [ ] Generic
        [ ] Indefinite   [ ] Non-referential   [ ] Specific

7. X. All my life I've been searching for <u>someone who would worship me, support me, and give me</u>
                                                                              A

    <u>the space I need to be myself and do my own thing</u>. Are you <u>that person</u>?
                                                                              B

    Y. Search no longer. I am <u>the one you've been dreaming of</u>. (Yeah, right.)
                                                  C

    A: [ ] Definite   [ ] Referential   [ ] Generic
        [ ] Indefinite   [ ] Non-referential   [ ] Specific

    B: [ ] Definite   [ ] Referential   [ ] Generic
        [ ] Indefinite   [ ] Non-referential   [ ] Specific

    C: [ ] Definite   [ ] Referential   [ ] Generic
        [ ] Indefinite   [ ] Non-referential   [ ] Specific

8. <u>They</u>'re having <u>a Stallone retrospective</u> at <u>the Vista</u> this week. Do <u>you</u> want to go?
    A   **B**   **C**   **D**

    A: [ ] Definite   [ ] Referential   [ ] Generic
        [ ] Indefinite   [ ] Non-referential   [ ] Specific

    B: [ ] Definite   [ ] Referential   [ ] Generic
        [ ] Indefinite   [ ] Non-referential   [ ] Specific

    C: [ ] Definite   [ ] Referential   [ ] Generic
        [ ] Indefinite   [ ] Non-referential   [ ] Specific

    D: [ ] Definite   [ ] Referential   [ ] Generic
        [ ] Indefinite   [ ] Non-referential   [ ] Specific

Name _____   **Section** _____   **Date** _____

9. So I'm waiting for <u>a cab</u>, and <u>this guy</u> comes up to me and tries to sell me <u>a Rolex</u> for twenty bucks!
                         A   B   C

    A: [ ] Definite   [ ] Referential   [ ] Generic
        [ ] Indefinite   [ ] Non-referential   [ ] Specific

    B: [ ] Definite   [ ] Referential   [ ] Generic
        [ ] Indefinite   [ ] Non-referential   [ ] Specific

    C: [ ] Definite   [ ] Referential   [ ] Generic
        [ ] Indefinite   [ ] Non-referential   [ ] Specific

Name _____   **Section** _____   **Date** _____

5.07   SEMANTIC ROLES IN HEADLINES

Headlines tend to be telescoped clauses, with some function words unexpressed. Certain noun phrases have been underscored in the headlines below (taken, sometimes adapted, from the *Los Angeles Times*).

A.   Above each underscored NP identify its semantic role in its clause by writing the abbreviation for the role above it:

A	= Agent	TH	= Theme/Patient	B	= Benefactive
E	= Experiencer	I	= Instrument	C	= Cause
R	= Recipient	TM	= Temporal	L	= Location

For any NP that you judge to play a role other than those listed above, propose a suggestive name for that role and explain it.

B.   For each underscored NP, add a second underscore if its grammatical relation is subject of the clause and a second and third underscore if its grammatical relation is object of the verb.

        A or C   **TH or E**   **L**

EXAMPLE: Small U.S. Studios Delight Audience at Moscow Fair.

1.   Network Fends Off Critics for Busting Embargo

2.   Actor Has Lived in the 'Hood

3.   Gay Men's Chorus Opens Doors in Europe

4.   Boyhood Favorites Still Leave Critic Reeling

5.   FBI Loses Lennon Papers Battle

6.   Disney Seeks U.S. Highway Funds for Expansion

7.   James Hawkins, Who Defended Family From Gangs, Dies at 80

8.   Shootings Mar 'BOYZ' Showings

9.   Beleaguered Governor Needs a Winner on Election Day

10.   Gates Tells Officials He'll Quit

11. <u>Gorbachev</u> Gives <u>Bush</u> <u>Assurance</u> on Soviet Reform

12. <u>U.S. Troops</u> Pull Out With <u>Warning</u> to <u>Iraq</u>

13. Opening <u>Ceremony</u> Plays on <u>Past</u> in Hopes of Igniting the <u>Present</u>

14. <u>INS</u> Issues New <u>Rules</u> for Foreign <u>Performers</u>

15. <u>Glaspie</u> Reportedly Misled <u>Congress</u> on Iraq Warning

Name _____   **Section** _____   **Date** _____

5.08   AGENTLESS PASSIVES IN ENGLISH

An agentless passive sentence is one which lacks a 'by + AGENT' constituent:

(a) ACTIVE SENTENCE: Melvin stole the baby's candy.

(b) AGENT PASSIVE: The baby's candy was stolen by Melvin.

(c) AGENTLESS PASSIVE: The baby's candy was stolen.

Note that in these examples, (a) and (b) have the same referential meaning, but (c) does not, since it conveys less information: it might be Melvin who perpetrated the dastardly deed or it might not—we aren't told.

English speakers use agentless passives in several situations. One is when the agent of the action is either unknown or irrelevant in the discourse. Another—and the focus of this exercise—is when the speaker wishes to avoid assigning responsibility or blame.

The following example illustrates this second use of the agentless passive:

Gary is talking to his boss, who is asking why a client hasn't received some important correspondence. Gary knows the reason: it was Bob's responsibility to take the mail to the post office Tuesday afternoon, and Bob forgot to do it. Gary doesn't want to get Bob in trouble or appear to be a "snitch," but on the other hand he doesn't want to lie to his boss. So rather than saying "Bob didn't take out the mail on Tuesday," he sidesteps the issue of responsibility by saying, "I don't think the mail was taken out on Tuesday." That way, the boss might or might not pursue the question of whose job it was to take out the mail, but at least he knows why the letter hasn't arrived—he won't suspect, for example, that the secretary never typed it.

For each of the examples that follow, give a context or circumstance in which a speaker can use the agentless passive in question to avoid assigning responsibility or blame. Indicate the speaker's motivation and the "protected" agent in each case. The last example is up to you—either your own plausible creation or one you've actually heard or read.

1. I indicated the corrections in red on the sheet I gave back to you, but it looks as if the changes were never made.

    CIRCUMSTANCE: _____

    _____

    MOTIVATION: _____

    _____

    PROTECTED AGENT: _____

    _____

2. Our troops achieved all of their military objectives. Unfortunately, forty civilians were killed or injured in the course of the operation.

    CIRCUMSTANCE: _____

    _____

    MOTIVATION: _____

    _____

    PROTECTED AGENT: _____

3.   Mommy, my bicycle got broken!

CIRCUMSTANCE: _____

_____

MOTIVATION: _____

_____

PROTECTED AGENT: _____

4.   I *know* there aren't any clean socks! The laundry hasn't been done for three weeks!

CIRCUMSTANCE: _____

_____

MOTIVATION: _____

_____

PROTECTED AGENT: _____

5.   I'll do whatever I can to save Fluffy, but I have to tell you that for her own good, she may have to be put to sleep.

CIRCUMSTANCE: _____

_____

MOTIVATION: _____

_____

PROTECTED AGENT: _____

6.   _____

_____

CIRCUMSTANCE: _____

_____

MOTIVATION: _____

_____

PROTECTED AGENT: _____

Name _____   **Section** _____   **Date** _____

5.09   NEGATIVE TRANSPORTATION IN ENGLISH

When a negative element moves from one position in a sentence to another, the meaning is often changed. For example,

(1)   I like peas, but I don't like carrots.
      A   **B**

If the negative moves from position B to position A, we get

(2)   I don't like peas, but I like carrots.

Clearly, (1) and (2) are different in meaning.

Sometimes, however, the referential meaning is not changed when the negative is moved. Consider

(3)   I think that Tom won't come.
      A   **B**

Moving the negative from position B to position A gives

(4)   I don't think that Tom will come.

Now it is possible that (4) has more than one meaning. It might be the case, for example, that someone has asserted that the speaker believes Tom will come, and the speaker responds with (4), probably with *don't* stressed, to contradict that assertion and indicate that in fact she has no opinion on the subject. The point is, however, that (4) *can* mean the same as (3), even though the negative has been "transported' from the embedded clause to the main clause.

A.   In the sentences below, the negative is in the "B" position. In each case, move the negative to the "A" position, writing out the new sentence you obtain. Then consider carefully the referential meanings of the pair of sentences you now have. For each pair, state whether the "before" and "after" sentences can or cannot mean the same thing.

1.   I think you can't possibly lift that weight.

_____

These sentences [ ] CAN   [ ] CANNOT mean the same thing.

2.   I deduced that the gun wasn't loaded.

_____

These sentences [ ] CAN   [ ] CANNOT mean the same thing.

3.   I regret I didn't take that course.

_____

These sentences [ ] CAN   [ ] CANNOT mean the same thing.

4. I suppose you're not very happy with me.

_____

These sentences [ ] CAN   [ ] CANNOT mean the same thing.

5. It's odd that Glenda doesn't play chess.

_____

These sentences [ ] CAN   [ ] CANNOT mean the same thing.

6. It's likely that Glenda doesn't play chess.

_____

These sentences [ ] CAN   [ ] CANNOT mean the same thing.

7. I realized that his pet giraffe wasn't healthy.

_____

These sentences [ ] CAN   [ ] CANNOT mean the same thing.

8. I believe they haven't left yet.

_____

These sentences [ ] CAN   [ ] CANNOT mean the same thing.

9. I believe that he didn't lift a finger to help.

_____

These sentences [ ] CAN   [ ] CANNOT mean the same thing.

10. I'm surprised that he didn't lift a finger to help.

_____

These sentences [ ] CAN   [ ] CANNOT mean the same thing.

B. For each original sentence in part A, insert the words "the fact (that)" in the appropriate place. (You may have to do some rearranging of the sentence.) For example, "I acknowledge that he's not too swift" becomes "I acknowledge the fact that he's not too swift." Likewise, "It's tragic that Schubert died so young" becomes "The fact that Schubert died so young is tragic."

Some of the sentences you obtain in this way will be grammatical, and others will not. Label each of your derived "fact" sentences as grammatical or ungrammatical.

1. _____

[ ] GRAMMATICAL   [ ] UNGRAMMATICAL

Name _____   **Section** _____   **Date** _____

2. _____

[   ] GRAMMATICAL   [   ] UNGRAMMATICAL

3. _____

[   ] GRAMMATICAL   [   ] UNGRAMMATICAL

4. _____

[   ] GRAMMATICAL   [   ] UNGRAMMATICAL

5. _____

[   ] GRAMMATICAL   [   ] UNGRAMMATICAL

6. _____

[   ] GRAMMATICAL   [   ] UNGRAMMATICAL

7. _____

[   ] GRAMMATICAL   [   ] UNGRAMMATICAL

8. _____

[   ] GRAMMATICAL   [   ] UNGRAMMATICAL

9. _____

[   ] GRAMMATICAL   [   ] UNGRAMMATICAL

10. _____

[   ] GRAMMATICAL   [   ] UNGRAMMATICAL

C. Compare the results of parts A and B. What correlations, if any, can you discover between these two apparently unrelated phenomena?

_____

_____

_____

_____

Name _____   **Section** _____   **Date** _____

5.10   ENGLISH METAPHORS 1

Many common expressions have arisen from a metaphorical use of other expressions, as with *dove* and *hawk* to refer to supporters and opponents of the Vietnam War. Identify and underscore at least one metaphorical expression in each sentence; then indicate the literal meaning of the term and the appropriateness of its extension to capture a phenomenon in the context in which it is used. The sentences are taken, slightly adapted, from *Time* magazine (July 22, 1991), in an article about France, written by James Walsh.

A. It is a culture abrim with connoisseurs.

_____

_____

B. De Gaulle, father of the Fifth Republic, used to cite France's prodigious number of cheeses.

_____

_____

C. Why all the buzz about discontent, social gloom and political drift, a crisis of faith and a fading sense of identity?

_____

_____

D. It sounds as unlikely as Cyrano de Bergerac fumbling his sword or groping for the *mot juste*.

_____

_____

E. Not since Baron Haussmann thrust his boulevards through rancid slums has Paris experienced such a fever of renewal.

_____

_____

F. Judging by the diagnoses in the press, a country that long prided itself on being the *lumière du monde* is awash in dark soul-searching.

_____

_____

G. There is the hangover from the gulf war, an episode that deflated the vaunted image of French power and influence.

_____

_____

H. What the country preserved over the centuries it now risks losing in the homogenizing vat of that mysterious entity called Europe.

_____

_____

I. The French seem to be losing their bearings, their ideals and dreams.

_____

_____

J. It is a bitter vintage, all the more so considering how high expectations were running.

_____

_____

K. Just last year France looked well placed to become more than the center of gravity of a newly ascendant Europe.

_____

_____

L. Paris was confidently pulling the strings of Europe.

_____

_____

M. The jewel of French assets in recent years has been stability.

_____

_____

N. Inflation was reined in, and a Socialist President guided France's fortunes with confident generalship.

_____

_____

O. A few people famous for crossing swords over the slightest trespass settled into a harmonious political dispensation.

_____

_____

P. Now the country seems to be suffering an outbreak of that endemic French affliction called *malaise*.

_____

_____

Name _____   **Section** _____   **Date** _____

Q. The symptoms are widespread public unease—a volatile mixture of boredom, anxiety, and irritation.

_____

_____

R. Change looks overwhelming to many of the French, eroding the old certainties that once defined Frenchness for everyone.

_____

_____

S. With a 38% approval rating, the bride of high office may be headed for divorce when she has barely assembled her trousseau.

_____

_____

T. But her summons to arms has fallen flat at a time when the treasury is tight.

_____

_____

Name _____   **Section** _____   **Date** _____

5.11   ENGLISH METAPHORS 2

The phrases and clauses below are taken (sometimes slightly adapted) from *The New Yorker* magazine's "In Brief" movie reviews. Each contains at least one familiar metaphorical use of a word. Identify a metaphorical use in each, and briefly explain the difference between the literal and the metaphorical use of the word.

1.   the kind of power that Kurosawa aims for

   _____

   _____

   _____

2.   the second half of "Dreams" is weak

   _____

   _____

   _____

3.   the fifth episode is a thin conceit

   _____

   _____

   _____

4.   she's too decent and too timid to explode

   _____

   _____

   _____

5.   Eugene O'Neill's play about a black man's disintegration

   _____

   _____

   _____

6.   ... was conceived in a semi-Expressionist style

   _____

   _____

   _____

7. Yet there isn't a breath of life in it

_____

_____

_____

8. a cold, clever period gangster movie

_____

_____

_____

9. the action unfolds in and around a city

_____

_____

_____

10. hushed and hypnotic, it makes you so conscious of its artistry

_____

_____

_____

11. this tale of a sorrowful, wisecracking starlet

_____

_____

_____

12. whose brassy, boozing former-star mother started her on sleeping pills

_____

_____

_____

13. his tone keeps slipping around

_____

_____

_____

Name _____   **Section** _____   **Date** _____

14.   She remains distant, emotionally atonal.

_____

_____

_____

15.   Marlon Brando, in his magnetic, soft-eyed youth

_____

_____

_____

16.   Atkinson's lethal genius at playing an articulate swine

_____

_____

_____

17.   who seems stripped down to pure flakiness

_____

_____

_____

18.   the movie ... dies on the screen

_____

_____

_____

19.   The shocks don't have much resonance

_____

_____

_____

20.   The novelty of the character's ethnicity wears off quickly, because everything else in the movie is secondhand

_____

_____

_____

Name _____   Section _____   Date _____

5.12   CLASSIFIERS IN MALAY/INDONESIAN

In English, we can generally place numbers directly before nouns: 'five books,' 'twenty-three rabbits,' 'one computer.' Sometimes, however, a different structure is necessary. We don't normally say 'two chalks' or 'three breads,' but 'two sticks (or pieces) of chalk,' and 'three slices (or pieces or loaves) of bread.'

Although in English it is relatively rare that nouns like *stick, piece* or *loaf* are required to count objects, in languages like Chinese, Vietnamese and Malay/Indonesian, such classifiers are the rule rather than the exception, and it is part of native speaker competence to know which of these to use with any particular noun.

Some classifiers are quite general in their applicability, while others are highly restricted and used with only a few lexical items. The choice of classifier is based on the semantic properties of nouns. The set of nouns counted with any particular classifier form a *lexical field*—a set of lexical items with identifiable semantic affinities.

This exercise will introduce you to six common classifiers in Malay/Indonesian. The data are given in standard Malay/Indonesian orthography. Note that <c> = [č], and <e> is usually [ə], sometimes [ɛ] (as in *ekor* [ɛkɔr]).

A.   Examine the data below. Extrapolating from these examples, determine the constitution of the lexical field of nouns used with each classifier illustrated. (You may be reminded of the popular TV game show in which contestants have to guess categories of objects, and clues consist of members of the category: "Knife, razor blade, axe, broken glass..." "Things that are sharp!")

1.   dua orang laki-laki   'two men'

     tiga orang guru   'three teachers'

     enam orang pemain bola sepak   'six football players'

     tiga orang perempuan   'three women'

     seorang tukang besi   'one blacksmith'

     empat orang Cina   'four Chinese people'

     CLASSIFIER: _____

     USED WITH: _____

2.   lima ekor burung   'five birds'

     tujuh ekor gajah   'seven elephants'

     lapan ekor labah-labah   'eight spiders'

     seekor buaya   'one crocodile'

     sepuluh ekor anjing   'ten dogs'

     lima puluh ekor kerbau   'fifty water-buffaloes'

     CLASSIFIER: _____

     USED WITH: _____

3.   sebatang rokok   'a cigarette'

     dua batang pensel   'two pencils'

     sepuluh batang jari   'ten fingers'

     lima puluh dua batang pokok   'fifty-two trees'

     empat puluh satu batang buluh   'forty-one bamboos'

| dua batang rokok | 'two cigarettes' |
| sembilan batang kapor | 'nine sticks of chalk' |

CLASSIFIER: _____

USED WITH: _____

4. | enam helai kertas | 'six pieces of paper' |
    | sehelai kain | 'a length of cloth' |
    | dua belas helai daun | 'twelve leaves' |
    | enam belas helai bulu | 'sixteen feathers' |
    | sebelas helai rumput | 'eleven blades of grass' |
    | lapan helai saputangan | 'eight handkerchiefs' |

CLASSIFIER: _____

USED WITH: _____

5. | tujuh buah kereta | 'seven cars' |
    | tujuh puluh buah rumah | 'seventy houses' |
    | tujuh belas buah sofa | 'seventeen sofas' |
    | tujuh puluh tujuh buah gunung | 'seventy-seven mountains' |
    | sebuah sekolah | 'one school' |
    | lima buah pulau | 'five islands' |
    | sembilan belas buah kedai | 'nineteen shops' |

CLASSIFIER: _____

USED WITH: _____

(*Hint:* Consider size and shape.)

6. | dua belas biji telor | 'a dozen eggs' |
    | enam biji peluru | 'six bullets' |
    | dua puluh satu biji permata | 'twenty-one jewels' |
    | tiga biji buah anggur | 'three grapes' |
    | tiga puluh lima biji benih | 'thirty-five seeds' |

CLASSIFIER: _____

USED WITH: _____

Name _____   **Section** _____   **Date** _____

B.   Translate noun phrases 1–8 using this glossary:

tikar	'floormat'	ikan	'fish'
kapal api	'steamship'	budak	'boy'
komputer	'computer'	bola pingpong	'pingpong ball'
tongkat	'walking stick'	buah duku	'duku' (small round Asian fruit)

1.   five floormats   _____

2.   twelve fish   _____

3.   forty steamships   _____

4.   eighteen boys   _____

5.   ninety-one computers _____

6.   a pingpong ball   _____

7.   two hundred walking sticks _____

8.   fifty-nine dukus   _____

C.   Classifiers in Malay/Indonesian can also be used as independent nouns. For example, *ekor* is the word for 'tail.' Take a guess as to what *orang* and *batang* mean when used as nouns.

orang _____   batang _____

Date

Name _____   **Section** _____   **Date** _____

5.13   ADJECTIVE CLASSES IN PERSIAN

Just as verbs are marked in the lexicon to indicate the kinds of subjects they allow, adjectives can be similarly marked to show the types of noun phrases they can modify.

Compared to many languages, English has rather loose restrictions on adjectives and the nouns they qualify. Thus, we can speak of a worried man or a worried look; a courageous parent, a courageous act or a courageous newspaper article; a sarcastic remark or a sarcastic teacher. Other languages can have tighter constraints on adjective-noun co-occurrences.

In the Persian data below, the starred NPs are ungrammatical. By comparing the acceptable and unacceptable phrases, you will be able to divide the adjectives in the data into two classes based on the kinds of nouns they can modify. (*Note:* The bound morpheme *-e/-ye* is required between a noun and an attributive adjective modifying it; this is not relevant to the present problem.)

1. mærd-e mehræban   'kind man'
    *name-ye mehræban   'kind letter'

2. *bæčče-ye biræhmane   'cruel child'
    hæmle-ye biræhmane   'cruel attack'

3. *hærfha-ye bahuš   'clever remarks'
    šagerd-e bahuš   'clever student'

4. *bæččegan-e mohæbbætamiz   'affectionate children'
    hærfha-ye mohæbbætamiz   'affectionate remarks'

5. *mærd-e mehræbanane   'kind man'
    hærf-e mehræbanane   'kind word'

6. mærd-e bašæræf   'honorable man'
    *ǰæng-e bašæræf   'honorable war'

7. bæččegan-e bamohæbbæt   'affectionate children'
    *hærfha-ye bamohæbbæt   'affectionate remarks'

8. ræftar-e sæfahætamiz   'foolish behavior'
    *pedær-e sæfahætamiz   'foolish father'

9. *mæqale-ye nafæhm   'stupid article'
    ræhbær-e nafæhm   'stupid leader'

10. *valedein-e sorudamiz   'joyful parents'
    mouqe'-e sorudamiz   'joyful occasion'

11. *mo'ællem-e tæ'neamiz   'sarcastic teacher'
    hærf-e tæ'neamiz   'sarcastic remark'

12.   pesær-e gostax   'rude boy'
       *goftar-e gostax   'rude speech'

13.   zæn-e biræhm   'cruel woman'
       *kar-e biræhm   'cruel deed'

14.   karha-ye bišærmane   'shameless acts'
       *zænan-e bišærmane   'shameless women'

15.   *soxæn-e doroštxuy   'harsh speech'
       qazi-ye doroštxuy   'harsh judge'

16.   *ræhbær-e šærafætmændane   'honorable leader'
       tæsmim-e šærafætmændane   'honorable decision'

17.   mærdom-e šadman   'joyful people'
       *mouqe'-e šadman   'joyful occasion'

18.   kæleme-ye dorošt   'harsh word'
       *mo'ællem-e dorošt   'harsh teacher'

19.   soxæn-e koframiz   'blasphemous speech'
       *ǰævan-e koframiz   'blasphemous young man'

20.   ræhbær-e kohnepæræst   'old-fashioned leader'
       *šælvar-e kohnepæræst   'old-fashioned trousers'

21.   *særbazan-e tæhævvoramiz   'courageous soldiers'
       karha-ye tæhævvoramiz   'courageous acts'

22.   *karha-ye bišærm   'shameless acts'
       zænan-e bišærm   'shameless women'

23.   *ǰæng-e ba'edalæt   'just war'
       ræhbær-e ba'edalæt   'just leader'

24.   *doxtær-e gostaxane   'rude girl'
       hærfha-ye gostaxane   'rude words'

A.   What is the relevant distinction between the two classes of adjectives in the data?

_____

_____

Name _____   **Section** _____   **Date** _____

B. Using the following chart, divide the adjectives into the two classes you have determined. Write the characterization of each class at the head of its column in the spaces provided.

	Class I	Class II
	_____	_____
	_____	_____
affectionate	_____	_____
blasphemous	_____	_____
clever	_____	_____
courageous	_____	_____
cruel	_____	_____
foolish	_____	_____
harsh	_____	_____
honorable	_____	_____
joyful	_____	_____
just	_____	_____
kind	_____	_____
old-fashioned	_____	_____
rude	_____	_____
sarcastic	_____	_____
shameless	_____	_____
stupid	_____	_____

C. Are there any morphological clues that allow you to predict which class an adjective will fall into? Explain.

_____

_____

_____

Name _____   **Section** _____   **Date** _____

5.14   SENTENCE-FINAL *ba* IN MANDARIN CHINESE

Chinese has a set of sentence-final particles that have different semantic and pragmatic functions. In this exercise, you will investigate one of these particles.

Examine the Mandarin sentences below, transcribed in Pinyin (see Appendix A). The second sentence of each pair is identical to the first, with the exception of the sentence-final *ba*. By noting the translations, you will be able to determine the function of *ba*. Your goal is to observe the "common thread" that runs through all the *ba* sentences and then provide a general statement that characterizes sentences with final *ba*. (It is *not* sufficient simply to list the different situations in which *ba* can be used, and the various associated translations.)

1.   A.   Wǒ-men   zǒu.

          I PLURAL leave

          'We leave.'

      B.   Wǒmen zǒu ba.

          'Let's leave.'

2.   A.   Dàjiā   hē   chá.

          Everyone drink tea

          'Everyone drinks tea.'

      B.   Dàjiā hē chá ba.

          'Have some tea, everyone.'

3.   A.   Wǒ gēn nǐ   qù bówùguǎn.

          I   with you go museum

          'I'll go to the museum with you.'

      B.   Wǒ gēn nǐ qù bówùguǎn ba.

          'I'll go to the museum with you, OK?'

4.   A.   Nǐ   shì Wáng Lǎoshī.

          you be Wang Teacher

          'You are Teacher Wang.'

      B.   Nǐ shì Wáng Lǎoshī ba.

          'You must be Teacher Wang.'

5.   A.   Zhèi-ge   cài hěn hǎo chī.

          this CLASSIFIER dish very good eat

          'This dish is very tasty.'

      B.   Zhèige cài hěn hǎo chī ba.

          'This dish is very tasty, don't you think?'

6.   A.   Nǐ   děng yi děng.

          you wait one wait

          'You wait a little while.'

      B.   Nǐ děng yi děng ba.

           'Why don't you wait a little while.'

    7.   A.   Tā   bú   huì   lái.

           s/he NEG likely come

           'S/He isn't likely to come.'

      B.   Tā bú huì lái ba.

           S/He isn't likely to come, wouldn't you agree?'

A.   Judging from the data, what is the function of sentence-final *ba*?

_____

_____

_____

B.   Does English have a uniform way of marking the same function? If so, what is it?

_____

_____

_____

C.   For examples 3 and 6 in A above, show how your analysis of the function of *ba* applies.

    3.   _____

_____

_____

_____

    6.   _____

_____

_____

_____

D.   Translate into idiomatic English:

    1.   Nǐmen bù gēn tā zǒu ba.

_____

    2.   Lǜ chá bù hǎo hē ba. (lǜ = 'green')

_____

Name _____   **Section** _____   **Date** _____

5.15   THE *shì ... de* CONSTRUCTION IN CHINESE

Consider the following two Mandarin Chinese sentences:

(a)   Wǒ péngyou zuótiān dào   le.

    I   friend   yesterday arrive

    'My friend arrived yesterday.'

(b)   Wǒ péngyou shì zuótiān   dào   de.

    I   friend   be yesterday arrive

    'My friend arrived yesterday.'

Both these sentences refer to a completed action in the past. They are translated identically, and have the same referential meaning. However, they are not interchangeable. Depending on the information structure of the discourse, only one of the two will generally be appropriate.

Note that (a) contains the function word *le* and (b) contains the words *shì* 'be' and the function word *de*. (Neither *le* nor *de* have been glossed.) By examining the following mini-dialogs and answering the questions that follow them, you will be able to discover when to use the *le* construction and the *shì ... de* construction in referring to completed action in the past.

1.   A: Nǐ   péngyou hái zài Xiānggǎng ma?

        you friend   still at Hong Kong QUESTION

        'Is your friend still in Hong Kong?'

    B: Bù. Tā zuótiān   zǒu   le.

        NEG s/he yesterday leave

        'No. S/He left yeaterday.'

2.   A: Nǐ   péngyou shì shénme shíhou dào   de?

        you friend   be what   time   arrive

        'When did your friend arrive?'

    B: Tā shì zuótiān dào   de.

        s/he be yesterday arrive

        'S/He arrived yesterday.'

3.   A: Nǐ shì zài nǎr   yùjiàn tā   de?

        you be at where meet   s/he

        'Where did you meet him/her?'

    B: Wǒ shì zài Xiǎo Běijīng yùjiàn tā   de.

        I   be at   little Beijing meet   s/he

        'I met him/her at Little Beijing.'

4.   A: Nǐ   chī le ma?

        you eat   QUESTION

        'Have you eaten?'

B: Wǒ zài Xiǎo Běijīng chī le wǎnfàn.

I   at little Beijing eat   supper

'I had supper at Little Beijing.'

5. A: Wǒ érzi zuótiān   shēng le.

I   son yesterday born

'My son was born yesterday.'

    B: Gōngxǐ,   gōngxǐ!

congratulations congratulations

'Congratulations!'

6. A: Nǐ shì něi   nián shēng de?

you be which year born

'What year were you born?'

    B: Wǒ shì yī jiǔ qī   wǔ nián shēng de.

I   be one nine seven five year born

'I was born in 1975.'

7. A: Wǒ mǔqin zuótiān   dào   le.

I   mother yesterday arrive

'My mother arrived yesterday.'

    B: Zhēn de ma?   Wǒ bù   zhīdào tā yào lái.

real   QUESTION I   NEG know she will come

'Really? I didn't know she was going to come.'

Tā shì yí ge   rén   lái de ma?

she be one CLASSIFIER person come   QUESTION

'Did she come alone?'

    A: Bú   shì. Tā bú shi yí ge   rén   lái de.

NEG be she NEG be one CLASSIFIER person come

'No. She didn't come alone.'

8. A: Nǐ zuótiān   zuò le xiē   shénme shì?

you yesterday do   PLURAL what   thing

'What did you do yesterday?'

    B: Wǒ qù le bówùguǎn.

I   go   museum

'I went to the museum.'

    A: Nǐ shì gēn shéi qù de?

you be with who go

'Who did you go with?'

    B: Wǒ shì gēn wǒ péngyou qù de.

I   be with I friend   go

'I went with my friend.'

Name _____   **Section** _____   **Date** _____

A. Syntactic analysis

   1. Examine all the examples above in which *le* appears. What is the rule for the position of *le* in these sentences or questions?

   _____

   _____

   2. Repeat for the *shì ... de* examples. What rule determines the position of *shì* and the position of *de*?

   _____

   _____

B. Pragmatic analysis

   1. Now examine each of the *shì ... de* examples in the mini-dialogs in terms of information structure. Alongside each example, indicate what, if any, information is *given, old* or *presupposed* at the time of utterance, and what stated or requested information is *new*.

   2. Repeat question 1 for the *le* examples.

   3. You should now be ready to state your generalization: In statements or questions about completed action in the past, when do Mandarin speakers use the *le* construction, and when do they use the *shì ... de* construction?

   _____

   _____

   _____

   _____

   _____

C. Translate the following dialog into Chinese:

   A: My mother's left.

   _____

   B: When did she leave?

   _____

   A: She left yesterday.

   _____

B: Did she leave with your friend?

_____

A: No, my friend didn't leave.

_____

Name _____   **Section** _____   **Date** _____

C H A P T E R

6

Historical and Comparative Linguistics

6.01 CLASSIFICATION OF SIMILARITIES

Despite the general arbitrariness of the relationship between a word and its referent, we observe that words referring to the same or similar things are sometimes similar in different languages. There are four basic explanations for such similarities:

1. *Genetic Relationship.* The similar lexical items may be reflexes of an earlier, common source in a common ancestor language.

2. *Borrowing.* One language may borrow a lexical item from another, or both may borrow similar items from an outside source or sources.

3. *Universal Tendencies.* In a very limited number of cases, observed similarities are the result of something universal in human physiology, psychology or perception. An oft-cited example is the observation that many languages, related or not, have an *m* in their word for 'mother,' presumably a consequence of the fact that the bilabial nasal is one of the first speech sounds nursing babies learn to produce. Diverse languages often have a high front vowel in words or morphemes denoting smallness or diminution: English *teeny;* Spanish *poco* 'some, a little,' *poquito* 'very little,' *poquitito* 'extremely small amount'—something about the [i] sound seems to convey a "small" feeling. Words that are onomatopoetic—i.e., that attempt to mimic actual sounds—also fall into this category. For example, words for the sounds made by cats, sheep and cows are often (but not always!) similar across languages.

4. *Coincidence.* If no other plausible reason presents itself, we have to conclude that the similarity is due to chance. Clearly, the probability of a chance resemblance is inversely proportional to the length of the word. It is highly unlikely that two seven-syllable words will be similar by coincidence; with short lexical items, chance resemblances can occur more frequently.

For each of the paired languages and lexical items below, determine the most plausible explanation for the similarity. In the space provided, write C for coincidence, UT for universal tendency, B for borrowing, or GR for genetic relationship. In the case of borrowing, also indicate the *source* of the borrowed item: Which language borrowed from which, or was there an *outside* source (or sources) involved?

In a few cases, you may have to make an educated guess as to the correct explanation. But you will usually be able to arrive at the most plausible answer by a process of deduction, using your knowledge of language families and language change, and assessing the likelihood that borrowing took place. (Some questions to ask yourself: What is the chance that speakers of the two languages were in contact? Was there political or cultural influence involved that would encourage the borrowing of words? Was it likely that the need arose in one or both languages to be able to refer to something "new" for which a convenient word didn't already exist?) One thing to bear in mind: *From the fact that two languages are genetically related, it does not necessarily follow that every observed similarity between them is a result of their genetic relationship!*

Note: In these data, words from languages that employ the Roman alphabet appear in their standard orthography (Mandarin Chinese is in Pinyin—see Appendix A), with occasional phonetic transcriptions in brackets. Words from other languages appear in transcription unless otherwise indicated.

1. Japanese: futtobooru   'football'

    English: football   _____

2. Hebrew: šalɔm   'peace; a greeting'

    Arabic: sala:m   'peace; a greeting'   _____

3. German: Haus [haws]   'house'

    English   house   _____

4. Hawaiian: aloha   'love; a greeting'

    Maori: aroha   'love; a greeting'   _____

5. Greek: ne   'yes'

    Korean: ne   'yes'   _____

6. English: Halleluyah

    Hebrew: halᵊluya   'Halleluyah'   _____

7. Portuguese: libro   'book'

    French: livre   'book'   _____

8. Persian: bæradær   'brother'

    English: brother   _____

Name _____   **Section** _____   **Date** _____

9.   English: tofu
     Chinese: dofu   'tofu'   _____

10. German: fünf   'five'
     Welsh: pump [pɪmp]   'five'   _____

11. Tok Pisin: yumi   'we (incl.)'
     English: you and me   _____

12. Anc. Greek: hüpo   'under'
     English: hypo-   'under' (prefix)   _____

13. Welsh: deg   'ten'
     Latin: decem   'ten'   _____

14. French: weekend [wikɛnd]   'weekend'
     English: weekend   _____

15. Persian: to   'you (sg. familiar)'
     Spanish: tu   'you (sg. familiar)'   _____

16. Norwegian: nei   'no'
     English: nay   _____

17. English: neuron
     Anc. Greek: neuron   'nerve, sinew'   _____

18. Russian: dva   'two'
     Malay: dua   'two'
     _____

19. Hebrew: ima   'mommy'
     Malay: emak   'mother'
     _____

20. Chinese: chá   'tea'
     Persian: čay   'tea'
     _____

21. German: Messer   'knife'
     Yiddish: mɛsɛr   'knife'
     _____

22. Polish: człowiek   'man'
     Czech: člověk   'man'
     _____

23. Japanese: naifu   'knife'
     English: knife
     _____

24. Mod. Greek: mitera   'mother'
     German: Mutter   'mother'
     _____

25. Hungarian: radio   'radio'
     Finnish: radio   'radio'
     _____

26. English: snow
     Dutch: sneeuw   'snow'
     _____

27. Arabic: ana   'I'
     Hebrew: ani   'I'
     _____

Name _____   **Section** _____   **Date** _____

28. Welsh: hi   'she'
    Hebrew: hi   'she'   _____

    _____

29. Yiddish: mɪdbɛr   'desert'
    Hebrew: midbar   'desert'   _____

    _____

30. French: os   'bone'
    Rumanian: os   'bone'   _____

    _____

31. Malay: kamus   'dictionary'
    Swahili: kamusi   'dictionary'   _____

    _____

32. Hungarian: grépfrút   'grapefruit'
    Turkish: grepfrut   'grapefruit'   _____

    _____

33. Persian: šeš   'six'
    Hebrew: šɛš   'six'   _____

    _____

34. Persian: xahær   'sister'
    Welsh: chwaer [xwaer]   'sister'   _____

    _____

35. English: egg
    Norwegian: egg   'egg'   _____

    _____

36. French: grand   'big, great'
    English: grand   _____

    _____

37. Yiddish: ɪz   'is'
    English: is
    _____

38. English: thou
    Icelandic: þu [θu]   'you (sg. familiar)'
    _____

39. Persian: mahi   'fish'
    Hawaiian: mahi-mahi   'kind of fish'
    _____

40. English: taboo
    Tongan: tapu   'forbidden'
    _____

41. Japanese: densha   'streetcar'
    Chinese: diànchē   'streetcar'
    _____

42. Chinese: gōngchang   'factory'
    Korean: koŋčaŋ   'factory'
    _____

43. Malay: orang utan   'person of the forest'
    English: orangutan
    _____

44. Malay: ini   'this'
    Persian: in   'this'
    _____

45. Japanese: anata   'you'
    Arabic: anta   'you (m. sg.)'
    _____

46. Malay: salam alaikum   'peace be upon you' (a greeting)
    Yiddish: šʌləm aleixɛm   'peace be upon you' (a greeting)
    _____

Name _____   **Section** _____   **Date** _____

6.02   PHONOLOGICAL CHANGE IN GREEK

This problem concerns a particular phonological development in Greek—the changes in the pronunciation of the Ancient Greek stops. The data below give you the ancient and modern pronunciations of some words common to both stages of the language. You'll notice many changes that took place along the way, but you should concentrate on what became of the original stops. (*Note:* The transcription is phonemic—that is, every symbol represents a different phoneme. Stress is phonemic in Greek and is indicated in the transcription, but it is not relevant to this problem.)

	Ancient Greek	Modern Greek	Gloss
1.	agapáo:	aɣapáo	'I love'
2.	glükǘs	ɣlikós	'sweet'
3.	diapʰtʰeíro:	ðiafθíro	'corrupt'
4.	düstükʰé:s	ðistixís	'unfortunate'
5.	grápʰo:	ɣráfo	'I write'
6.	tʰéatron	θéatro	'theater'
7.	blápto:	vlápto	'I harm'
8.	karpós	karpós	'fruit'
9.	badízo:	vaðízo	'I walk'
10.	ptósis	ptósi	'fall'
11.	pʰtʰorá	fθorá	'destruction'
12.	pʰoberós	foverós	'fearful'
13.	kʰtʰés	xθés	'yesterday'
14.	tekʰníte:s	texnítis	'craftsman'

A.   On the chart below, indicate the position of each of the Ancient Greek stops.

	Labial	Alveolar	Velar
Voiceless Aspirated			
Voiceless Unaspirated			
Voiced Unaspirated			

B.   For each ancient stop, indicate the corresponding sound in Modern Greek. Your answers should consist of statements of the form *A > B, where *A is an ancient stop and B is its modern reflex.

_____

_____

_____

_____

C. Now generalize from the individual sound changes you identified in part B. How did whole *classes* of sounds change in the journey from Ancient to Modern Greek?

_____

_____

_____

_____

Name _____   **Section** _____   **Date** _____

6.03   PHONOLOGICAL CHANGE IN PERSIAN

Below you will find transcriptions of some Persian words which contain short vowels. The modern Iranian pronunciation is given alongside the pronunciation at an earlier stage of the language.

Examine the differences between the earlier and modern pronunciations, and then answer the questions that follow.

	Earlier Persian	Modern Persian	Gloss
1.	guft	goft	's/he said'
2.	zærtušt	zærtošt	'Zoroaster'
3.	šæbækæ	šæbæke	'network'
4.	sift	seft	'stiff'
5.	sipurdæn	sepordæn	'to deposit'
6.	giriftæ	gerefte	'taken'
7.	gurusnæ	gorosne	'hungry'
8.	nigæh	negæh	'look'
9.	zindæ	zende	'alive'
10.	muslim	moslem	'Muslim'

A.   State all the sound changes that are evident from the data. Determine whether each change is *unconditioned* (taking place across the board, independent of environment) or *conditioned* (occurring only in certain environments). For the conditioned changes, identify the environment in which they took place.

_____

_____

_____

_____

_____

_____

_____

_____

_____

_____

_____

_____

B.   Diagram the Persian short vowel system at the two different stages of the language represented by the data.

EARLIER SHORT VOWELS   **MODERN SHORT VOWELS**

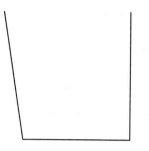   

C.   Referring to the diagrams you drew in B, what generalizations can you state about the sound changes you've identified?

_____

_____

_____

_____

_____

_____

Name _____   **Section** _____   **Date** _____

6.04   COMPARATIVE ROMANCE 1

Examine this list of cognates in three Romance languages, Spanish, Italian and French, and answer the questions below.

Note: The data are given in the standard orthography for each of the languages. In all of these words, <c> = [k].

	Spanish	Italian	French	Gloss
1.	acto	atto	acte	'act'
2.	óptico	ottico	optique	'optic'
3.	obturador	otturatore	obturateur	'shutter'
4.	selectiva	selettiva	sélective	'selective'
5.	flota	flotta	flotte	'fleet'
6.	eléctrico	elettrico	électrique	'electric'
7.	abdomen	addome	abdomen	'abdomen'
8.	apto	atto	apte	'apt'
9.	último	ultimo	ultime	'last'
10.	octubre	ottobre	octobre	'October'
11.	antagonista	antagonista	antagoniste	'antagonist'
12.	septiembre	settembre	septembre	'September'
13.	carta	carta	carte	'card'
14.	correcta	corretta	correcte	'correct'
15.	adoptar	adottare	adopter	'to adopt'
16.	súbdito	suddito	———	'subject'
17.	obtener	ottenere	obtenir	'to obtain'
18.	sospechar	sospettare	suspecter	'to suspect'
19.	letra	lettera	lettre	'letter'
20.	optimista	ottimista	optimiste	'optimist'

A.   The data give clear evidence of a phonological change involving adjacent consonants that took place in the development of one of the languages. Which language was this?

_____

B.   Make a "before and after" list of all the sound changes that took place in this language as part of the process you've identified. Your goal is to isolate the *parts* of the words in the data that have changed, and thus "boil down" the data to the essentials.

Before the Change	After the Change

C. Examining the sound changes you've isolated in the previous question, come up with a *general statement of the process*. Your statement should not include specific cases, yet must cover all (and only!) the sound changes in the data that were part of this process. You may want to use the words "assimilate" or "assimilation" in your answer. (*Assimilation* is the general term for the phonological process by which one of two neighboring sounds changes to become more like the other.)

_____

_____

_____

_____

D. Assimilation can be *partial* or *complete*, and *progressive* or *regressive*. The former pair of terms refers to whether the sound change results in partial similarity or complete identity; the latter refers to the direction of influence—whether the first sound influenced the second or vice versa. Characterize the process you've identified using these terms:

The process is an example of _____, _____ assimilation.

E. Phonological processes sometimes result in *lexical mergers*—two originally different words or morphemes that have become identical. Is there any evidence for lexical mergers in the data? Explain.

_____

_____

_____

F. Based on your analysis of the data you've seen and not on any prior knowledge of these languages, can you fill in the missing members of the cognate sets below with reasonable confidence? Explain how sure you can be of the answer in each case.

Spanish	Italian
contacto	_____
_____	ottava

_____

_____

_____

_____

Name _____   **Section** _____   **Date** _____

6.05   COMPARATIVE ROMANCE 2

A. Study the following list of cognates in Spanish, Italian and Portuguese, paying particular attention to final vowels. Then answer the questions that follow. *Note:* These data are given in phonetic transcription. The Portuguese transcription reflects Brazilian pronunciation current in Rio de Janeiro.

	Spanish	Italian	Portuguese	Gloss
1.	libro	libro	livru	'book'
2.	fama	fama	famə	'fame'
3.	sentro	čentro	sẽtru	'center'
4.	grande	grande	grə̃ǰi	'big'
5.	kwatro	kwattro	kwatru	'four'
6.	alto	alto	awtu	'tall'
7.	kanta	kanta	kə̃tə	'sings'
8.	digo	diko	ǰigu	'I say'
9.	fwerte	fɔrte	fɔxči	'strong'
10.	famosa	famoza	famɔzə	'famous'
11.	nweβe	nɔve	nɔvi	'nine'
12.	alta	alta	awtə	'tall'
13.	seðe	sɛde	sɛǰi	'seat'
14.	base	baze	bazi	'base'
15.	karo	karo	karu	'dear'
16.	bale	vale	vali	'is worth'
17.	fiesta	fɛsta	fɛštə	'party'
18.	latina	latina	lačinə	'Latin'
19.	dentista	dentista	dẽčištə	'dentist'
20.	tanto	tanto	tə̃tu	'so much'

1. As evidenced by the data, list the individual sound changes that have taken place in the final vowels of Portuguese. Assume that the Spanish and Italian final vowels, which agree in these data, represent the sounds from which the Portuguese final vowels evolved. You should come up with three statements of the form "*A > B in final position."

_____

_____

_____

_____

_____

2. Fill in the following vowel charts to illustrate this phonological process graphically. On each chart, simply indicate the positions of the three vowels that are involved in the process.

Before the Change

	Front	Central	Back
High			
Mid			
Low			

After the Change

	Front	Central	Back
High			
Mid			
Low			

3. Now write a single statement that covers all three of the sound changes you've identified. Your statement should not make reference to specific vowels, but should be a *linguistically significant generalization* that refers to classes of vowels.

_____

_____

_____

_____

4. The phonological process you've identified is a natural and expected one, and has happened in many languages. It would be rare to find a language with the reverse process, i.e., *B > A instead of *A > B in the same environment. Why is the original process natural and the reverse one unusual? (*Hint:* Consider what the process means in terms of your vocal apparatus, and why this should be a natural occurrence at the end of a word.)

_____

_____

_____

_____

_____

_____

Name _____   **Section** _____   **Date** _____

B. Now focus your attention on the Portuguese *affricates*. What sound changes have taken place in Portuguese that resulted in these affricates? Again, assume that the corresponding sounds in Spanish and Italian represent the sounds from which these affricates evolved. Find two such sound changes, and then find the single generalization that captures both of them. Were these changes *conditioned* (taking place only in specific environments) or *unconditioned* (independent of environment)?

_____

_____

_____

_____

_____

C. The Portuguese word for 'I could' is spelled *pude*. Assume that this spelling represents the earlier pronunciation of the word before the sound changes you have identified took place. Show by means of phonetic transcription how this word is pronounced today. Then show step-by-step how this pronunciation evolved. (You may be reminded of the type of synchronic phonology problem in which you are required to show how phonological rules apply to an underlying form to yield the correct surface form.)

_____

_____

_____

_____

_____

_____

_____

_____

Name _____   Section _____   Date _____

6.06   YIDDISH AND GERMAN COMPARATIVE PHONOLOGY

Yiddish and Modern German are closely related genetically. Although there is a fair amount of mutual intelligibility between Yiddish and German speakers, the two languages differ significantly in their phonology, morphology and syntax. (The biggest difference, however, lies in the lexicon—Yiddish, unlike German, has borrowed heavily from Hebrew and Aramaic, and to a lesser extent from Slavic and Romance.)

The data below show you some cognates in Modern German and Yiddish. The German data are given both in standard orthography and phonetic transcription; the Yiddish equivalents are given in transcription only.

In the German transcription, the vowels ü and ö are like ʊ and ɔ respectively, but are *front* rather than back. The unstressed vowels in the final syllables of both languages have been transcribed with a ə; the actual pronunciation varies somewhat. You may ignore these vowels, which are not relevant to the problem.

Compare the Yiddish and German cognates, paying particular attention to the vowel differences, and then answer the questions that follow.

	German		Yiddish	Gloss
	Spelling	*Transcription*		
1.	mit	mɪt	mɪt	'with'
2.	Hemd	hɛmt	hɛmd	'shirt'
3.	süss	züs	zis	'sweet'
4.	sie	zi	zi	'she'
5.	Flöte	flötə	flet	'flute'
6.	erst	ɛrst	ɛršt	'first'
7.	körper	körpər	kɛrpər	'body'
8.	öl	öl	el	'oil'
9.	dick	dɪk	dɪk	'thick'
10.	Mädel	medəl	medəl	'girl'
11.	hübsch	hüpš	hɪpš	'pretty'
12.	dienen	dinən	dinən	'serve'
13.	höchst	höçst	hɛxst	'highest'
14.	Flügel	flügəl	fligəl	'wing'
15.	Wähler	velər	velər	'voter'
16.	kürzer	kürtsər	kɪrtsər	'shorter'

A.   List the correspondences between the German and Yiddish vowels that are present in the data. (For the German data, be sure to use the transcription, not the spelling! Ignore ə.) Then, based on these vowel correspondences, reconstruct a plausible set of proto-vowels from which the present-day Yiddish and German vowels in the data can be derived.

German Vowel	Yiddish Vowel	Proto-Vowel

B. State the phonological changes have taken place in German and/or Yiddish to yield the modern vowels. Your list should consist of statements of the form *A > B, where *A is a proto-vowel and B is its modern reflex. Were these changes unconditioned, or did they take place in specific environments only?

_____

_____

_____

_____

_____

_____

_____

Name _____ **Section** _____ **Date** _____

C. Classify each vowel that appears on the list you constructed in part A according to the following criteria:

High, mid or low?

Front or back?

Tense or lax?

Round or non-round?

Include in your analysis the following three additional vowels not found on your list: o, u, a.

EXAMPLE: /i/ high
front
tense
non-round

D. Based on the classification you did in C, characterize the following set of "umlaut" vowels in German:

ü   Ü   ö   ɔ̈

That is, what characteristics of these four vowels set them apart from the other vowels you analyzed in part C and define them as a class?

_____

_____

_____

_____

E. Now examine each of the rules you wrote in part B in light of the analysis you did in part C. That is, look at each rule of the form *A > B, make note of the analysis you did for vowels A and B, and determine which features have changed. What simple generalization neatly sums up all the individual sound changes you've discovered?

_____

_____

_____

Name _____   **Section** _____   **Date** _____

6.07   PHONOLOGICAL CHANGES IN BORROWED ITEMS

When a language borrows a word, it usually adapts the pronunciation to its own phonological system. Thus, for example, although the Spanish term *burrito* is used by many non-Spanish-speaking Americans to refer to a popular item in Mexican cuisine, its pronunciation is usually anglicized—the first vowel is reduced to a schwa, the strongly-trilled Spanish *rr* becomes an English *r*, the intervocalic *t* becomes a voiced flap, and the final vowel is diphthongized:

Sp. [buřito]   Eng. [bəriDoʷ]

Similarly, many Japanese enjoy playing *gorufu,* wearing *jinzu,* and having *dezato* at the end of their meals.[1]

Observing what happens to borrowed items can yield information about the phonology of the borrowing language. That is what you will be doing in this exercise, which concerns Arabic borrowings in two unrelated languages, Persian and Malay/Indonesian (MI).

Arabic has had a strong influence on many languages of Asia and Africa. On Persian, the influence has been profound: more than half the lexicon of Modern Persian has been borrowed from Arabic. MI has not absorbed Arabic terms quite so extensively, but the Arabic element in its vocabulary is nevertheless significant.

In the data below, you will find twenty Arabic words, each of which has been borrowed by both Persian and MI. The Persianized and Malayanized loan forms have some interesting differences. Compare these forms with their sources, and then answer the questions that follow.

Notes:

1. The data are transcribed phonemically in modern Standard Arabic, Persian and MI. If you are not familiar with some of the symbols used in the Arabic, you will find them explained in Appendix B.

2. MI and Persian borrowed from Arabic at different times in their history; however, you can regard the Arabic transcriptions as being fairly representative of the language when both the Persians and Malays borrowed these terms, since Standard Arabic has been extremely conservative phonologically.

3. The Persian alterations to the non-low vowels are the result of a phonological change that took place in Persian after the time of borrowing. (See problem 6.03.)

4. The glosses given are for identification purposes only, and are not necessarily exact for all three languages.

	Arabic	Persian	MI	Gloss
1.	badan	bædæn	badan	'body'
2.	salam	sælam	salam	'peace'
3.	ḍarb	zærb	darab	'strike; multiply'
4.	ðaːhir	zaher	lahir/zahir	'apparent; visible'
5.	zamaːn	zæman	zaman	'time, period'
6.	hudhud	hodhod	hudhud	'hoopoe' (bird)
7.	ħalaːl	hælal	halal	'religiously permissible'
8.	θaːbit	sabet	sabit	'fixed, constant'
9.	ðikr	zekr	zikir	'remembrance'

[1] Golf, jeans, dessert

	Arabic	Persian	MI	Gloss
10.	ðuhr	zohr	zuhur/luhur	'midday; noon prayer'
11.	ħa:ḍir	hazer	hadir	'present'
12.	baħθ	bæhs	bahas	'debate'
13.	di:n	din	din	'religion'
14.	ṣubħ	sobh	subuh	'daybreak'
15.	ṣabr	sæbr	sabar	'patient'
16.	ða:t	zat	zat	'essence; vitamin'
17.	ǰa:hil	ǰahel	ǰahil	'ignorant'
18.	maǰlis	mæǰles	maǰlis	'assembly'
19.	siħr	sehr	sihir	'magic'
20.	la:zim	lazem	lazim	'necessary; usual'

A. For each of the eighteen Arabic consonants in the data, list the correspondences in Persian and MI. Two of these have already been done for you.

	Arabic	Persian	MI
1.	m	m	m
2.	ḍ	z	d
3.	_____	_____	_____
4.	_____	_____	_____
5.	_____	_____	_____
6.	_____	_____	_____
7.	_____	_____	_____
8.	_____	_____	_____
9.	_____	_____	_____
10.	_____	_____	_____
11.	_____	_____	_____
12.	_____	_____	_____
13.	_____	_____	_____
14.	_____	_____	_____
15.	_____	_____	_____
16.	_____	_____	_____
17.	_____	_____	_____
18.	_____	_____	_____

Name _____   **Section** _____   **Date** _____

B. Based on how the Arabic consonants have been adapted in the borrowing languages, which Arabic phonemes in the data can you conclude are not found in Persian? Which are not found in MI?

NOT FOUND IN PERSIAN:

_____

_____

NOT FOUND IN MI:

_____

_____

C. In borrowed items, Persian *s* and *z* each correspond to how many different phonemes in Arabic? List the correspondences.

Persian *s* corresponds to _____ Arabic phoneme(s), namely

_____.

Persian *z* corresponds to _____ Arabic phoneme(s), namely

_____.

D. The Arabic alphabet has a different letter to correspond to each Arabic consonant phoneme. Persian uses a modified version of this alphabet for its orthography. Items borrowed from Arabic are for the most part spelled exactly as they are in Arabic, with no change to accommodate Persian phonology.

Suppose you are a beginning student of Persian, and you hear the word *zærbolmæsæl,* which you have reason to suspect is an Arabic loanword. You want to look the word up in a dictionary. As a result of the two fricatives, how many possible spellings do you have to consider? Explain.

_____

_____

_____

_____

E. Arabic makes a phonemic distinction between its two low vowels. Have the borrowing languages kept this distinction? Explain and illustrate.

_____

_____

_____

_____

F. Based on the data, it is clear that Arabic allows final consonant clusters. What can you conclude in this regard about the two borrowing languages? Explain carefully how Persian and MI deal with the original Arabic consonant clusters. (*Note:* If you find that one or the other language does something to break up such clusters, you must state *exactly* what happens. It is not enough, for example, to say, "A vowel is inserted.")

_____

_____

_____

_____

_____

_____

_____

Name _____   **Section** _____   **Date** _____

6.08   PROTO-SEMITIC CONSONANT RECONSTRUCTION

The following data consist of a list of cognates in three Semitic languages: Biblical Hebrew, Biblical Aramaic, and Classical Arabic. Examine the consonant correspondences carefully, and determine what consonants the data lead you to reconstruct for the hypothetical parent language, Proto-Semitic. You should be able to reconstruct 25 of the 29 consonants usually associated with the proto-language.

Notes:

1.   The data are transcribed phonemically, and the effect of certain phonological rules (e.g., schwa-insertion in Hebrew and Aramaic) is not indicated. If you are not familiar with some of the symbols used, see Appendix B.

2.   Each cognate set shows items derived from the same *root*, which in Semitic consists entirely of consonants (usually three). However, the forms do not necessarily come from corresponding *stems,* which involve vowels, prefixes and suffixes, and gemination (long or "doubled" consonants). For this reason, you shouldn't try to reconstruct the original vowels based on these data. Stick to the consonants!

3.   The glosses given are for identification purposes only, and are not necessarily exact for all three languages.

	Hebrew	Aramaic	Arabic	Gloss
1.	di:n	di:n	di:n	'judgment; religion'
2.	zma:n	zman	zama:n	'time'
3.	za:ha:b	dhab	ðahab	'gold'
4.	ṭo:b	ṭa:b	ṭa:b	'good'
5.	ʕa:mo:q	ʕami:q	ʕami:q	'deep'
6.	ša:lo:m	šla:m	sala:m	'peace'
7.	zeru:ʕ	zraʕ	zuru:ʕ	'seed'
8.	šalo:š	tla:t	θala:θ	'three'
9.	pešer	pšar	fassara	'interpret(ation)'
10.	do:r	da:r	daur	'generation; period'
11.	yikto:b	yiktub	yaktub	'he writes'
12.	ṣda:qa:	ṣidqa:	ṣadaqa	'charity'
13.	ʔereṣ	ʔarʕa:	ʔarḍ	'earth'
14.	qa:ṭalti	qiṭlet	qataltu	'I killed'
15.	ħeleq	ħla:q	xala:q	'share'
16.	ba:ʕa:	bʕa:	baɣa:	'he asked for'
17.	zebaħ	dbaħ	ðabħ	'sacrifice; slaughter'
18.	gbu:ra:	gbar	ǰabr	'might; man'
19.	ṣa:par	ṣipar	ṣafara	'he whistled'
20.	ʕereb	_____	ɣarb	'evening; west'
21.	ħemer	ħmar	xamr	'wine'
22.	ṣerur	ʕar	ḍarr	'enmity, foe; harm'
23.	šeleg	tlag	θalǰ	'snow'
24.	šali:ṭ	šali:ṭ	sali:ṭ	'ruler; firm, mighty'

A. First, reconstruct the "easy" proto-consonants—that is, the ones from cognate sets where there is no variation in the corresponding consonants. Indicate the numbers of the examples in the data that support your reconstruction. One set has already been done for you.

Hebrew	Aramaic	Arabic	Proto-Semitic	Examples
m	m	m	*m	2, 5, 6, 21

Name _____   **Section** _____   **Date** _____

B. Next, do the same for the more interesting cases where there is evidence of sound change. You will only need to consider *unconditioned* sound changes—ones in which the given change took place in all environments.

You will find that in several cases, you may have to ignore the "majority rules" principle of reconstruction; this is largely a consequence of the fact that the data for this problem have been restricted to three languages.

Hebrew	Aramaic	Arabic	Proto-Semitic	Examples

C. Finally, list the consonant changes that have taken place in each language. Your list should consist of statements of the form *A > B, where *A is a proto-consonant and B is its reflex in the given language. Based on your analysis, which, if any, of these languages has retained more of the original consonants of Proto-Semitic than the others? Explain.

Hebrew	Aramaic	Arabic

Name _____   **Section** _____   **Date** _____

6.09   COMPARATIVE RECONSTRUCTION IN SPIIKTUMI

Below you will find twenty cognate sets in four languages of the little-known Spiiktumi family. Your task is to reconstruct the etymons (original forms) in proto-Spiiktumi for each of the cognate sets in the data, and to state the sound changes that have taken place in each daughter language.

Examine the data below and answer the questions that follow.

(´ indicates stress.)

	W	X	Y	Z
1.	pámut	pánti	pámüti	pámut
2.	sít	sído	šíðo	síd
3.	denubó	dembó	denuβó	denubó
4.	lelúk	lerúge	lerúɣe	lelúg
5.	sudán	sudáno	suðáno	sudã́
6.	únik	úŋga	úniɣa	únig
7.	čomús	čomúsi	čomǘši	šomús
8.	láhuk	láhka	láuka	láhuk
9.	banubín	bambíni	banüβíni	banubí̃
10.	elujǐl	erǰila	erüǰila	elužíl
11.	láhuk	ráhgo	ráuɣo	láhug
12.	héfum	héfmo	héfumo	héfũ
13.	sehúbat	sehúbda	sehúβaða	sehúbad
14.	tehigém	tehgémo	teiɣémo	tehigẽ́
15.	yúnup	yúmbi	yúnüβi	yúnub
16.	jǔt	jǔda	jǔða	žúd
17.	famagí	faŋgí	famaɣí	famagí
18.	časinokóm	časiŋkómo	čašinokómo	šasinokṍ
19.	sudá	sudá	suðá	sudá
20.	kahihánom	kahhámmo	kaihánomo	kahihánṍ

Some helpful hints:

Although there is no "cookbook" method of approaching problems like this, there are a few general guidelines that may help you arrive at a solution.

1. It is often useful to make a list of the sound correspondences in the daughter languages. For example,

A	B	C	D	Examples	
b	b	b	b	9, 13	
b	b	β	b	3, 9	
p	b	β	b	15	etc.

When all the daughters agree, as in the first line, it is usually the case that the etymon is the same as the reflexes and there has been no change. When there is disagreement, your best bet is to go by the "majority rules" principle unless there is evidence to the contrary; this minimizes the number of independent sound changes you need to posit.

2. The sound changes you propose should account for all the variation in the data. Bear in mind that chronological ordering may play a role here: you should consider the possibility that the output of an earlier sound change served as input to a later one.

3. The sound changes you propose should be plausible and natural. With experience, you will be able to judge whether a proposed sound change is natural or not without much trouble. While you are in the process of gaining that experience, keep in mind that sound changes you have already seen in one language will very likely crop up again and again in other languages, related or not. As a general rule, sound changes with an assimilition or other ease-of-articulation basis are usually natural ones.

A. Reconstruct the original forms of each of these words in the parent language, proto-Spiiktumi.

1. _____

2. _____

3. _____

4. _____

5. _____

6. _____

7. _____

8. _____

9. _____

10. _____

11. _____

12. _____

13. _____

14. _____

15. _____

16. _____

17. _____

18. _____

19. _____

20. _____

Name _____ **Section** _____ **Date** _____

B. State the sound changes that occurred in each daughter language, referring whenever possible to classes of sounds. Point out any instances of chronological ordering. Also state whether each change is conditioned or unconditioned; for conditioned sound changes, state precisely under what conditions the change occurred.

CHANGES IN W	CHANGES IN X

CHANGES IN Y	CHANGES IN Z

LOOKING AT LANGUAGES

C. On the basis of the sound changes you have proposed for the daughter languages, is there any reason to group two or more of them into a subfamily? Give evidence to support your answer.

_____

_____

_____

_____

D. Do [u] and [ü] contrast in language Y, or are they in complementary distribution? Give evidence to support your answer.

_____

_____

_____

E. Is nasalization distinctive in language Z? Again, give evidence to support your answer.

_____

_____

_____

F. Find an example in the data of a *lexical merger*—two words that were originally distinct but later became identical.

_____

_____

_____

C H A P T E R

7

Dialect, Register, and Style

7.01 DIALECTS OF ENGLISH

In certain phonological, lexical or syntactic features, each of the expressions below is particularly characteristic of a regional or social dialect. Among the dialects that may be represented are African-American Vernacular English; New York City English; Southern American English; Cockney English; Standard British English; Chicano English. For each expression, identify in the first column the dialect group whose speech the sample most consistently suggests. In the second column, identify two features from the expression that are characteristic of that group. In the third column, provide the colloquial Standard American English (SAE) equivalent for the dialect feature identified.

1. [ðə sʌn, i ops tə bi wɪf əm bof, ɪz mʌm n̩ ɪz dæd] *The son, he hopes to be with both, his mom + his dad*
   The sun, e ops to be wif ombof,
2. [hi pʰæs də tʰičər hu wəz sɪtn̩ æt hə dɛs]
3. [hɪm n̩ mi wəz frɛnz ɪn ði armi] *Him and me was friends in the army*
4. [i boʔ ə pʰaʔ ə flawəz fər ɪz mʌm, uz ɪn aspəʔəl] *I brought a ___ pot ___ of flowers for his mom, - in* *hospital*
5. [ɪz ɪt ə nu blu bayk ovə dɛ:] *Is it a new blue bike over there,*
6. [dæt sodər an ðə flɔr ɛnt mayn, ɪts hʌz ɔ° pʰiDəz] *That ___ and the ___* *ain't mine,* *(isn't)*
7. [dɛn i wɛn tə bay spɛčəl čuz fər də wɛDin] *its herself)* *Then I went to buy special cars for de wedding*
8. [ðə læmps ər an ə fɔθ flɔ, niə di ɛləveDə] *The lamps are on a fourth floor, near the elevator*
9. [mɪni a:v ma: frɛnz wɪl se ðæt ðer tʰa:rd] *Mini*
10. [ɪz ɪt ə mɪs wɪlyəmz hu ɔwez bi wərkən hiə] *Is it a Miss Williams who was be working here*
11. [hi wetəd ɪn ə kʰyu fə ədišənəl pʰɛtrəl fə ðə lɔri] *He waited in a ___ additional petrol for* *the lorry,*
12. [ši yuzd ə tʰɔč tə faynd ðə tʰɪn əv bɪskəts ɪn ðə but]
   She used a torch to find the tin of biscuts in the boot.

Dialect	Feature Name	SAE Equivalent
1. Cockney English	dropping "h"	The son hopes to be with both his mom and dad

Dialect	Feature Name	SAE Equivalent
2. African-American Vernacular English	deletion of word final stops	He passed the teacher who was sitting at his desk
3. African-American Vernacular English	ʌ	He and I were friends in the Army.
4.		
5. NYC	dropping /r/	Is it a new blue bike over there?
6.		
7.		
8. Bostonian	ɔ sound/drop /r/	The lamps are on the fourth floor near the elevator.
9.		
10.		
11. English		He waited in a additional petrol for the lorrey.
12. English		She used a torch to find the tin of biscuits in the boot.

Name _____   Section _____   Date _____

7.02   ISOGLOSSES

An isogloss is a line drawn on a map marking the boundary within which or up to which a particular linguistic feature occurs. On maps representing occurrences of several features, each type of marker represents a particular feature; larger markers represent speakers in several communities.

A.   Examine Map A, which identifies the locations in which respondents used the expression *I want off* (where speakers of other dialects might say *I want to get off*). On the map, draw the isogloss that represents the northern and eastern limits of that phrase.

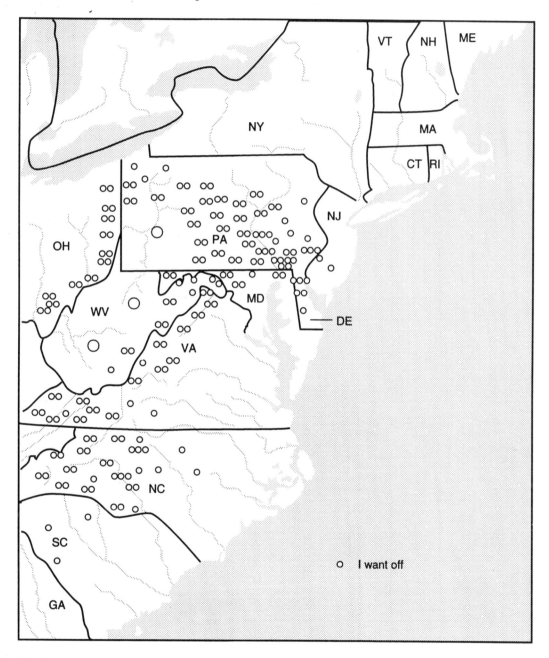

MAP A
Distribution of *I want off* in the Eastern States
Source: Kurath 1949

B. Map B indicates the locations where respondents used various expressions (other than *saw*) for the past tense of *see*. Using different colors for each feature, draw (a) the isogloss that represents the northern limits of *seed*. Then, noting that *see* occurs in three separate areas, draw (b) an isogloss representing the southern limits of *see* in the north and (c) and (d) the two isoglosses that completely enclose *see* in the Middle Atlantic states and the south. (*Note:* In drawing certain isoglosses, it may be useful to exclude isolated occurrences of a feature, especially when they occur far away from where the isogloss would otherwise be drawn.)

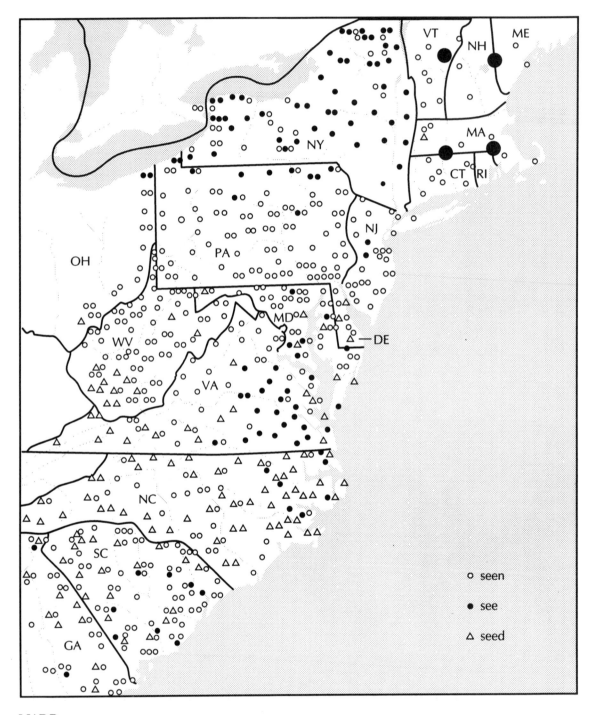

MAP B
Words for Past-tense of *see* in the Eastern States
Source: Atwood 1953

Name _____   **Section** _____   **Date** _____

C. Map C indicates the locations in the Eastern United States where respondents used various expressions for 'bastard.' Draw the isoglosses that represent: (a) the southern limits of *ketch colt;* (b) the entire area for *stolen colt;* (c) the southern limits of *come-by-chance;* (d) the northern limits of *woods colt.* (Again, it may be useful to exclude isolated occurrences.)

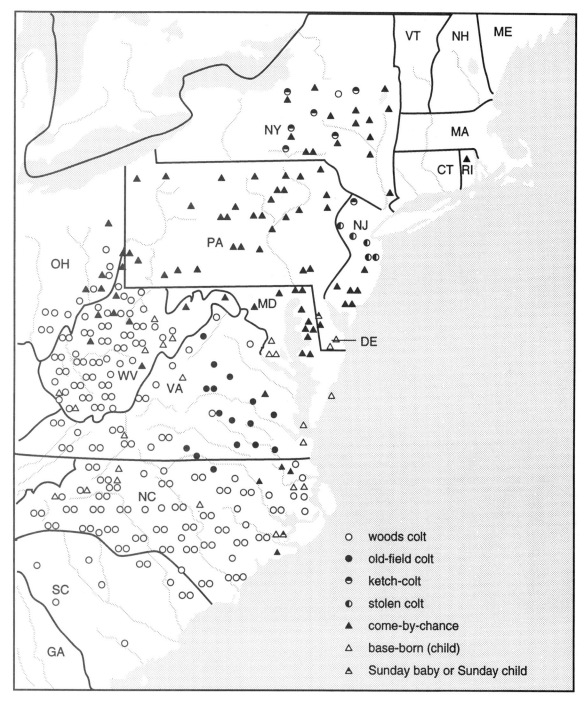

MAP C
Words for 'bastard' in the Eastern States
Source: Kurath 1949

D. Besides the standard form *saw,* some regions use only a single regional form, while others have several forms. Using Map B and the isoglosses as a guideline, describe in words what usages are found in each of the following locations:

1. Pennsylvania _____

_____

2. Maryland _____

_____

3. West Virginia _____

_____

4. No. Carolina and So. Carolina _____

_____

5. New England _____

_____

E. Now, using Map C and the isoglosses, describe the geographical distribution of each of the following features:

1. *woods colt* _____

_____

2. *come-by-chance* _____

_____

3. *bastard* _____

_____

F. What do the isoglosses you have drawn suggest about the tidiness of dialect boundaries?

_____

_____

_____

Name _____   **Section** _____   **Date** _____

7.03   PRONUNCIATION OF *-ING* IN NEW YORK CITY

Below is a line graph representing the pronunciation of *-ing* as /ɪn/ in words like *working* and *talking* among white adult New York City residents; the speakers are classed into four socioeconomic status groups and the graph represents pronunciation in three situations of use. Examine the graph and answer the questions below.

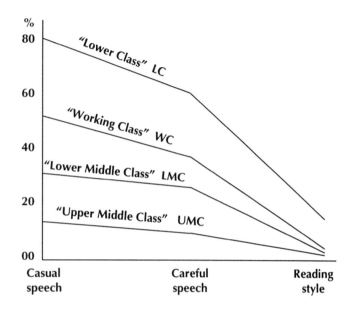

Source: William Labov, *The Study of Nonstandard English*

A. Referring to the Lower Class group as LC, the Working Class group as WC, the Lower Middle Class group as LMC, and the Upper Middle Class group as UMC, list the socioeconomic status groups in order of increasing frequency of pronunciation of /ɪn/

1. in casual speech: _____

2. in careful speech: _____

3. in reading style: _____

B. Which group alters its pronunciation the *most* in moving from one situation/style to another?

_____

Which the *least?* _____

C. In which situation of use is the speech of the four groups most *similar* with respect to this feature?

_____

In which the most *dissimilar?* _____

D. What generalization can be made about the relationship between the pronunciation of /ɪn/ among the social groups and across the situations?

_____

_____

E. If you knew that a particular white adult resident of New York City pronounced -*ing* as /ɪn/ about 30% of the time in some situation but you did not know which situation it was, explain why you would or would not have a basis for gauging which of the four socioeconomic status groups that person belonged to.

_____

_____

_____

_____

F. Repeat question E for someone using /ɪn/ about 70% of the time:

_____

_____

_____

_____

G. For any speech situation, what information does the graph provide about the range of variation across speakers *within* a particular socioeconomic status group?

_____

_____

Name _____   **Section** _____   **Date** _____

7.04   LEXICAL DOMAINS AND INFORMALITY

Read through the list of adjectival words and expressions below, all of which can be related to the notion of 'disorder.' Then answer the questions, selecting your answers from the list. You may use the same expression in answer to several questions if appropriate.

bedraggled	careless	chaotic	confused
deranged	disheveled	disorderly	frumpy
grubby	haphazard	haywire	indiscriminate
irregular	jumbled	messy	mixed up
muddled	negligent	out of kilter	out of place
out of whack	random	ruffled	rumpled
scattered	screwed up	seedy	shabby
shoddy	slipshod	sloppy	slouchy
slovenly	squalid	sordid	tacky
topsy-turvy	tousled	unarranged	unkempt
unmethodical	unorganized	unsystematic	untidy

A. Identify four expressions usually associated with 'disorder' in *personal appearance,* and list them from least (1) to most (4) formal:

1. _____   3. _____

2. _____   4. _____

B. Identify four expressions usually associated with 'disorder' in *physical surroundings,* and list them from least to most formal:

1. _____   3. _____

2. _____   4. _____

C. Identify four expressions usually associated with 'disorder' in *workmanship,* and list them from least to most formal:

1. _____   3. _____

2. _____   4. _____

D. Identify four expressions usually associated with 'disorder' in *mental state,* and list them from least to most formal:

1. _____   3. _____

2. _____   4. _____

E. List four expressions usually associated with 'disorder' more generally and list them from least to most formal:

1. _____   3. _____

2. _____   4. _____

F.   Identify and list four expressions that you regard as slang, at least as they are used in certain situations:

1. _____   3. _____

2. _____   4. _____

G.   Identify and list four expressions that you regard as particularly formal:

1. _____   3. _____

2. _____   4. _____

H.   Can you make any generalization about the expressions you listed in F and G? That is, can the slang and formal expressions be distinguished on the basis of their form?

_____

_____

_____

Name _____   **Section** _____   **Date** _____

7.05   SLANG

"Slang" is a familiar but notoriously tough register to define. Commentators agree that slang occurs in circumstances of extreme informality and serves to "spice up" language. In recent decades, slang has moved unusually quickly into relatively formal channels (such as weekly newsmagazines), especially in discussion of such popular topics as computers, sports, criminal behavior, medical and nursing practice, the drug scene, and life in the fast lane. Slang terms are consequently often found in movie and music reviews, lifestyle pieces, and "people" columns.

While some older slang terms continue in use (*jabber, jackass, malarkey, meal ticket*), many have lost their edge compared to more current slang terms, like *grody, get it on, gross out,* and *grunge; nerd* and *nickel; zilch, zit,* and *zap.*

A. Examine a single issue of a current newsweekly or pop culture magazine, and provide six examples of slang terms, with a gloss for each, and a notation of its lexical category. Put an asterisk after those terms that you believe you will be able to find in your desk dictionary in the sense that you have glossed; then verify your expectation and place a "D" after glosses that are in fact listed in your dictionary.

EXAMPLE: "grody"   adjective   'disgusting, bizarre'
                      "get it on"   verb phrase   'have sexual intercourse'

	Term	Lexical Category	Gloss
1.	_____	_____	_____
2.	_____	_____	_____
3.	_____	_____	_____
4.	_____	_____	_____
5.	_____	_____	_____
6.	_____	_____	_____

Name and date of magazine: _____

Name of dictionary: _____

B. Provide six slang terms frequently heard on your campus, with their lexical category and a gloss.

	Term	Lexical Category	Gloss
1.	_____	_____	_____
2.	_____	_____	_____
3.	_____	_____	_____
4.	_____	_____	_____
5.	_____	_____	_____
6.	_____	_____	_____

C. Provide a list of six slang terms (plus lexical category and gloss) used by some campus group (for example, band, fraternity, computer science majors) that you are familiar with but which are not widely understood by people outside that group.

	Term	Lexical Category	Gloss
1.	_____	_____	_____
2.	_____	_____	_____
3.	_____	_____	_____
4.	_____	_____	_____
5.	_____	_____	_____
6.	_____	_____	_____

D. Examine the lists you have provided in B and C and indicate several common arenas in which slang seems to arise on your campus (for example, course names, body parts, personal hygiene).

_____

_____

E. Examine the lists you have provided in B and C and indicate which lexical categories seem to be most open to slang terms.

_____

F. Choose a single "subculture" (for example: computers, drugs, music) and list four slang words that originated in that subculture but are commonly understood by outsiders nowadays.

Subculture: _____

1. _____   3. _____

2. _____   4. _____

G. For the italicized words in the items below (taken from *Time* and *Newsweek*), label those that you judge to be slang by writing *S* in the column marked "Slang?" Note with Yes (Y) or No (N) in the "Listed?" column whether the items are listed in your desk dictionary and do the same in the "Label?" column to indicate whether or not they are labeled *slang*. Then check the frontmatter of your dictionary for its definition of slang, and give that definition below. (If no discussion of slang appears in the frontmatter, consult the entry for "slang" in the alphabetical listings.)

_____

_____

_____

_____

Name _____   Section _____   Date _____

Finally, decide whether your dictionary should have marked the word or sense as "slang" in accordance with *its own* guidelines; write "I" for inconsistent or "C" for consistent in the fourth column.

	Slang?	Listed?	Label?	Con/Incon?
1. *wall-to-wall* reruns				
2. too *off the wall*				
3. *remote-control* medicine				
4. just plain *screwy*				
5. the *low-impact* story line				
6. *laid-back* respect				
7. teen *fanzine* favorites				
8. the *tensomething* crowd				
9. to pickle *veggies*				
10. popular among *foodies*				
11. naked babe *nukes* G-men				
12. Ice Cube, the *rapper*				
13. diatribes against *whitey*				
14. *touchy-feely* comedy				
15. a *trek* from the Bronx				
16. his emotional *chops*				
17. a local *superpig*				
18. her fathomless *ditsiness*				
19. a kind of *road movie*				
20. a fleet of *copmobiles*				
21. these *delicious* desperadoes				
22. a *blitz* of nutrition advice				
23. the latest dietary *bugaboo*				
24. there's *life after* croissants				
25. *forget* red meat				

Name _____   **Section** _____   **Date** _____

7.06   NATURAL VS. LITERARY CONVERSATION

Below are excerpts from three representations of conversation: from a novel, a play, and a linguistic transcription of an actual conversation. Notice the common and distinguishing linguistic characteristics of these three conversational registers.

1. FICTIONAL CONVERSATION [from Tom Wolfe's *The Bonfire of the Vanities* (Farrar, Straus, Giroux, 1987)].

> "Craaaaasssssssh!" said Maria, weeping with laughter. "Oh God, I wish I had a videotape a that!" Then she caught the look on Sherman's face. "What's the matter?"
> "What do you think that was all about?"
> "What do you mean, 'all about'?"
> "What do you think he was doing here?"
> "The *land*lord sent him. You remember that letter I showed you."
> 'But isn't it kind of odd that—"
> "Germaine pays only $331 a month, and I pay her $750. It's rent-controlled. They'd love to get her out of here."
> "It doesn't strike you as odd that they'd decide to barge in here—right now?"
> "Right now?"
> "Well, maybe I'm crazy, but today—after this thing is in the paper?"
> "In the *paper*?" Then it dawned on her what he was saying, and she broke into a smile. "Sherman, you *are* crazy. You're paranoid. You know that?"
> "Maybe I am. It just seems like a very odd coincidence."
> "Who do you think sent him in here, if the landlord didn't? The police?"
> "Well ..." Realizing it did sound rather paranoid, he smiled faintly.

2. SCREENPLAY CONVERSATION [From *My Left Foot* by Shane Connaughton and Jim Sheridan (Faber and Faber, 1989)].

INT. LIVING ROOM. DAY

MRS. BROWN *and* MR. BROWN *listen to* CHRISTY *and* DR. COLE.

Mr. Brown:	She's working with him on a Saturday now?
Mrs. Brown:	She has to work with him on her day off. She's doing this voluntarily.
Mr. Brown:	She's a great girl altogether.
Mrs. Brown:	I wish we could afford to pay her.
Mr. Brown:	You were always from the other end of town, Maisie. You're getting it for nothing and you want to pay for it.
Mrs. Brown:	I have me pride as well as you, mister.
Mr. Brown:	I think you're jealous.
Mrs. Brown:	(*Considered*) Do you think that's our Christy up there?
Mr. Brown:	What do you mean?
Mrs. Brown:	Does that sound like our Christy?
Mr. Brown:	It sounds a lot better.
Mrs. Brown:	Not to me it doesn't.

3. ACTUAL CONVERSATION. Friends Marguerite (M), Rob (R), and Bobby (B), discussing word processing and computers before dinner. Initial Cap for sentence start; CAPS or Í for stress/emphasis; : for lengthened vowel; [ ] for overlapping turns; ⌐L for latched turns; — for incomplete intonation unit; .. for short and ... for longer pause; ((comments)); / ?? / for inaudible syllables.

B: Is TA:Ndy—I-B-M comPA:Tible?

M: ... I: don't KNOW,

B: ⌈ .. Well it's —

R: ⌊ .. More importantly, ⌋ does it ha:ndle WO:RDstar?

M: .. No. And and a LO:T of — She SAID that — Consumer Reports says there's a lo:t of problems with WO:RDstar — that it doesn't DO:,

         ... a lot of things that you wa:nt it to be A:BLE to do: that it WO:N

         ⌈ in the study, and SHE: has the one that ⌉ goe:s with .. TA:Ndy —

B: ⌊ Tha:t is riDI: culous ⌋

M: that that's much BE:Tter⌐

R: ⌐Do you know what the NA:ME ⌈ of it is?

B: ⌊ / ?? / ⌋

M: ... U:h — .. Í: don't know — something ... MA:Gnavox, .. Í: don't know ... ((1 sec.)) u:h .. ((laughs))

B: His MA:Ster's voice

M: ... Something LI:KE that, ... but that's not I:T is it.

         That's what it SOU:NDS like.

         ... ((1.2 sec.)) SO:MEthing VOI:CE, .. something ... vo:x,

         ... vo:x PO:Puli ((laughs))

R: ((laughs)) ... no I don't know what it I:S.

M: ... Vox DE:I.

A. List features of the transcribed conversation that do not occur in either of the literary representations of conversation.

_____

_____

_____

_____

_____

_____

B. Specify several ways in which the representation of conversation in a novel differs from that in a dramatic script (or screenplay).

_____

_____

_____

_____

_____

_____

Name _____   **Section** _____   **Date** _____

C. Explain how the circumstances of literary production influence the representation of conversation in ways that make it different from natural conversation.

_____

_____

_____

_____

_____

_____

Name _____   **Section** _____   **Date** _____

7.07   COLLOQUIAL WRITING

The passage below has been shortened and slightly adapted from a "My Turn" column in *Newsweek* magazine (by Scott Shuger, July 8, 1991). Make two lists, one identifying those linguistic features of the passage that make the writing style "colloquial" or conversational, and the other identifying those features that mark it as planned and edited, the way writing, but not conversation, typically is. Consider such things as pronouns, conjunctions, prepositions, contractions, adjectives, conjoining, subordination, speech acts, semantic roles.

Were you happy with John Sununu when you learned that he had used your tax dollars to go on ski vacations and stamp-buying expeditions to Christie's? Were you delighted with Oregon Sen. Mark Hatfield when you found out that he has received nearly $15,000 in gifts from one university and special admissions considerations for his children? Of course not. The displeasure you feel when you learn about these things and bigger scandals is the key to the fundamental reform this country is screamingly in need of: more news about what our taxes are buying. That's fundamental because politicians take being looked at badly, but they take looking bad worse.

Sununu and Hatfield realized you'd be furious if you knew what they were up to. But they were also betting you wouldn't find out. And the way things are now set up, that's a good bet.

A.   Conversational features:

_____

_____

_____

_____

_____

_____

_____

_____

_____

_____

_____

_____

B.   Planned and edited features:

_____

_____

_____

_____

_____

_____

_____

_____

_____

_____

_____

_____

Name _____   **Section** _____   **Date** _____

7.08   RECIPE REGISTER

Observe the syntax of recipes, as exemplified in these three examples, adapted slightly from *The New James Beard* (Knopf, 1981). Among other features, note the use of prepositions and articles, the modality (or mood) of verbs, and the use of direct objects with typically transitive verbs.

1.   SAUTEED BRAINS

Parboil the brains as in preceding recipe. Drain and dry. Dip them in flour, then in beaten egg, and then in freshly made bread crumbs. Saute quickly in hot butter until golden brown on both sides. Season with salt and pepper and serve with lemon wedges.

2.   SAUTEED MARINATED BRAINS

Parboil the brains. Cool and cut in thick slices. Marinate for several hours in a mixture of 1/2 cup olive oil, 3 tablespoons lemon juice, 1/4 teaspoon Tabasco, 1 teaspoon salt, and 1 tablespoon each chopped parsley and chopped chives. Remove from marinade, dip in flour, beaten egg, and fresh bread crumbs, and saute in hot oil until golden brown.

3.   CIOPPINO

1 quart clams	2 teaspoons salt
1 cup dry white or red wine	1 teaspoon freshly ground pepper
1/2 cup olive oil	1 pound crabmeat
1 large onion, chopped	1 pound raw shrimp, shelled
2 cloves garlic, chopped	2 tablespoons finely chopped fresh basil
1 green pepper, chopped	3 tablespoons chopped parsley
4 ripe tomatoes, peeled, seeded, and chopped	[plus other ingredients]

Steam the clams in the 1 cup white or red wine until they open—discard any that do not open. Strain the broth through two thicknesses of cheesecloth and reserve.

Heat the olive oil in a deep 8-quart pot and cook the onion, garlic, pepper, and mushrooms for 3 minutes. Add the tomatoes and cook 4 minutes. Add the strained clam broth, tomato paste, and 2 cups red wine. Season with salt and pepper and simmer for about 20 minutes. Taste and correct seasoning. Add the basil and the fish, and just cook the fish through about 3 to 5 minutes. Finally, add the steamed clams, crabmeat, and shrimp. Heat just until shrimp are cooked. Do not overcook. Sprinkle with parsley and serve.

A.   *Verbs*

1.   What mood are most of the verbs expressed in?

_____

2.   Underline all verbs in other moods.

3.   Provide an example of a sentence made up solely of two verbs linked by a conjunction.

_____

4.   What is the mood of the two conjoined verbs in question 3? _____

B. *Prepositions*

List three prepositional phrases in the data and three phrases that would usually be introduced by a preposition in conversational English but lack it here.

Prepositional phrases	Phrases lacking prepositions
1. _____	4. _____
2. _____	5. _____
3. _____	6. _____

C. *Articles*

List five noun phrases in the data that lack an article where conversational English would typically have one.

1. _____   4. _____

2. _____   5. _____

3. _____

D. List four simple adverbs in the data and characterize their semantic content:

1. _____   3. _____

2. _____   4. _____

Semantic content of recipe adverbs: _____

_____

E. Identify four verbs usually transitive that lack direct objects in the recipes above. Why does this register often use transitive verbs intransitively?

_____

_____

_____

F. What other syntactic features strike you as characteristic of this register?

_____

_____

_____

G. In what way might it be useful to distinguish two subregisters of recipes?

_____

_____

_____

Name _____   **Section** _____   **Date** _____

H. Write a brief description characterizing the register of recipes.

_____

_____

_____

_____

_____

I. Name two other registers you are familiar with that share some of these characteristics, and specify the shared features.

_____

Name any other registers that share *all* the features you have identified for recipe register.

_____

Name _____   **Section** _____   **Date** _____

7.09   THE SYNTAX AND LEXICON OF PERSONAL ADS

Examine the personal ads below, adapted from a daily newspaper.

CUDDLER, OUTDOORS LOVER Tall, cute, SWM, 46, N/S, educ. New to Pasadena area seeks youthful, affectionate, playful, nurturing fem to share life with. Do you enjoy getting away from it all & long to build a happy relationship? Attitude more important than age, race, looks. Height & weight proportional plz. P/P nice but not neces.

TRAVEL Woman with sofa, frplc & passprt seeks man to share Sunday paper, capuccino at home, travel and adventure abroad. Attrctv, educ. D/W/F, seeks humorous, n/s, loving, articulate man 48+.

RESPECT & CONSIDERATION. Do you know a petite Jewish gal, 30sh, looks like Ms. America, with a heart like my mother's? Please tell her a healthy, unencumbered, comfortable, trilingual, traditional Jewish man wants her for his soulmate.

QUIET EVENINGS AT HOME. Attractive, professional, single Filipino lady, 35, never been married, honest, has great sense of humor, one-man woman, no smoking, drinking or drugs, looking for possible serious relationship. Photo pls.

Looking for that special someone to share my life with. Me: 48, SWJM, self employed, successful, stable, honest, sincere, non smoke/drug. You: SWF, age open, sincere, honest.

DINING Sensitive SWM 39, tall, successful, out-going, wishes to meet good looking lady, 25 — 35 for possible relationship.

BEACH WALKS, DINING Physician (Anesthesiologist), Bus. Man (Owner of Co.), 40+, Ambitious, Sweet, Generous, Shy, Oriental Gentleman, No Games, Seeks Vry Honest, Kind, Sweet, Beautiful, Attractive Female, 20 — 30, for Sharing Good Life &/or Future Committed Relationship. Photo, Telephn # & Description to:

Identify the linguistic features that characterize personal ads register, including the use or absence of personal pronouns; whether the ads are written in the first person (*I, you*) or third person (*he, she*), and what marks person when pronouns are absent; whether they are consistent in the use of person (or use both first- and third-person pronouns); what information is offered and omitted about the writer and potential respondent; what information is abbreviated; conventions about the use of nouns, verbs, adverbs, adjectives, and articles that characterize this register.

Information offered and abbreviated:

_____

_____

_____

_____

_____

_____

_____

_____

Linguistic characteristics:

1. Frequent lexical categories

   _____

   _____

2. Infrequent lexical categories

   _____

   _____

3. Personal pronouns used

   _____

   _____

4. Subjects and verbs

   _____

   _____

Name _____   Section _____   Date _____

7.10   INVOLVED VERSUS INFORMATIONAL REGISTERS

Certain linguistic features (including those in Set A below) tend to co-occur frequently in texts belonging to registers that reflect considerable personal *involvement*. Other linguistic features (including those in Set B) tend to co-occur with unusual frequency in texts representing registers whose primary focus is on *information* rather than involvement.

Set A (*INVOLVED FEATURES*)

first-person pronouns	second-person pronouns
contractions (*I'm, doesn't*)	emphatics (*really, so*)
hedges (*kind of, maybe*)	*be* as a main verb
wh-clauses (That's *why he sings*)	private verbs (*think, know*)

clausal coordination (*She went and he stayed*)

zero subordinators (*She said ∅ he cried*)

Set B (*INFORMATIONAL FEATURES*)

frequent nouns	frequent prepositions
longer words	lexical variety

attributive adjectives (*young* people)

Below are two passages from an article about Axl Rose and his rock band Guns N' Roses. Passage I is Rose's spoken responses to an interviewer in his hotel room (the article doesn't provide the interviewer's questions). Excluding the bracketed words (which were supplied editorially), the passage contains 196 words. Passage II is the interviewer's written analysis of Rose and the band. It contains 195 words. [From "Run n' Gun" by Robert Hilburn. *Los Angeles Times/Calendar,* July 21, 1991.]

I.   Interview with Axl Rose:

I know people are confused by a lot of what I do, but I am too sometimes.   1

That's why I went into therapy.   2

I wanted to understand why Axl had been this volatile, crazy, whatever, for years.   3

I was told that my mental circuitry was all twisted ... in terms of how I would deal with stress because   4

of what happened to me back in Indiana.   5

Basically I would overload with the stress of a situation ... by smashing whatever was around me...   6

I used to think I was actually dealing with my problems, and now I know that's not dealing with it at   7

all.   8

I'm trying now to [channel] my energy in more positive ways ... but it doesn't always work.   9

You get a lot of teaching in high school about going after your dreams and being true to yourself, but   10

at the same time [teachers and parents] are trying to beat you down.   11

It was so strict in [our house] that everything you did was wrong.   12

There was so much censorship, you weren't allowed to make any choices.   13

Sex was bad, music was bad.   14

I eventually left, but so many kids stay [in that environment].   15

I wanted to tell them ... that they can break away too.   16

II.   Writer's analysis of Guns N' Roses

Rose, 29, has been speaking slowly and thoughtfully for more than an hour, outlining the   1
frustrations of his small-town Indiana childhood...   2

Just a week before the shows here on the band's first tour in three years, Rose made news by   3
going onstage in his "homecoming" concert in Indianapolis and decrying the forces—including   4
parents and school—that he believes can rob young people of their individuality and aspirations...   5

But the Los Angeles–based group's best music is a provocative and affecting exploration of fast-   6
lane temptations and consequences.   7

At the center, Rose is a charismatic performer with an exciting edge of spontaneity—the most   8
compelling and combustible superstar in American hard rock since Jim Morrison...   9

You sense in his music and manner a genuine tug of war between healthy and destructive urges—   10
a contest that personalizes for the audience its own struggle over issues as fundamental, and often as   11
paralyzing, as lifestyle, career and relationships. Reflecting in the hotel room on his Indianapolis   12
speech, Rose echoes the classic underdog sentiments that have been a dominant theme in rock ever   13
since James Dean, in "Rebel Without a Cause," articulated youthful anger and pain for the first   14
generation of rockers.   15

A.   Underline all attributive adjectives (*mental* circuitry) and double underline all predicative adjectives (*it was* strict) in Passage I.

B.   Do the same for Passage II.

C.   What function do attributive adjectives serve in texts?

_____

D.   What function do predicative adjectives serve in texts?

_____

E.   Why would you expect to find predicative adjectives occurring more frequently in spoken texts than in written texts?

_____

_____

F.   Above each of these adverbs in Passage I, mark its adverbial function (**T** for time, **P** for place, **M** for manner, **S** for speaker's stance): *sometimes* (line 1); *actually* (7); *now* (7, 9); *always* (9); *eventually* (15). List any other adverbs you find in the passage, and also mark them appropriately.

_____

_____

Name _____   **Section** _____   **Date** _____

G. Repeat question F for these adverbs in Passage II: *slowly* (1); *thoughtfully* (1); *here* (3). List any other adverbs you find in the passage, and mark their function.

_____

_____

H. On the basis of your answers to F and G, how would you characterize the *differences* between common adverbial functions in conversation and in edited writing?

_____

_____

I. The number of occurrences for particular features is provided below for one or both passages. Fill out the chart by supplying the missing frequency counts. In those cases where space is provided beneath the blank, list as many examples of that feature as is indicated by the number in parenthesis and give the number of the line in which the example occurs.

	Passage I	Passage II
Set A (INVOLVED FEATURES)		
first-person pronouns	_____	0
second-person pronouns	_____	1
zero subordinator	_____	0
(Two) _____		
private verbs	_____	3
(Four) _____		
contractions	_____	0
(Three) _____		
emphatics	_____	0
(Three) _____		
be *as a main verb*	_____	2
(Five) _____		

	Passage I	Passage II
Set B (INFORMATIONAL FEATURES)		
nouns	25	58
prepositions	24	27
long words (three or more syllables)	15	
(Six; no proper nouns)		
lexical variety	126/196	137/195
attributive adjectives		18
(Three)		

J. On the basis of the comparisons above, determine which passage is more involved and which passage is more informational.

More involved: _____   More informational: _____

Name _____   **Section** _____   **Date** _____

7.11   FORMAL AND COLLOQUIAL REGISTERS IN PERSIAN

Among the styles of Modern Persian are two that are often termed formal and colloquial. Formal Persian (FP) is the usual language of books, magazines and newspapers, as well as of radio and television news-broadcasts, formal speeches, sermons, etc.; Colloquial Persian (CP) is the language of everyday conversation. The two registers are part of the linguistic repertoire of all educated speakers of Persian, who unconsciously switch from one to the other as the situation demands. In this exercise you will discover a few of the phonological, morphological and syntactic differences between formal and colloquial style.

The sentences below are given in both their FP and CP versions. Compare them carefully, and then answer the questions that follow. The data are given in phonetic transcription; parentheses indicate optional elements.

1. FP: mæn æli-ra mibinæm.
    CP: mæn æli-ro mibinæm.
    'I see Ali.'

2. FP: æli šoma-ra mibinæd.
    CP: æli šoma-ro mibine.
    'Ali sees you.'

3. FP: mæryæm an ketab-ra miforušæd.
    CP: mæryæm un ketab-(r)o miforuše.
    'Maryam is selling that book.'

4. FP: an xane bozorg æst.
    CP: un xune bozorg-e.
    'That house is big.'

5. FP: nader midanæd ke iræǰ mæriz æst.
    CP: nader midune ke iræǰ mæriz-e.
    'Nader knows that Iraj is sick.'

6. FP: æbolfæzl miguyæd ke in zæn irani æst.
    CP: æbolfæzl mige ke in zæn iruni-e.
    'Abolfazl says that this woman is Iranian.'

7. FP: mohsen pul-ra be šoma midehæd.
    CP: mohsen pul-(r)o be šoma mide.
    'Mohsen gives the money to you.'

8. FP: kodam ketab asan æst.
    CP: kodum ketab asun-e.
    'Which book is easy?'

9. FP: mæn be xane miayæm.

    CP: mæn miam xune.

          'I'm coming home.'

10. FP: soheyl be ketabxane miræved.

    CP: soheyl mire ketabxune.

          'Soheyl is going to the library.'

11. FP: æli mitævanæd be širaz berævæd.

    CP: æli mitune bere širaz.

          'Ali can go to Shiraz.'

12. FP: mæn mitævanæm išan-ra bebinæm.

    CP: mæn mitunæm išun-(r)o bebinæm.

          'I can see him/her (deferential).'

13. FP: mæn an-ra be xane miaværæm.

    CP: mæn un-(r)o miaræm xune.

          'I'm bringing it home.'

14. FP: æbolfæzl ketabha-ra be dæftær mibæræd.

    CP: æbolfæzl ketab(h)a-ro mibære dæftær.

          'Abolfazl is carrying the books to the office.'

A. First examine the Formal Persian sentences by themselves, and do a morphemic analysis: isolate all the morphemes present in the FP sentences and give their meanings or functions. (In this problem you need not account for the function of the postposition *-ra* or for the meaning or function of the verb prefixes—just include these among your listing of morphemes.) Group the morphemes you find according to the categories indicated below.

Nouns

Name _____   **Section** _____   **Date** _____

Pronouns	Adjectives

Verb Stems	

Verb Prefixes	Verb Suffixes	Others

B. Now identify the morphemes in your list that assume a different form in CP. Make another list of these FP/CP pairs.

EXAMPLE:	FP	CP
	an	un

C. Examine your list of FP/CP pairs. Some of the variation you have identified can be accounted for by a general phonological rule. State this rule, and indicate which FP/CP pairs it accounts for.

_____

_____

_____

_____

_____

_____

D. Under what circumstances may the *r* in the CP morpheme *-ro* be omitted? State your rule as generally as possible.

_____

_____

E. Circle the numbers of the sentences in the data that exhibit a *syntactic* difference between the FP and CP forms. Determine what these sentences have in common. Then propose a syntactic rule that will account for the difference. Your rule can take the form of a transformation that assumes the FP version represents the underlying word order.

_____

_____

_____

_____

_____

_____

F. Translate into both FP and CP:

I know that Maryam is bringing the money to the hospital.

(*Note:* Although you haven't seen the word for 'hospital,' there is enough information in the data for you to correctly guess the Persian translation!)

FP: _____

CP: _____

C H A P T E R

8

Writing

8.01   ENGLISH NOTICES

Notices like the following are sometimes seen on bulletin boards and other posting-places on college campuses:

1.   Class cancelled today.

2.   Applications for Assistant Librarian position now being accepted.

3.   Sean. Meet me here at 8 tonight. Erica

A.   Explain why each of the three notices above is vague or ambiguous.

1.   _____

    _____

    _____

2.   _____

    _____

    _____

3.   _____

    _____

    _____

B.   What is it about how writing differs from speaking that makes these messages vague or ambiguous?

_____

_____

_____

_____

C.   What is the difference between using the word *here* and using the word *today* that makes the one but not the other ambiguous on a notice board? Why is it that neither one is typically ambiguous in speech?

_____

_____

_____

_____

D.   What have you noticed about the situational similarity of messages on bulletin boards and messages on telephone answering machines? In what ways are the circumstances of composition on such machines more like writing than speaking?

_____

_____

_____

_____

E.   Collect several examples from bulletin boards or telephone answering machines in which some very common English expressions (*today, here, now,* etc.) are ambiguous or vague.

_____

_____

_____

_____

Name _____   **Section** _____   **Date** _____

8.02   18TH CENTURY WRITTEN VS. SPOKEN ENGLISH

Daniel Defoe, author of *Robinson Crusoe*, wrote of a visit he made to Somerset, about 150 miles southwest of London, in the first quarter of the eighteenth century.

... when we are come this Length from London, the Dialect of the English Tongue, or the Country-way of expressing themselves, is not easily understood. It is the same in many Parts of England besides, but in none in so gross a Degree as in this Part. As this Way of boorish Speech is in Ireland called, *"The Brogue upon the Tongue,"* so here it is named *Jouring.* It is not possible to explain this fully by Writing, because the Difference is not so much in the Orthography, as in the Tone and Accent; their abridging the Speech, *Cham*, for *I am*; *Chil*, for *I will; Don*, for *do on*, or *put on;* and *Doff*, for *do off*, or *put off;* and the like.

[Continuing, Defoe tells of a pupil reading aloud from the Bible.]

I sat down by the Master, till the Boy had read it out, and observed the Boy read a little oddly in the tone of the Country, which made me the more attentive; because, on Inquiry, I found that the Words were the same, and the Orthography the same, as in all our Bibles. I observed also the Boy read it out with his Eyes still on the Book, and his Head, like a mere Boy, moving from Side to Side, as the Lines reached cross the Columns of the Book: His Lesson was in the *Canticles of Solomon*; the Words these;
    'I have put off my Coat; how shall I put it on? I have washed my Feet; how shall I defile them?'
    The Boy read thus, with his Eyes, as I say, full on the Text:
    'Chav a doffed my Coot; how shall I don't? Chav a washed my Feet; how shall I moil 'em?'
    How the dexterous Dunce could form his Mouth to express so readily the Words (which stood right printed in the Book) in his Country Jargon, I could not but admire.

[First published 1724–7; cited from Tucker, 61–2.]

Defoe's astonishment that his "dexterous Dunce" read aloud in a "Country Jargon" reveals his view of the relationship between writing and speaking—for example, about which one should be based on which.

A.   Discuss the implications of Defoe's position, structuring your essay as follows:

1. Describe Defoe's conception of the relationship between spelling and pronunciation as revealed in this anecdote. Did he think spellings should be independent of local pronunciations?

    _____
    _____
    _____
    _____
    _____

2. If written English is to be relatively uniform across different regional dialects, could a system be devised in which spellings and pronunciations are relatively close? Explain and give examples to support your answer.

    _____
    _____
    _____
    _____
    _____

3. If, as Defoe wished, spelling *and* pronunciation were to be uniform, would people of different regions be forced to bring their pronunciation into harmony with standardized spellings, or could spelling vary to reflect local pronunciations and still serve the purposes that writing serves in the English-speaking world? (Things to consider: Even if a dictionary noted different spellings, which region's spelling would be alphabetized as the entry? And which region's spellings would be used in newspapers, and for laws, tax records, and information on how to use medicines and assemble bicycles?)

_____

_____

_____

_____

_____

_____

4. Finally, assess the soundness of Defoe's lament. Defoe claimed the boy was both "dexterous" and a "Dunce." In what way was the boy dexterous? Does this dexterity indicate that he was a dunce or an accomplished reader? Why?

_____

_____

_____

_____

B. Examine the Defoe passage again, and identify at least six ways in which the patterns of capitalization and punctuation in the early eighteenth century differ from the familiar patterns of today. What advantages do you see in today's system over the earlier one? What advantages did the earlier system have over today's?

_____   _____

_____   _____

_____   _____

_____

_____

_____

Name _____   **Section** _____   **Date** _____

8.03   MALAY/INDONESIAN SPELLING SYSTEMS

Malay and Indonesian are two dialects of the same language. Up until the late 1960s, however, the romanized orthography was significantly different for the two varieties, stemming from the fact that the Malays and Indonesians learned the Roman alphabet from their respective colonial overlords—the British in the case of Malaysia, the Dutch in Indonesia. In the early 1970s, the spelling systems in the two countries were finally unified.

Examine the following data. The first two columns illustrate some of the earlier spelling conventions—one column gives the older Malay spellings, the other gives the corresponding older Indonesian versions. The third column gives the newer, unified spelling. The fourth and fifth columns give the phonetic transcriptions and glosses.

1.	pulau	pulau	pulau	[pulau]	'island'
2.	tjakap	chakap	cakap	[čakap]	'speak'
3.	djalan	jalan	jalan	[ǰalan]	'road, way'
4.	dendang	dendang	dendang	[dəndaŋ]	'raven'
5.	achirnja	akhir-nya	akhirnya	[axirña]	'finally'
6.	zalim	dzalim	zalim	[zalim]	'cruel'
7.	sjarikat	sharikat	syarikat	[šarikat]	'company'
8.	jang	yang	yang	[yaŋ]	'which'
9.	dendang	dendang	dendang	[dendaŋ]	'song'
10.	masjhur	mashhur	masyhur	[mašhur]	'famous'
11.	kadi	kadhi	kadi	[kadi]	'Muslim religious officer'
12.	djalan2	jalan2	jalan-jalan	[ǰalanǰalan]	'(various) ways'
13.	berdjalan2	berjalan2	berjalan-jalan	[bərǰalanǰalan]	'stroll'
14.	leher	leher	leher	[leher]	'neck'
15.	air	ayer	air	[air]	'water'

Now answer the following questions:

A. Which column gives the older Malay spellings, and which the older Indonesian ones? How do you know?

_____

_____

_____

B. Who do you think had the harder time adapting to the new system, the Malaysians or the Indonesians? Or was the burden equally shared? Give examples to support your position.

_____

_____

_____

_____

_____

_____

C. In what way(s) is the new spelling system superior to each of the old ones? Give examples.

_____

_____

_____

_____

_____

_____

D. What, if any, are the *disadvantages* of the new system compared to the old ones?

_____

_____

_____

E. Is the new system free of ambiguity? That is, does each written symbol in the new system have a unique pronunciation? Explain. Compare the situation in the two older systems.

_____

_____

_____

_____

Name _____   Section _____   Date _____

8.04   ITALIAN SPELLING

A. Examine the following Italian words, given in both Italian spelling and phonetic transcription. Then answer the questions that follow.

	Italian spelling	Phonetic transcription	Gloss
1.	circa	[čirka]	'about'
2.	chicco	[kikko]	'grain'
3.	quota	[kwɔta]	'height'
4.	cella	[čɛlla]	'cell'
5.	chiosco	[kyɔsko]	'booth'
6.	cinque	[čiŋkwe]	'five'
7.	accetta	[ačč etta]	'ax'
8.	quindici	[kwindiči]	'fifteen'
9.	chiedere	[kyɛdere]	'to ask'
10.	ciocco	[čɔkko]	'log'
11.	cui	[kwi]	'whom'
12.	quercia	[kwɛrča]	'oak tree'
13.	socio	[sɔčo]	'member'
14.	ciuco	[čuko]	'donkey'
15.	cocco	[kɔkko]	'coconut'
16.	schivo	[skivo]	'shy'
17.	chiusa	[kyuza]	'lock'
18.	accetta	[ačč etta]	'accepts'
19.	qualche	[kwalke]	'some, any'
20.	cuocio	[kwɔčo]	'I cook'
21.	vecchio	[vɛkkyo]	'old'
22.	cucire	[kučire]	'to sew'
23.	scalea	[skalea]	'staircase'
24.	chiamo	[kyamo]	'I call'
25.	chela	[kɛla]	'claw'
26.	acquoso	[akkwozo]	'watery'
27.	porcellino	[porčellino]	'piggy'
28.	questo	[kwesto]	'this'
29.	cherubino	[kerubino]	'cherub'
30.	chierico	[kyeriko]	'clergyman'

1.   Your goal is to explain fully, based on the above examples, how the sounds [k] and [č] are spelled before vowels and glides in Italian.

You will need to refer to the Italian vowel system, which is as follows:

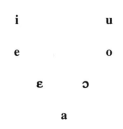

    i   u

     e   o

      ɛ   ɔ

       a

Filling in the following chart will help you organize your data and see the patterns more clearly. Indicate the spelling for each phonetic sequence that exists in Italian. (Two of the sequences do not exist.) In certain cases, more than one spelling is possible.

[či] _____ [ki] _____ [kyi] _____ [kwi] _____

[če] _____ [ke] _____ [kye] _____ [kwe] _____

[čɛ] _____ [kɛ] _____ [kyɛ] _____ [kwɛ] _____

[ča] _____ [ka] _____ [kya] _____ [kwa] _____

[čo] _____ [ko] _____ [kyo] _____ [kwo] _____

[čɔ] _____ [kɔ] _____ [kyɔ] _____ [kwɔ] _____

[ču] _____ [ku] _____ [kyu] _____ [kwu] _____

2. Now summarize your findings by giving the required spelling rules for [k] and [č]. Be as general as possible.

   EXAMPLE: [k] is spelled _____ before_____ vowels.

_____

_____

_____

_____

_____

_____

B. Fill in the blanks:

Italian spelling	Phonetic transcription	Gloss
1. china	_____	'slope'
2. cima	_____	'summit'

Name _____   **Section** _____   **Date** _____

Italian spelling	Phonetic transcription	Gloss
3. _____	[često]	'basket'
4. ciao	_____	'So long!'
5. _____	[kyaro]	'light'
6. taciuto	_____	'withheld'
7. _____	[kwiɛto]	'quiet'
8. _____	[poko]	'little'
9. _____	[pokissimo]	'very little'
10. _____	[skermo]	'screen'

Italian uses the letter *g* to spell the sounds [g] and [ǰ], on principles similar to those for [k] and [č].

Fill in the blanks as above.

Italian spelling	Phonetic transcription	Gloss
1. _____	[garbo]	'grace'
2. _____	[girba]	'skin'
3. _____	[ǰakka]	'jacket'
4. giammai	_____	'never'
5. _____	[ǰorǰo]	'George'
6. giusto	_____	'right, fair'
7. _____	[gepardo]	'cheetah'

C. We can say a spelling system is *unambiguous* if the phonetic form of a word is always determinable from its orthography. Judging from what you've seen of the Italian spelling system, compare English and Italian in this respect.

1. Some English spellings are notoriously ambiguous. For example, you see the English surname *Hough* in a magazine article, but you've never heard it pronounced. Indicate all the possibilities that English allows:

a.   It could be _____[hu]_____ as in ___through [θru]___.

b.   It could be _____ as in _____.

c.   It could be _____ as in _____.

d.   It could be _____ as in _____.

e.   It could be _____ as in _____.

2.   As far as can be deduced from the data, how ambiguous is the Italian spelling system? Is the pronunciation always clear from the written form of the word, or are there cases of uncertainty? Using the data, explain and illustrate.

_____

_____

_____

_____

Name _____   **Section** _____   **Date** _____

8.05   WRITING SYSTEMS: MODERN GREEK

The Modern Greek alphabet consists of 24 letters, with the same distinction between upper and lower case as there is in the Roman alphabet. This problem will familiarize you with the upper-case (capital) letters, and some of the sounds they represent.

A. Compare these Modern Greek words, written in "all caps," with their phonetic transcriptions. (Stress has not been indicated.) In these words, there is a one-to-one correspondence between orthographic and phonetic symbols, so you should have no difficulty in pairing each letter with its sound. Then fill in the chart that follows, giving the phonetic value of each letter. These data will allow you to determine only one sound—the most common one—for each written symbol. But bear in mind that for certain letters, other phonetic manifestations are possible depending on the environment. (Note: The combinations p̂s and k̂s function as single phonemes in Greek.)

ΠΟΛΥΚΑΤΑΣΤΗΜΑ	[polikatastima]	'department store'
ΔΙΟΡΘΩΝΩ	[ðiorθono]	'I correct'
ΓΡΑΦΟΜΗΧΑΝΗ	[ɣrafomixani]	'typewriter'
ΨΕΚΑΖΕΤΕ	[p̂sekazete]	'you sprinkle'
ΞΕΒΓΑΖΩ	[k̂sevɣazo]	'I rinse'

A _____ B _____ Γ _____ Δ _____ E _____ Z _____ H _____ Θ _____

I _____ K _____ Λ _____ M _____ N _____ Ξ _____ O _____ Π _____

P _____ Σ _____ T _____ Y _____ Φ _____ X _____ Ψ _____ Ω _____

B. *Digraphs* are combinations of two letters used to represent a single sound, as English sh for [š]. Determine what digraphs are present in the following data, and give their phonetic values:

ΜΠΟΡΟΥΜΕ	[borume]	'we can'
ΝΤΡΕΠΟΜΑΙ	[drepome]	'I am ashamed'
ΓΚΡΕΜΙΖΕΙ	[gremizi]	'he pulls down'
ΥΙΟΘΕΤΗΜΕΝΟΙ	[ioθetimeni]	'adopted (m. pl.)'

_____

_____

_____

_____

_____

C. 1. List the ways that the sound [i] can be spelled in Modern Greek.

_____

2. Speculate on how it came about that Modern Greek has so many ways to spell the same sound.

_____

_____

_____

Name _____   **Section** _____   **Date** _____

8.06 WRITING SYSTEMS: MODERN HEBREW

The Hebrew alphabet consists of 22 symbols for consonants. Two of these are usually "silent" in Modern Hebrew, often serving to indicate that a word or syllable begins with a vowel sound. Some letters have several pronunciations, the correct choice of which is usually predictable from the phonology, morphology and lexicon of the language. Among these ambiguous letters are several that serve double duty as vowels.

In the chart below, forms in parentheses are "final" letters, variants used exclusively at the end of a word.

א	silent, ʔ	ל	l
ב	b, v	מ(ם)	m
ג	g	נ(ן)	n
ד	d	ס	s
ה	h, final a	ע	silent, ʔ
ו	v, u, ɔ	פ(ף)	p, f
ז	z	צ(ץ)	t͡s
ח	x	ק	k
ט	t	ר	r
י	y, i, ε	ש	š, s
כ(ך)	k, x	ת	t

Aside from the three vowel symbols derived from consonants, vowels are not indicated in ordinary Hebrew texts. Thus the sequence כתב can stand for any of the following: (Note that Hebrew is read from right to left.)

katav	'he wrote'
kᵊtɔv	'write!' (m. sg. imp.)
kitεv	'he wrote a lot'
katεv	'write a lot!' (m. sg. imp.)
kᵊtav	'writing, script'

In dictionaries, in material for children and non-native speakers, and also in adult texts when there is danger of ambiguity, a series of "vowel points" (sometimes in conjunction with the consonants *v* and *y*) and other symbols originally invented to fix the pronunciation of Biblical Hebrew texts are used to differentiate vowels and determine the values of certain consonant symbols.

For this exercise, you will need to recognize the following consonant distinctions and vowel symbols:

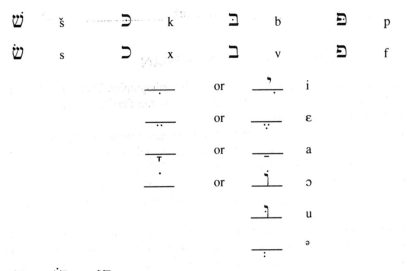

Thus, בָ ba, בוֹ bɔ, בִי bi, etc.

A. For the letters כ, ב and פ, formulate a generalization explaining the function of the internal dot.

_____

_____

_____

_____

B. The following Hebrew words are given both in their ordinary and "pointed" forms. Give the phonetic transcription in each case.

שלום	שָׁלוֹם	_____	'hello, goodbye, peace'
כשר	כָּשֵׁר	_____	'ritually fit or proper'
פורים	פּוּרִים	_____	(a Jewish holiday)
יום כפור	יוֹם כִּפּוּר	_____	(a Jewish holiday)
תל אביב	תֵּל אָבִיב	_____	(place name)
ירושלים	יְרוּשָׁלַיִם	_____	(place name)
עדן	עֵדֶן	_____	(Biblical place name)
אדם	אָדָם	_____	(Biblical character)
שטן	שָׂטָן	_____	(Biblical character)

Name _____   **Section** _____   **Date** _____

8.07   WRITING SYSTEMS: PERSIAN

Persian uses a modified version of the Arabic writing system for its orthography. There are 32 letters, 28 of which are borrowed from Arabic; four letters were added to represent the Persian sounds not found in Arabic, namely *p, g, č,* and *ž*. The writing runs from right to left.

The six vowels of Persian—*i, u, a, e, o, æ*—are incompletely represented in the orthography. The first three are always written; *e* is written only at the end of a word; *o* and *æ* are indicated very rarely. (There are diacritic symbols written above and below the script that can indicate all these vowels, but these are used only in special circumstances—dictionaries, children's books, etc.) Most of the vowels that do appear in writing are represented by certain consonants doing double duty as vowels, much the same as the English letter *y*.

This problem introduces you to twelve Persian letters. Most of these are joined to each other continuously in writing; a few are never joined to the following letter. (Bear in mind that the "following" letter is the one to the *left*!) The chart below shows you the various ways each of these can appear in a word; the most extreme case of variation is with *h*, where there are four quite distinct shapes.

Note: Following a non-joining letter, the next letter is in the initial form unless it is the last letter of the word, in which case it is in the isolated form.

Sound	Shapes				Remarks
	In Isolation	*Initial*	*Medial*	*Final*	
See remarks.	ا	ا	ـا	ـا	Used for [a]. Not joined to following letter. Initially, indicates word begins with a vowel.
b	ﺏ	ﺑ	ـﺒـ	ـﺐ	
p	ﭖ	ﭘ	ـﭙـ	ـﭗ	
t	ﺕ	ﺗ	ـﺘـ	ـﺖ	
r	ﺭ	ﺭ	ـﺮ	ـﺮ	Not joined to following letter.
s	ﺱ	ﺳ	ـﺴـ	ـﺲ	
š	ﺵ	ﺷ	ـﺸـ	ـﺶ	
f	ﻑ	ﻓ	ـﻔـ	ـﻒ	
n	ﻥ	ﻧ	ـﻨـ	ـﻦ	
v	ﻭ	ﻭ	ـﻮ	ـﻮ	Used for [u]. Not joined to following letter.
h	ﻩ	ﻫ	ـﻬـ	ـﻪ	In final position, used to indicate *e*.
y	ﯼ	ﯾ	ـﯿـ	ﯽ	Used for [i]. Notice when the dots disappear!

A. By comparing the following Persian words with the chart, you will be able to match them up with their pronunciations and glosses. As you analyze each word, keep in mind that with the exception of ﯼ, *the dots remain intact in all positions* even though the shape of the letter may change.

Write the letter of the transcription that corresponds to each written word in the space provided.

1. _____ور_____   _____   a. pošt   'back'

2. _____ﻩﺍﺭ_____   _____   b. tup   'ball'

3. _____ﻥﺍﻥ_____   _____   c. behtær   'better'

4.	باب	_____		d.	nan	'bread'
5.	سه	_____		e.	bab	'chapter'
6.	سی	_____		f.	særšir	'cream'
7.	بیش	_____		g.	orupa	'Europe'
8.	توپ	_____		h.	ru	'face'
9.	هوش	_____		i.	šiše	'glass'
10.	اوف	_____		j.	ensani	'human'
11.	این	_____		k.	huš	'intelligence'
12.	است	_____		l.	æst	'is'
13.	پشت	_____		m.	ræhbær	'leader'
14.	ناهار	_____		n.	navban	'lieutenant'
15.	شیشه	_____		o.	nahar	'lunch'
16.	ناوبان	_____		p.	biš	'more'
17.	تنور	_____		q.	uf	'ouch!'
18.	فشار	_____		r.	tænur	'oven'
19.	روانی	_____		s.	behešt	'paradise'
20.	رهبر	_____		t.	fešar	'pressure'
21.	بهتر	_____		u.	pišræft	'progress'
22.	سرشیر	_____		v.	rævani	'psychological'
23.	اروپا	_____		w.	rah	'road'
24.	اشاره	_____		x.	ešare	'sign'
25.	تهران	_____		y.	tabestan	'summer'
26.	نیستی	_____		z.	tehran	'Tehran'
27.	بهشت	_____		aa.	si	'thirty'
28.	انسانی	_____		bb.	in	'this'
29.	تابستان	_____		cc.	se	'three'
30.	پیشرفت	_____		dd.	nisti	'you're not'

Name _____   **Section** _____   **Date** _____

B. Fill in the blanks below:

Orthography	Pronunciation	Gloss
1. _____	ba	'with'
2. _____	bi	'without'
3. فارس	_____'Persian'	
4. _____	tab	'warmth'
5. پاریس	_____	_____
6. _____	šah	'Shah'
7. _____	sup	'soup'
8. ایران	_____	_____

Name _____   **Section** _____   **Date** _____

8.08   WRITING SYSTEMS: KOREAN HANGUL

Hangul, the Korean alphabet, appeared in 1446 after having been commissioned by King Sejong. It is a phonemic writing system, well adapted to the structure of the language it transcribes. This exercise will acquaint you with several vowel and consonant symbols, and the way they are put together to write Korean syllables.

A. By carefully analyzing the following Korean words in their Hangul orthography and comparing them with their phonetic transcriptions, you should be able to isolate the five vowel and eight consonant symbols present in these data.

1. 공   [koŋ]   'ball'
2. 말   [mal]   'language'
3. 아무   [amu]   'any'
4. 덕분   [təkpun]   'favor'
5. 박   [pak]   'Park' (surname)
6. 누님   [nunim]   'older sister'
7. 로   [ro]   'to'
8. 번   [pən]   'time'
9. 삼   [sam]   'three'
10. 식사   [šiksa]   'meal'
11. 눈   [nun]   'snow'
12. 우리   [uri]   'we'
13. 일상   [ilsaŋ]   'daily'
14. 맏   [mat]   'first'
15. 부인   [puin]   'lady'
16. 사람   [saram]   'person'
17. 아니   [ani]   'no'
18. 국   [kuk]   'soup'
19. 비서   [pisə]   'secretary'
20. 사무   [samu]   'office work'
21. 구   [ku]   'nine'

1. List the symbols you have identified, grouping them by consonants and vowels. For each one, give its phonetic value or values according to the data.

	Symbol	Phonetic Value(s)
Consonants	_____	_____
	_____	_____
	_____	_____
	_____	_____
	_____	_____
	_____	_____
	_____	_____
	_____	_____
Vowels	_____	_____
	_____	_____
	_____	_____
	_____	_____
	_____	_____

2. With the exception of o each symbol you have identified stands for a single phoneme in Korean. For those phonemes having more than one allophone present in the data, explain carefully how these allophones are distributed. In other words, what determines how the written symbol is pronounced?

_____

_____

_____

_____

_____

_____

3. Explain the use of o. Is this symbol ambiguous in context, or is its pronunciation always clearly determined?

_____

_____

_____

_____

Name _____   **Section** _____   **Date** _____

B.   Fill in the blanks:

1. 부모   _____   'parents'

2.   [tari]   'bridge'

3.   [əməni]   'mother'

4. 서울   _____   (place name)

5. 건물   _____   'building'

6.   [pusan]   (place name)

7. 기숙사   _____   'dormitory'

8.   [paŋsoŋ]   'broadcasting'

9.   [kolmok]   'streetcorner'

10. 사무실   _____   'office'

Name _____   Section _____   Date _____

8.09   WRITING SYSTEMS: JAPANESE HIRAGANA

Japanese is considered to have one of the most complex writing systems in the world. In addition to *kanji*—characters borrowed from Chinese and used for most roots of nouns, verbs, adjectives and adverbs—there are two distinct systems of *kana*, sound-based syllabic symbols. The more important of these, *hiragana*, is used for native Japanese and Chinese-origin words and grammatical morphemes for which the 2,000-some-odd *kanji* in common use are not suitable; *hiragana* can also substitute for *kanji* in various situations. The other syllabic system, *katakana*, is used mainly for borrowed words of non-Chinese origin, and to transcribe foreign names. There are also two somewhat different forms of romanization, or *roomaji*, used on public signs and for certain abbreviations. Literacy in Japanese entails fluency in all four of these systems, along with the ability to switch back and forth among them instantaneously; all four systems can in fact be used in the same written sentence.

This exercise will introduce you to twenty of the 103 hiragana symbols (46 basic and 57 derived or compound symbols).

A.   Analyze the following twelve Japanese words, given in *hiragana* and *roomaji*. (Note: <sh> = [š].) Then isolate the twenty different hiragana symbols they contain and give the pronunciation of each.

1.	さす	sasu	'thrust; indicate'
2.	のき	noki	'eaves'
3.	あした	ashita	'tomorrow'
4.	やがて	yagate	'soon'
5.	うら	ura	'back'
6.	みこし	mikoshi	'portable shrine'
7.	もらう	morau	'receive'
8.	かがみ	kagami	'mirror'
9.	です	desu	'be'
10.	こけし	kokeshi	'wooden doll'
11.	だから	dakara	'therefore'
12.	げき	geki	'drama'

Hiragana symbols found in these words, with their pronunciations:

1. _____   2. _____   3. _____   4. _____

5. _____   6. _____   7. _____   8. _____

9. _____   10. _____   11. _____   12. _____

13. _____   14. _____   15. _____   16. _____

17. _____   18. _____   19. _____   20. _____

B. Now answer the following questions:

1. Examine the *hiragana* for the syllables *ko, no* and *mo*. Is the phonetic similarity among these sylla-bles reflected in their *hiragana* symbols? If so, how?

_____

_____

2. Now examine the *hiragana* for the syllables *ko, ka* and *ki*. Is the fact that all three syllables contain the sound [k] reflected in the *hiragana*? If so, how?

_____

_____

3. Is *hiragana* an alphabet? Why or why not?

_____

_____

_____

4. Judging from these data, are there any *parts* of individual *hiragana* symbols that have identifiable functions? If you find there are, be as general as possible in your analysis, and refer to *classes* of sounds. (*Hint:* Consider ``.)

_____

_____

_____

_____

_____

_____

5. Here is the Japanese word for 'afternoon' written in *hiragana*. The syllabic symbols it uses are not among the ones you isolated above. Nevertheless, you should be able to figure out how it is pro-nounced:

   ここ   Pronunciation: _____

Name _____   **Section** _____   **Date** _____

C.   The following Japanese words are familiar to many westerners. Transcribe them into *roomaji*.

すし   _____

すきやき   _____

きもの   _____

さけ   _____

さしみ   _____

からて   _____

Name _____   Section _____   Date _____

8.10   CHINESE CHARACTERS 1: PICTOGRAPHS, IDEOGRAPHS, AND IDEOGRAPHIC COMPOUNDS

Many people are under the impression that Chinese characters are simply stylized pictures or diagrams of the objects or ideas they represent. Although in fact the vast majority of Chinese characters can *not* be so analyzed, a relatively small number do conform to this popular notion. In this exercise you will be introduced to a few of these purely 'pictorial' characters. (Mandarin pronunciations are given in the Pinyin romanization—see Appendix A.)

A. Pictographs

The Chinese characters that derive from pictures of the objects they represent have mostly evolved to the point where the visual connection between character and object is no longer obvious:

馬	mǎ	'horse'
魚	yú	'fish'
豕	shǐ	'swine'
人	rén	'person'
variant: 仁		
女	nǚ	'woman'
子	zǐ	'child'

In a few cases, the evolutionary process that derived the modern characters can be inferred, and then confirmed historically:

mù 'eye':   目

Here are some examples of the relatively rare group of Chinese characters that may still bear somewhat of a resemblance to the things they represent. Try to match each character up with its Mandarin pronunciation and meaning. Don't be surprised if the answers aren't entirely obvious! (Hint: It may help to look for drops of rain, people under an umbrella, a field divided into sections, and a swinging, saloon-type door.)

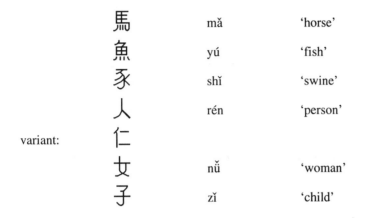

口	_____	a.	sǎn	'umbrella'
木	_____	b.	tián	'field'
山	_____	c.	mén	'door'
雨	_____	d.	mù	'tree, wood'
川	_____	e.	kǒu	'mouth'
田	_____	f.	yǔ	'rain'
傘	_____	g.	chuān	'river'
門	_____	h.	shān	'mountain'

346   LOOKING AT LANGUAGES

B. Ideographs

A small group of Chinese characters are simple diagrams that "point to" the idea or relationship in question. Match these characters up with their pronunciations and meanings:

中 _____   a. yī   'one'

下 _____   b. èr   'two'

二 _____   c. sān   'three'

一 _____   d. shàng   'above'

上 _____   e. xià   'below'

三 _____   f. zhōng   'middle, center'

C. Ideographic compounds

In this group of Chinese characters, two or more meaningful elements are combined to yield a compound character whose meaning is derived from the meanings of the components.

1. Examine the following compound characters, and match them with their pronunciations and meanings. (In a few cases you will have to make an educated guess as to which of several possible alternatives is correct.) You should already know the meanings of most of the components from having worked section A above. Here is the additional information you will need:

日 'sun'

月 'moon'

言 'speech'

宀 'roof'

明 _____   a. chuǎng   'force one's way in'

好 _____   b. ān   'safe, tranquil; peace'

信 _____   c. dāi   'slow-witted, dull'

林 _____   d. míng   'bright, clear'

家 _____   e. jīng   'brilliant, shiny'

闖 _____   f. hǎo   'good'

安 _____   g. lín   'forest'

晶 _____   h. xìn   'believe'

呆 _____   i. jiā   'household'

Name _____   **Section** _____   **Date** _____

2. For each of these characters, explain briefly how the meaning of the whole is related to the meanings of the component parts.

chuǎng: _____

_____

_____

ān: _____

_____

_____

dāi: _____

_____

_____

míng: _____

_____

_____

jīng: _____

_____

_____

hǎo: _____

_____

_____

lín: _____

_____

_____

xìn: _____

_____

_____

jiā: _____

_____

_____

Name _____   **Section** _____   **Date** _____

8.11   CHINESE CHARACTERS 2: PHONETIC COMPOUNDS

It is a common misconception that Chinese characters are based exclusively on the meaning of the word represented. Actually, about 95 percent of contemporary characters have a partial phonetic basis—although given phonological change over the centuries, this is not always evident today.

An example will illustrate the basic principle. The word for 'horse' is mǎ, with the following pictographic character: 馬. (See previous exercise.) Now another Chinese word, mā 'mother' is similar in pronunciation—only the tone is different. Given the phonetic similarity, the character for mǎ 'horse' was *borrowed* to serve as the character for mā 'mother.' However, something had to be done to differentiate the two—otherwise an unacceptable ambiguity would be created in the written language. To distinguish the two characters, a component was added to the character for 'mother' that would give a clue to its meaning. This component is 女, which as an independent character stands for 'woman.' Thus we now have the following two characters:

馬	mǎ	'horse'
媽	mā	'mother'

The first is a pictograph deriving from a stylized picture of the object represented; the second is a *phonetic compound*, with a component (on the left in this case) giving a clue to the meaning, and another component (on the right) giving a clue to the pronunciation. (Note that the character for 'mother' is *not* an ideographic compound—if it were, its meaning would probably be 'mare'!)

In phonetic compounds, the element giving a clue to the meaning is called the *signific, determinative* or *radical*[1]. The element that can hint at the pronunciation is called the *phonetic*.

In each of the following groups of compound characters, one element is common throughout the group. For each group, draw the common element in the space provided. Then determine whether it is the *signific* or the *phonetic*. If the former, make an educated guess as to its general meaning; if the latter, give the range of phonetic values in contemporary Mandarin that are represented in the data. (The romanization used here is the Pinyin system—see Appendix A.)

1. 請   qǐng   'please'

    清   qīng   'clear'

    睛   jīng   'eyeball'

    情   qíng   'emotion'

    晴   qíng   'good weather'

Common element: _____

[ ] Signific.   Meaning: _____

[ ] Phonetic.   Values: _____

[1]The term "radical" is not precisely equivalent to the other two, but the difference does not concern us here.

2. 淋   lín   'drenched'

   漂   piāo   'float'

   灣   wān   'bay, gulf'

   淚   lèi   'tears'

   注   zhù   'pour'

Common element:

[   ] Signific.   Meaning: _____

[   ] Phonetic.   Values: _____

3. 國   guó   'country, nation'

   園   yuán   'garden'

   圖   tú   'picture, map'

   圍   wéi   'surround, enclose'

   圈   quān   'encircle'

Common element:

[   ] Signific.   Meaning: _____

[   ] Phonetic.   Values: _____

4. 刨   bào   'plane'

   跑   pǎo   'run'

   雹   báo   'hail'

   飽   bǎo   'full'

   苞   bāo   'bud'

Common element:

[   ] Signific.   Meaning: _____

[   ] Phonetic.   Values: _____

Name _____   **Section** _____   **Date** _____

5. 肪   fáng   'fat'

    芳   fāng   'fragrant'

    坊   fāng   'lane'

    訪   fǎng   'visit'

    房   fáng   'dwelling'

Common element:

[   ] Signific.   Meaning: _____

[   ] Phonetic.   Values: _____

6. 疤   bā   'scar'

    痘   dòu   'smallpox'

    疼   téng   'ache, pain'

    癲   diān   'insane'

    病   bìng   'sick'

Common element:

[   ] Signific.   Meaning: _____

[   ] Phonetic.   Values: _____

APPENDIXES

The Pinyin Transcription System for Mandarin Chinese

All the Mandarin examples in this book have been transcribed in *pinyin* (except for the phonology problems of Chapter 2).

In the People's Republic of China, *pinyin* is the official system for representing Mandarin in the roman alphabet. It is the standard used for names in Western media, and it is employed extensively in Chinese language education.

Pinyin uses all the letters of the English alphabet except *v,* adding to these only *ü.* Tone marks, although seldom indicated, are the familiar ones: ¯, ´, ˇ, ` for tones 1 through 4 respectively (see problem 2.17).

Listed below with their phonetic equivalents are *those symbols that differ significantly from the identical phonetic notation, or that require special comment.*

Pinyin	Phonetics	Comments and Examples
p, t, k	$[p^h]$, $[t^h]$, $[k^h]$	Aspirated voiceless stops. (p̱īngp̱āng, 'table tennis')
b, d, g	[p], [t], [k]	Unaspirated voiceless stops. (Ḇěijīng)
h	[h], [x]	Varies between [h] and [x], tending towards [x] with emphasis. (H̱únán)
z	$[\widehat{ts}]$	Unaspirated voiceless affricate. (Máo Ẕédōng)
c	$[\widehat{ts}^h]$	Aspirated voiceless affricate. (c̱àidān, 'menu')
x	[ç]	Palatal; as in German *ich,* English *hue.* (Dèng X̱iǎopíng)
j	$[\widehat{tç}]$	Palatal; closest English sound is the *j* of *jeans,* but unvoiced. (Běij̱īng)
q	$[\widehat{tç}^h]$	Palatal; closest English sound is the *ch* of *cheese,* with aspiration. (tàijíq̱uán 'tai chi chuan')
sh	[ʂ]	Retroflex; an *š*-like sound articulated with the tip of the tongue curled up and back towards the palate. (S̱hànghǎi)
zh	$[\widehat{tʂ}]$	Retroflex; closest English sound is the *j* of *jerk,* but unvoiced. (Ẕhōngguó 'China']
ch	$[\widehat{tʂ}^h]$	Retroflex; closest English sound is the *ch* of *churn,* with aspiration. (c̱hǎomiàn 'fried noodles')
r	[r]	Retroflex; in final position very much like an American *r,* in initial position has a hint of a simultaneous [ž] sound. (èṟ 'two,' ṟén 'person')

Pinyin	Phonetics	Comments and Examples
ng	[ŋ]	Appears only in syllable-final position. (Shànghǎi)
e	[ɤ]	When syllable-final and not preceded by *i, u,* or *ü*. A mid, back, unrounded vowel, close to [ə]. (Máo Zédōng)
en, eng	[ən], [əŋ]	(Zhōu Ēnlái, Dèng Xiǎopíng)
er	[ər] or [ar]	Depending partly on tone. (èr 'two')
i	[ɿ]	After the dental sibilants (*s, z, c*). A dental apical vowel. (Sìchuān)
i	[ɭ]	After the retroflex consonants (*sh, zh, ch, r*). A retroflex apical vowel; closest English sound is the *ir* of *shirt*. (chī 'eat')
ian	[iɛn]	(chǎomiàn 'fried noodles')
ie	[iɛ]	(qiē 'cut')
iu	[io]	(jiǔ 'wine')
o	[ɔ]	Does not occur after *a* or before *ng*. (wǒ 'I')
ong	[ʊŋ]	(Máo Zédōng)
u	[ü]	
uan	[üɛn]	After the palatals *x, j, q,* and *y*. (qù 'go,' yuán 'garden,' xué 'study')
ue	[üɛ]	
ui	[uei]	(duì 'correct')
un	[uən]	(kùn 'surround')

Notes:

1. *i* has three pronunciations. For the values of *i* following dental sibilants and retroflex consonants, see above; the pronunciation of these unfamiliar vowels is best learned from a native speaker. In other environments *i* is simply [i].

2. Syllable-initial *i* and *u* are respelled *y* and *w* respectively before a following vowel, e.g. *uàng → wàng, iǎn → yǎn*. If no vowel follows, *y* is inserted before the *i* (*īng → yīng*) and *w* before the *u* (*ǔ → wǔ*). *y* is also inserted before initial *ü* (see below).

3. *ü* is written as an ordinary *u* after the palatals *x, j, q*; syllable-initial *ü* becomes *yu*. *ü* appears in *pinyin* only after *n* and *l;* only in these environments do [u] and [ü] contrast, e.g. *lù* 'road,' *lǜ* 'green.'

B

Transcription of Semitic Consonants

In the transcription of Arabic, Aramaic and Hebrew in this book, several phonetic symbols may be unfamiliar to you. These are explained below.

q	a voiceless uvular stop
ħ	a voiceless pharyngeal fricative: a strong *h*-like sound, pronounced with pharyngeal (throat) constriction
ʕ	a voiced pharyngeal fricative, usually regarded as the voiced counterpart of ħ
ś	an *s*-like sound found in Biblical Hebrew and Biblical Aramaic, the exact pronunciation of which is uncertain. Perhaps palatalized.
ç	A dot below a consonant, e.g. *ṭ*, indicates that the consonant is pronounced with a secondary articulation in which the back of the tongue is raised towards the velum. Such consonants are said to be *velarized* or *emphatic*.
ə, a	ultra-short vowels, as in Biblical Hebrew z^əma:n, laʕ^aqo:r

C

Language Index

	Problems	Pages
Natural Languages		
Akan	2.18	95
Arabic	2.02, 2.09, 2.11, 3.10, 3.11, 6.07, 6.08	57, 73, 77, 131, 133, 273, 277
Aramaic	6.08	277
Chinese	2.16, 2.17, 4.16, 5.14, 5.15, 8.10, 8.11	91, 93, 197, 247, 249, 245, 349
English	1.01, 1.02, 1.03, 1.04, 1.05, 1.06, 1.07, 1.08, 1.09, 2.05, 2.12, 2.13, 2.14, 2.15, 3.03, 3.04, 3.09, 3.16, 4.01, 4.02, 4.03, 4.04, 4.05, 4.06, 4.07, 4.10, 4.14, 5.01, 5.02, 5.03, 5.04, 5.05, 5.06, 5.07, 5.08, 5.09, 5.10, 5.11, 7.01, 7.02, 7.03, 7.04, 7.05, 7.06, 7.07, 7.08, 7.09, 7.10, 8.01, 8.02	1, 3, 7, 9, 11, 13, 15, 17, 21, 63, 81, 83, 85, 87, 111, 117, 129, 149, 153, 155, 159, 161, 163, 165, 167, 177, 191, 207, 209, 211, 215, 217, 219, 223, 225, 227, 231, 235, 285, 287, 291, 293, 295, 299, 303, 305, 309, 311, 319, 321
French	4.08, 6.04	171, 263
German	4.13, 6.06	187, 269
Greek	2.11, 3.14, 4.14, 6.02, 8.05	77, 141, 191, 259, 329
Hawaiian	1.14	37
Hebrew	1.17, 2.09, 3.01, 4.17, 6.08, 8.06	45, 73, 107, 201, 277, 331
Hindi	2.04	61
Icelandic	2.11	77
Italian	2.07, 4.14, 6.04, 6.05, 8.04	69, 191, 263, 265, 325
Japanese	2.03, 2.08, 2.15, 2.19, 4.09, 4.10, 8.09	59, 71, 87, 99, 175, 177, 341
Korean	8.08	337
Lakota	1.16, 3.06	41, 123
Latin	3.07	125
Malay/Indonesian	3.02, 3.13, 5.12, 6.07, 8.03	109, 139, 239, 273, 323
Old English	2.06	65

Bibliography

Abas, Lutfi, and Awang Sariyan, eds. 1988. *Kamus Pelajar* [Student Dictionary] (Petaling Jaya, Malaysia: Delta).

Adams, Douglas Q. 1987. *Essential Modern Greek Grammar* (New York: Dover).

Atwood, E. Bagby. 1953. *A Survey of Verb Forms in the Eastern United States* (Ann Arbor: University of Michigan Press).

Boas, Franz, and Ella Deloria. 1941. *Dakota Grammar* (Washington, DC: U.S. Govt. Printing Office).

Brown, Francis, S. R. Driver, and C. A. Briggs. 1907. *A Hebrew and English Lexicon of the Old Testament* (Oxford: Clarendon Press).

Burke, David. 1988. *Street French: How to Speak and Understand French Slang* (New York: John Wiley).

Ch'en, Ta-tuan, Perry Link, Yih-jian Tai, and Hai-tao Tang. 1987. *Chinese Primer* (Princeton: Chinese Linguistics Project, Princeton University).

Chang, Namgui, and Yong-chol Kim. 1989. *Functional Korean* (Elizabeth, NJ: Hollym International).

Cheng, Chin-Chuan. 1973. *A Synchronic Phonology of Mandarin Chinese* (The Hague: Mouton).

Cohen, A. 1946. *The Five Megilloth* (London: Soncino Press).

Davies, Basil, and Cennard Davies. 1980. *Catchphrase: A Course in Spoken Welsh* (Penygroes, Wales: Sain (Recordiau) Cyf.).

Halkin, Abraham S. 1970. *201 Hebrew Verbs* (New York: Barron's).

Harris, Martin, and Nigel Harris, eds. 1988. *The Romance Languages* (New York: Oxford University Press).

Haïm, S. 1961. *The One-Volume Persian–English Dictionary* (Tehran: Béroukhim).

Henshall, Kenneth G., and Tetsuo Takagaki. 1990. *A Guide to Learning Katakana and Hiragana* (Rutland, VT: Charles E. Tuttle).

Jónsson, Snæbjörn. 1927. *A Primer of Modern Icelandic* (London: Oxford University Press).

Jones, T. J. Rhys. 1977. *Living Welsh* (London: Hodder and Stoughton).

Jorden, Eleanor Harz. 1963. *Beginning Japanese* (New Haven: Yale University Press).

Kurath, Hans. 1949. *A Word Geography of the Eastern United States* (Ann Arbor: University of Michigan Press).

Lazard, Gilbert. 1957. *Grammaire du Persan contemporain* (Paris: Klincksieck).

Li, Charles N., and Sandra A. Thompson. 1981. *Mandarin Chinese: A Functional Reference Grammar* (Berkeley: University of California Press).

Luschning, C. A. E. 1975. *An Introduction to Ancient Greek* (New York: Charles Scribner's Sons).

Melzi, Robert C. 1976. *The New College Italian & English Dictionary* (New York).

Moscati, Sabatino, ed. 1980. *An Introduction to the Comparative Grammar of the Semitic Languages* (Wiesbaden: Otto Harrassowitz).

Murray, Janette, ed. 1989. *Lakota: A Language Course for Beginners* (Guilford, CT: Audio-Forum).

Nathanail, Paul, ed. *New College Greek and English Dictionary* (Lincolnwood, IL: National Textbook Co.).

Obolensky, Serge, Panagiotis S. Sapountzis, and Aspasia Aliki Sapountzis. 1988. *Mastering Greek* (New York: Barron's).

Okrand, Marc. 1985. *The Klingon Dictionary* (New York: Pocket Books).

Park, B. Nam. 1988. *Mastering Korean* (New York: Barron's).

Peng, Tan Huay. 1980–1983. *Fun with Chinese Characters,* 3 vols. (Singapore: Federal Publications).

————. 1987. *Chinese Radicals,* 2 vols. (Union City, CA: Heian International).

Perrot, D. V. 1951. *Swahili* (London: Hodder and Stoughton).

Redden, J. E., N. Owusu, and Associates. 1963. *Twi Basic Course* (Washington, DC: Foreign Service Institute).

Rona, Bengisu. 1989. *Turkish in Three Months* (Edison, NJ: Hunter).

Rood, David S. 1975. "The Implications of Wichita Phonology." *Language 51:* 315–337.

Rosenthal, Franz. 1968. *A Grammar of Biblical Aramaic* (Wiesbaden: Otto Harrassowitz).

Shibatani, Masayoshi. 1990. *The Languages of Japan* (Cambridge: Cambridge University Press).

Snell, Robert, and Simon Weightman. 1989. *Hindi* (London: Hodder and Stoughton).

Tiwari, R. C., R. S. Sharma, and Krishna Vikal. n. d. *Hindi–English Dictionary* (New York:Hippocrene Books).

Tucker, Susie I. 1961. *English Examined.* (Cambridge: Cambridge University Press).

Underhill, Robert. 1976. *Turkish Grammar* (Cambridge, MA: MIT Press).

Wehr, Hans. 1976. *A Dictionary of Modern Written Arabic,* J. Milton Cowan, ed. (Ithaca, NY: Spoken Language Services).

Weinreich, Uriel. 1967. *College Yiddish* (New York: YIVO Institute for Jewish Research).

Windfuhr, Gernot L., and Shapour Bostanbakhsh. 1980. *Modern Persian, Intermediate Level I* (Ann Arbor: Dept. of Near Eastern Studies, University of Michigan).

Yoshida, Yasuo, ed. 1973. *Japanese for Today* (Tokyo: Gakken).